D0856999

THE WOMAN TAKEN
IN ADULTERY
and
THE POGGENPUHL FAMILY

The Woman Taken in Adultery

and

The Poggenpuhl Family

Theodor Fontane

Translated, with Notes, by
GABRIELE ANNAN

With an Introduction by
ERICH HELLER

The University of Chicago Press

Chicago and London

The University of Chicago Press, Chicago 60637
The University Of Chicago Press, Ltd., London

Library of Congress Cataloging in Publication Data

Fontane, Theodor, 1819–1898.
  The woman taken in adultery and The Poggenpuhl family.

  Translation of L'Adultera and Die Poggenpuhls.
  I. Fontane, Theodor, 1819–1898. Die Poggenpuhls.
English.   II. Title.
PZ3.F7347Wo   1979   [PT1863]   833'.8   78–31371
ISBN 0–226–25680–4

CONTENTS

INTRODUCTION

Theodor Fontane—The Extraordinary Education of a Prussian Apothecary

Erich Heller

"It is not far from the estuary of the Rhône, in the region—roughly—between Toulouse and Montpellier, where the Western border of the Gascogne meets the foothills of the Cévennes. This relatively small part of the earth was the homeland of my ancestors, both from my father's and mother's side. They lived in neighboring districts, and because two profoundly different kinds of people exist within this narrow space, it surely is not surprising that *mes ancêtres* reflect these differences. They persisted in my parents despite the fact that their families, long since, had transplanted themselves into the Mark Brandenburg. My father was a big, impressive Gascognian, full of *bonhomie*, fantasies and humor, a *causeur*, fond of telling stories and, when he was completely at ease, tall stories—'Gasconnades.' My mother, on the other hand, was a child of the Southern Cévennes, a slender, delicate woman with black hair, eyes like coal, energetic, selfless, a strong character, and of so passionate a nature that my father used to say of her: 'If she had stayed where she came from, the wars of the Cévennes would rage to this very day.' "

By the "wars of the Cévennes" Fontane *père* meant the uprisings, in 1638, of the Huguenots (although his wife was far from being a religious fanatic.) The son's *Years of my Childhood* (*Meine Kinderjahre*), from which this passage comes, appeared in 1894, when he was seventy-five years old. Fontane rightly called it "an autobiographical *novel*" for his ancestors were to a large extent Germans after Jacques François

Some sections of this Introduction were published in the *Times Literary Supplement*, 20 October 1978, pp. 1222–24.

Fontaine, a Calvinist who manufactured stockings in Nîmes, left France in 1694 and settled in Germany.

Theodor Fontane's grandfather was the first who officially dropped the *i* in "Fontaine." He had a successful career at the courts of the Prussian king Friedrich Wilhelm II and Queen Luise. A contemporary court diarist wrote of him, "A Herr Fontane, painter by trade, has become Cabinet secretary to the Queen; he paints badly, but speaks French well." His grandson, born in 1819, would no longer enjoy such linguistic distinction. He was to become a very good writer, but his French was poor. True, his father, son of the bad painter and his second wife, a Westphalian woman, was christened Louis Henri, but as the beloved amateur teacher of his son, who had inherited but hardly ever used "Henri" as his first Christian name, he must have badly neglected French in his rather improvised syllabus. Although the family pronounced their name without sounding the *e*, the French nasal pronunciation was heard only "on Sundays and holidays," as Theodor's son Friedrich (who became his father's publisher) once remarked.

It seemed advisable to give this sketchy account of Fontane's genealogy because much, far too much, has been made—in explaining his artistry or, in accordance with political fashion, in justifying his being neglected—of his "purely" French descent. The fact is that there is nothing "pure" in his family history. At the same time it is very strange that the most "Gallic" among the German writers of the late nineteenth century had such tenuous links not only with the French language but also with French literature. It would be useless to seek a place for him in a literary mode fashioned by Stendhal, Balzac, and Flaubert; and this is not a matter of comparative importance but of essential difference. The truth is that Germany's first modern "realist" novelist before Thomas Mann (first not in time, for—well, yes, there were Freytag and Spielhagen and Gutzkow before him—but in rank) would read the books of his French predecessors or contemporaries, if he read them at all, in German translations, and this despite his father's veneration of Napoleon. Old Fontane's love of the heroic and the adventurous was altogether excessive. In his apothecary's existence it took the form of gambling and led to his bourgeois Waterloo: he lost his pharmacy in Swinemünde by the Baltic sea (where he had moved from Neuruppin in the Mark Brandenburg, birthplace of his son Theodor) and finally also lost his wife, who left him because she could not bear the perpetual threat of financial ruin.

Indeed, one of the most dramatic lessons in history that young Henri Theodor received from his father, and later described with belletristic artistry and humorous affection, would take the form of a scene in which the father played the part of a flank man in a Napoleonic military detachment while the boy was the commanding officer. "Latour d'Auvergne," the son would call out, and father, standing to attention, would answer in his basso profondo voice, "Il n'est pas ici." "Où est-il donc?" "Il est mort sur le champ d'honneur." This was how Latour's comrades, by daily repeating the scene, honored the memory of the man whom Napoleon designated "le premier grenadier de France." Theodor Fontane would never forget such pedagogy, neither its subjects nor its methods, and would come to detest the dry pedantry of orthodox school instruction. In the most moving chapter of *Years of my Childhood*—an insertion of a much later episode, his last visit at his father's solitary house in the country—the old man would talk about his school days in Neuruppin: "I was embarrassed sometimes how much more I knew than the teachers, except of course Horace and the irregular verbs. There was, for instance, old Starke. His hobby horse was Aristotle; and what Aristotle had long since forgotten, Starke knew. But what *really* mattered, *that* he didn't know. Our schools teach us the wrong things. Nobody will convince me that this isn't so. People don't learn what they ought to learn."

Napoleon and Latour notwithstanding, old Fontane's heroes were not necessarily French. At least one was Prussian. In another passage of *Years of my Childhood*—this time a true childhood memory—Fontane describes his father's living room in Swinemünde. The sofa was its most important piece of furniture—at least to the apothecary himself, who would lie down on it for his prolonged after-lunch naps (a habit that no doubt contributed to the failure of the pharmacy). Above the sofa there hung a much-treasured heirloom: an engraving with the caption "Frédéric le Grand retournant a Sanssouci après les manoeuvres de Potsdam, accompagné de ses généraux." It was reportedly a very sound sleep that was guarded by so dependable a warrior; and young Fontane stood before this picture again and again, gazing intently into the eyes of the Prussian king, and did so "with a premonition, perhaps, that he would become my own favorite hero."

Napoleon and Frédéric le Grand (in the king's preferred writing of his name), France and Prussia, "Fontaine" and Brandenburg: there is nothing unusual in this combination—however surprising it may seem in other contexts. In the "French Colony" in Prussia—the Fontanes belonged to it—it was commonplace. This French Colony—the most important concentration in Germany of the Calvinist French expatriates, the Huguenots—came into being in 1685 when Friedrich Wilhelm, the Grand Elector of Brandenburg, opened his country to the French refugees who fled after Louis XIV had revoked the religiously tolerant Edict of Nantes of 1598. They were even treated in a privileged way and developed into a state within the state, culturally and economically prosperous and politically loyal. Fontane, who joked that every third Berliner was a Frenchman, described the members of the Colony as puritanically stiff, earnest and ambitious—more Prussian than the Prussians. He might have said it of himself. He certainly used every puritanical cliché when he gave his exceedingly negative impressions of his first visit to "lascivious" Paris, and called Prussia his true home in a poem he wrote in 1885 to celebrate the two-hundredth birthday of the French Colony. He was sixty-six then and his novelistic masterpieces, *Effi Briest* and *Der Stechlin* were still to be written. This is what makes it so difficult to write a well-proportioned biography of Fontane. For what he said of his father, may well be said of him: "What he was in the end, was his real self."

Before his late liberation as a writer, Fontane's professional career was varied and most insecure. In consequence, he postponed for five years marrying the woman to whom he had become engaged in 1845, and often reproached himself for making her life so uncomfortable. What, then, was his profession? To begin with, he followed in his father's footsteps and was apprenticed to several apothecaries. But he knew this could not be for life. In his spare time, illicitly extended now and then, he wrote, rehearsing many genres: poetry, story, epic, journalism. His early fictional writings brought him the attention of some of the literary celebrities in Berlin (none of them destined to attain to the rank in German literary history that is now justly and safely assigned to him), and he was invited to join a literary circle, whimsically called "The Tunnel above the Spree" (the Spree is the river that flows through Berlin). There the young apothecary recited his first ballads, which faithfully accepted as their model the creations of the German masters of the genre: Bürger and Schiller and Goethe. He earned much applause from "The Tunnel" and through its members came to know many literary personalities even outside the club.

In 1844 he was invited by a friend, wealthier than he, to join him on a trip to England. During these two weeks in London he was in a state of perpetual enchantment and never quite "recovered" from it. Not even the mounting criticism of England's social conditions, an indignation widespread and culminating a year later in Friedrich Engel's book about the wretchedness of the English proletariat, damped his enthusiasm for the country in which he breathed the air of the great world and of political freedom. Although he was to say on one occasion that the Frenchman in him was responsible for his style, the *Plauderton*, the causerie, the conversational lightness, no French writer had any strong influence on him, certainly none that would be comparable to the impression made by Shakespeare, Scott, Thackeray, Dickens, or Byron—leaving aside the role that in later years the ballads of Scotland and the history and landscapes of England and "beyond the Tweed" would play in forming his imagination, a role almost as important as that of the Mark Brandenburg.

He would visit England again; indeed in 1855 it seemed

that he might settle there permanently. He had terminated, six years before, his uncongenial and tedious activities as a pharmacist and, to finance his married life, accepted in 1850 a position in the "Literary Cabinet," the central agency for controlling the press set up within the Prussian Ministry of the Interior. He obtained this highly "reactionary" appointment (he later referred to it as having sold himself) despite the fact that, as the Berlin correspondent of the liberal *Dresdner Zeitung,* he supplied the Saxon newspaper with "horror stories" of the lawless police regime that had replaced the rule of the honest and law-abiding Prussian army. When the editor rejected one of his articles in praise of the old Prussian militarism, Fontane, rather than continue "to please those *par force* democrats," made his peace with that arbitrary police government by joining its censorship "cabinet."

If we remember that he had played the revolutionary on the Berlin barricades in March 1848—a somewhat confused role that he himself described with considerable *vis comica:* how he tried single-handedly and in vain to break into a church ("Protestant churches are always locked") in order to ring the bells and thus rouse the masses ("All great events begin with the ringing of bells"); and how later that day he seized a gun from the stage properties of an undefended theater (it was probably used "fifteen years before in the popular comedy *Seven Girls in Uniform*") and filled it with so much powder that it became blocked rather than loaded; and how in the midst of the turmoil his father arrived and the two went to drink coffee in a peaceful garden restaurant—if we remember all this, without omitting the less facetious journalistic contributions he made at the time to the revolutionary cause, we can appreciate that he earned the reputation of an *unsicherer Kantonist,* a politically unreliable character. But his love of Prussia—the "good Prussia"—was unshakable, and so was his admiration of England despite the sobering effect that the years spent in the country (from September 1855 until January 1859) had upon his initial enthusiasm. There too, he moved in official business: as the founder and director of a German-English Press Office, a Prussian propaganda center. It lasted only six months, but Fontane stayed in England as the foreign correspondent of a variety of German newspapers.

Years of uncertainty, restlessness, and failure followed upon his return to Berlin in 1859; yet he gradually emerged as a literary figure. He began to write his *Wanderungen durch die Mark Brandenburg* in the belief that this austere part of the German lands with its richly aristocratic history had not yet found its "singer." The "song" was to become longer and longer, until in 1882 it filled four volumes. What he later said of the style in which he undertook those "walks" applies to many more of his writings—as it does to the works of his Austrian counterpart Adalbert Stifter: "It was my proud intention to describe the seemingly most insignificant things with the most detailed precision and thus to raise them to a certain artistic level, indeed to make them *interesting* by means of the kind of simplicity and transparency that appears to be easy but is most difficult to achieve." During the years following his return from London, he also published the journalistic exploits of his "travelsome" time in Britain, *From England* and *Beyond the Tweed*, but he could still not afford to become a "free writer," a vocation he described as ranking in respectability next to that of "traveling showman"; and so eventually, in 1860, he joined the staff of the archconservative Berlin *Kreuzzeitung*, a journal that Nietzsche regarded as representing the "German spirit" at its most hideous.

Yet Fontane later justified this alliance by saying that "all serious people who show dependability, constancy, character, and (which is all right with me) a little fanaticism and obstinacy—that all such people are conservatives; the rest is nothing but quicksand." Before long, however, his own conservatism ceased to be dependable. He felt "chained" to the *Kreuzzeitung*, and in a letter to his wife—it made her apprehensive of yet another spell of economic instability—called the newspaper intolerably "brutal," masking with Christian rhetoric its own "inhumanity." Indeed, he left the *Kreuzzeitung* in 1870 to become the drama critic of the more liberal *Vossische Zeitung*. In this new function he, the descendant of French Protestants, courageously rejected a play by the firmly established and all but unassailable Karl Gutzkow on account of his crude anti-Catholicism. And although, in his very first review, he had written approvingly of the patriotic demonstrations with which an audience, eager for the war against France, responded to the national liberation oratory of Schiller's *Wilhelm Tell*, he later praised a decidedly "unpatriotic" play that caused one of the most notorious scandals of the Berlin theater: Gerhart Hauptmann's *Before Sunrise (Vor Sonnenaufgang)*. Thus the critic Fontane helped to inaugurate the naturalist revolution in German drama.

During the war against France, Fontane's work as a critic, hardly begun, was interrupted by his short but eventful trip, as a reporter, to the French theater of war, where he was arrested in October 1870. He was suspected of being a Prussian spy, but was soon released at the intervention, it is said, of Bismarck himself. In December of the same year he was back in his seat in the Berlin theater. *Prisoner of War (Kriegsgefangen)* is the literary product of his martial adventure. It is free of any chauvinism, so much so that it became the first book of Fontane's that was translated into French. But he was still not simply a man of literature. Only after a brief and uncongenial appointment as First Secretary of the Berlin Academy of Arts did he decide that he could no longer play any part in the "totally confused machinery" of the state or its more or less official representations and, to the rancorous dismay of his wife, at last hazarded the career of an independent writer.

"The novel," he said in the fall of that decisive year, "is my only solace in these disconsolate days.... Working at it, I know for sure that I cannot be anything else but a writer." The historical novel in question, a work of long gestation, was hardly received as promising a novelist of genius. *Before the Storm (Vor dem Sturm)* was its title, its subject an episode from the uprising of Prussia against Napoleon in 1812–13, and its sentiments were "religious, moral, and patriotic." The author himself said so. Who would have expected such unambiguously pious attachments from the loyal son of a Napoleonbesotted father or from a writer who, after his "prostitution" in the service of the Prussian "Literary Cabinet" and the "religious, moral, and patriotic" *Kreuzzeitung*, had at last asserted his freedom? But he also described the theme of the novel as something more subtle and important: "A great idea, a great moment, breaks into very simple human conditions." The delineations of "simple human conditions" did not meet with universal applause. One influential critic found it all rather silly. Dramatic tension, he asked? Perhaps; but only if one is prepared patiently to wait for resolutions brought about by an outing in a coach or by setting the table or by going to bed.

Certainly, such "simplicities" may be too simple, but the theme itself, just as the historical subject, is reminiscent of *War and Peace*, and although clashes between the commonplace and "the great moment" are not new in the literature of the nineteenth century, this theme is, by virtue of his temperament and artistic disposition, Fontane's very own, just as it was Chekhov's; and there *is* something Chekhovian in this citizen of the Mark Brandenburg, son of the apothecary from Neuruppin and Swinemünde. (As the incongruity between spectacular deeds and mediocre doers, between the heroic measure of the suffering and the unheroic character of the sufferers, it has become one of the most terrible themes of our age.)

After *Before the Storm* there were to be many novels and novellas: eighteen, to be exact. Among the novellas his artistically most accomplished work is *Irretrievable (Unwiederbringlich)*. When the first novel of his newly-won freedom appeared in 1878, Fontane was fifty-nine; at the time of *Irretrievable*, seventy-three—and his greatest works were still to come. This may be unique in the history of literature. Tolstoy was ten years younger than Fontane, but *Before the Storm* was published ten years after *War and Peace*, not to count the years by which *Anna Karenina* is older than Fontane's novel of adultery *Effi Briest*. The latter appeared in the same year as *The Poggenpuhl Family (Die Poggenpuhls)*:—in 1896, when Fontane was seventy-seven. It seems both incredible that *Effi Briest* was written by so old a man and clear that Fontane could not possibly have written it when he was younger. For in his younger days he was given to uttering firm convictions and having "opinions," different ones at different times. He held no beliefs for any length of time, and sometimes not even the same beliefs at the same moment. It has justly been said of him that there is no political advocate in the warring world of politics who could not support his advocacy with one or other of the many contradictory utterances of Fontane's.

"The bourgeois is terrible," he would say, and would praise the proletariat for being incomparably more genuine, more vital, and more truthful. It accords with this—but far less with his wholly admiring poem on Bismarck that is inscribed on the tomb of the "Iron Chancellor" only half admired by him—that he called Gerhart Hauptmann's most revolutionary drama, *The Weavers (Die Weber)*, a "splendid achievement" that would inaugurate "a new epoch" in German literature. But he is offended by the crass social criticism of Turgenev and Zola, objecting to their "naturalism" because it is "too pessimistic." But since he himself, the "realist," is pessimistic enough, or at least extremely skeptical with regard to "human nature," one cannot help suspecting that what he means by the pessimism of the "naturalists" is their tendency to look upon the good manners of style as a violation of truth, the truth that comes to light through "revolutions" in art as well as in politics. And revolutions, he writes, "are usually initiated by the rabble, by adventurers, or by madmen." Yet instantly he exclaims, "But what would have become of us without revolutions!" This is the same Fontane who earlier pronounced that there could not be *any* social order without the masses being kept down by fear or religion, by the regimen of powerful governments, secular or ecclesiastical: "Any attempt to do without the great overlords of the world," he concluded, "can safely be regarded as having failed once and for all."

In other words, Fontane was a born novelist, even if this birth took place late in his life. What, then, did the art of the novel and his advancing years teach him that he had not learned as a journalist, as an author of travelogues, or even as a maker of poems and ballads? He himself rather naively believed that it was respect for what *is* rather than a hankering for what ought to be, the almost passive readiness to let life speak for itself rather than tell it how it should behave, to allow every character—no, not the right to his own deeds and convictions, but the unquestionable privilege of his existence. Fontane discovered that he was a novelist—and with some of his works he was a great novelist—when after years of uncomfortably upholding contradictory "ideologies," he arrived at the exact point at which Turgenev confessed that he felt always lost when challenged to say what he "in his own person" felt or believed about this or that without being given the chance of shifting the responsibility to the exchanges, the dialogue, of imaginary characters: "As for myself, it has always seemed to me that I might just as well, and with equal right, maintain the opposite of what I was saying." This is—almost word by word—what one of Fontane's most impressive and lovable creations, Dubslav von Stechlin in *Der Stechlin*, says after having ventured a definite opinion: "And if I had said the opposite, it would be equally right"—which does not prevent the old man from being obstinately and delightfully sure about certain principles of morality. Still, it was Keats who said that "the poetical Character has no character. It has as much delight in conceiving an Iago as an Imogen. What shocks the virtuous philosopher delights the chameleon Poet." The "chameleon" in the poet certainly did shock, for instance, Kierkegaard and—in one of the greatest inner dramas of literary history—Tolstoy.

Dubslav's words are Fontane's own: "And if I had said the opposite, it would be equally right." To be sure, this would be incongruous and even perverse when uttered by the critic sitting in judgment of performances in the theater, or by the maker of moral or political decisions; yet it is "dubiously," "dialectically," "metaphysically" true in the mouth of one who is about to become a very considerable novelist. Is this the *Erkenntnis*, the knowledge, that Fontane meant when he quoted Goethe's belief that the work of the *good* poet or writer reflect not some vague and partial intuition but the measure

of his knowing insight? Is this what made the critic into a
novelist, into a writer who said of his art that it was
"psychography and criticism" and, coming from the dark
ground of creativity, was ordered, pruned and trimmed in
the sobering light of day? Very likely. It was the *Erkenntnis*,
Turgenev's insight, that the truth of a novel, of any work of
art, is far beyond the truths of convictions and opinions.
These are at all times mere fragments within the ultimate
justification of the whole—or indeed its senselessness. ("Was
soll der Unsinn"—"What on earth is it all about?"—was what
Fontane's soul every so often muttered to itself.)

In *Effi Briest* it is certainly Fontane himself speaking—or at
least the part of himself that is ineradicably "Prussian"—
when Instetten, Effi Briest's husband, in making up his mind
to challenge his wife's lover to a duel, insists on the necessity
of the social order being protected by the power of established morality. Yes, Fontane himself—or what is left of the
self once it has withdrawn, leaving the stage to the interplay
of opposing natures and convictions. But has this self ever
really and literally withdrawn? Or is speaking like this only
an aesthetic *façon de parler?* Is not most literature critique,
critique of life? And if so, who *is* the critic? Most of Fontane's
works are certainly a critique of the moral ideas and social
institutions of the epoch, to the same degree that they *reflect*
their increasing instability. This much he has in common with
Ibsen, Zola, Shaw (or rather, they with him) or even with
Schnitzler (how much of Fontane's most "modern" book,
Schach von Wuthenow, is there in the early Schnitzler!). Yet
there is an important difference. For while Fontane's sympathy and affection lie with tradition, he knows of its historical fragility *and* its ethical dubiousness. Is this pure "and"
correct? Should it not be "and *therefore . . .*"? The question
would be almost senseless when speaking of Zola or Shaw.
For them, what is historically outlived, is morally objectionable; and insofar as this is so, it is to the detriment of their
artistic rank. This was certainly not so—or not simply so—in
the case of Fontane. Hence his social criticism is far less vigorous than theirs. Again and again, it is as if the critic stood

still for a while before leaving behind the old, just as someone departing from an accustomed place might, however many things he disliked there, turn round with tears in his eyes as it vanishes from view.

Therefore, with Fontane, it is an extreme victory of the novelist's art when he who speaks the author's mind (or speaks what was the author's mind just before he wrote it) is at the same time denied the reader's sympathies; when the author deflects the flow of the reader's emotions away from the man the author deems to be in the right (or did so before the novel took shape). It is what happened to Tolstoy—in a much more acute distress of the spirit—when his imagination and affection compelled him to leave to God the judgment that he himself, in his novel, had intended to pass on Anna Karenina's sin. In both cases this rout of moral righteousness at the hands of the affectionate imagination is even in excess of that artistic objectivity—the objectivity of Nature herself—as it has been stated with grim brilliance by Schopenhauer: "Nature," he said, "does not do as bad writers do when they show a knave or a fool and set about it so full of clumsy purpose that behind every such figure we see the writer himself disavowing their minds and words, and warning us with a raised finger: 'This is a knave, this is a fool: do not listen to what he says!'" Fontane, in his engagingly modest ways, goes beyond this. *Do* listen to Instetten's words, he seems to say, but *don't like him.* (Thomas Mann, who in more than one way is much indebted to Fontane, accomplished the same in *The Magic Mountain* with his famous pair of antagonists: Naphta, who is nearly always right and nearly always objectionable, and Settembrini, who, by comparison, is shallow and nearly always likable.)

In the sixteenth chapter of Fontane's *Years of my Childhood*, during that excursion into the future that tells of the son's last visit to his father, there occurs a scene that is not only, like the whole chapter, deeply moving but, in its apparently perfunctory way, allows us a glimpse of the novelist's moral problem. The old man, chatting away, suddenly comes upon "the thing" that must have caused him continual moral uneasiness: his professional and financial failure, his fatal passion for gambling, his inability to support his family:

"Please, Father, let's not talk about it. Don't you know that it is now all the same to us?"
"Maybe to you, but not to your mother."
"She has put up with it."
"Put up with it. You see, my boy, that's her way of accusing me, and of course the old woman is right. This is what I tell myself day after day . . ."
"You take it too much to heart, Father. It's harder for you than for us."
"Possibly, possibly. And it would be even harder if I didn't also tell myself: It's the circumstances that make the man."
"I remember your saying this even when we were still children. And it is certainly right."
"Yes, right it is . . . But it doesn't quite put one's mind at ease. A little, but not entirely."

"A little, but not entirely." The human world as character and circumstance: this is the universe of the novelist, the definition of his art. At the height of his power it was Fontane's ambition that everything presented in his writing should emerge with that "naturalness and necessity" that Schopenhauer demanded of great literature. Fontane even went one step further: *one* step; the next might lead into the territory of the amoral. It was his intention that differences between "big" and "small" or "good" and "bad" were not to be endowed with particular emphasis. What mattered was "objective reality," "the circumstances." Fontane spoke with Stifter's voice when in a letter he confessed that he did not think highly of such differences: he treats with the same affection every particle of "reality," and says even more: "If it so happens that I come upon something really great, I don't make many words about it. Greatness speaks for itself. It needs no artistic support to make an effect." Although this aesthetic mood is appealing, it is nonsensical—as appealing and nonsensical as Stifter's much-quoted assertion (it was polemically aimed at the dramatist Hebbel and his Hegelian themes of historical grandeur) that the eruption of a volcano is not "greater" than a milk pot boiling over; for both are expressions of the same natural law. There would be no classical literature—no Iliad, no Odyssey, no Oedipus, no Lear and no Faust—if poets had heeded the implied prescription. Rather were they inclined to obey Nietzsche's injunction that of great things they ought to speak greatly (even if one wishes for more moderation when it comes to the Zarathustra tone of Nietzsche himself).

But what Fontane very probably had in mind is that beloved—and utopian—principle of "equal poetic justice" for *all* things, the principle of realism itself. In this declared—but happily never practiced, indeed impracticable—radicalism, Fontane went so far as to question the reputation that a celebrated realist writer of the epoch, Gottfried Keller, enjoyed as a "stylist." Of course, he admitted, the Swiss writer did have "style" in the sense that he was unable to write a line that would not instantly be recognized as his. Yet Fontane meant "style" in a different sense. For he wanted to believe that the style of a work was true only if it was "objective," that is, the more it was the object itself that appeared to say what it was without its identity being veiled by peculiarities or idiosyncracies of the author's manner. If this were so, indeed if this could possibly be achieved by *any* style, Fontane himself would be the archsinner. It has even been said—by an admirer of Fontane's—that his last novel, *Der Stechlin* (he was seventy-six when he began to write it), is so riotous in old-age "sinning" and the "method," the "style," the "Fontane tone" so omnipresent that the contours of individual characters are hopelessly blurred, so that one might easily exchange many roles without affecting the organization—or disorganization—of the work. This is not true. For the characters of the novel are far from indistiguishable; their characteristics are merely subdued for the sake of their harmonization.

The musical allusion is not out of place. The "instruments" for which *Der Stechlin* has been written, are those of a chamber orchestra. No doubt, louder, more "characteristic" effects can be produced by trombones and kettledrums, but this is not to say that to finer ears the viola d'amore has no distinct personality whose voice could not be distinguished from the sound of the fiddle. One year before his death in 1898, Fontane described the novel to his publisher as "uneventful": "In the end an old man dies and two young people marry—this is about all that happens on five hundred pages." What mattered to him, was the *Mache*, the way the novel is made. Fontane even placed an admiring exclamation mark behind the word: *Die Mache!* Indeed, it is the indefinable quality of its "manufacture," the love, the verbal music, the very mind and humor of wisdom that transmute the lazy "circumstances" into a dynamic order that carries within itself a whole ensemble of aesthetic and ethical discriminations. The "circumstances" that according to Fontane *père* were to be blamed for everything—a belief that, as he confessed, would yet not allow the morally troubled soul to feel at ease ("a little, but not entirely")—are wholly freed of their overcrowded "factual" causality and have ample room for guilt and redemption in the art of the mature artist.

"Der Stechlin" is the name of a little lake in a wooded corner of Fontane's native Mark Brandenburg. It is mysteriously joined to "the other world" outside, as Fontane puts it in that letter, and in all its smallness reflects the great events from beyond the woods of the province. "When in Iceland or on Java a mountain spits fire and the earth trembles, the Stechlin bubbles up and forms funnels and whirlpools." In truth, the lake and the people living by its shore are capable of subtler responses; for put like this, the lake's symbolic role would be too obvious. Fontane's description was meant for the publisher. To the reader the superb book insinuates itself by the most discreet persuasiveness and sympathy. The sympathy is above all for the main character: Dubslav von Stechlin, a Prussian aristocrat. Although the aristocracy in Fontane's novels is by no means immune from his ironically critical and even satirical treatment—the ever more tenuous and often vacuous idea of honor, catastrophically upheld by this declining class, is one of his recurring *motifs*—it is yet true to say that he never ceased to be fond of what he regarded as the aristocratic virtues, the cast of mind elsewhere associated with "the gentleman." It certainly reflects upon the unhappy history of modern Germany that the grand swan song by a burgher writer for the Prussian nobility, *Der Stechlin*, is separated by only a few years from the novel of the decline and fall of the German burgherdom, Thomas Mann's *Buddenbrooks*.

"This is about all that happens on five hundred pages." What Fontane said in 1897 about *Der Stechlin* he could not possibly have said about a novel the very old writer for more than a decade dreamed of writing, and for which he made many notes and studied documents. It was to be called *The Like-dealers* (*Die Likedeeler*) and would have gone far back into history, much, much farther than *Before the Storm*, indeed would have been set in times in which the writer's imaginative engagement was bound to be stronger than his inclination to acquire the historical erudition necessary for depicting them: in the early fifteenth century, among pirates of noble character and revolutionary intentions, not unlike the *Robbers* of the young Schiller, "like-dealers," communist distributors of the treasures conquered in audacious feats of seafaring. They were the terror of the Baltic and the North Sea under the leadership of Klaus Störtebeker, and their end was a mass execution in Hamburg. Indeed, this story would have called for a more voluminous instrumentation than *Der Stechlin* and, as a great historical "phantasmagory," could not have been played by a chamber orchestra of words: the trombones and kettledrums would probably have come into their own. This, at least, is what the plan suggests. But it suggests even more: the ambition of an old man to recapture the emotions of youth as he evoked them in *Years of My Childhood*.

There he describes how, during the boy's time in and near Swinemünde, he would seek out the cave where Störtebeker and his pirates reportedly used to hide, and how the child, lying in its deepest recess, would be overcome by sublime feelings while the leaves of the beech trees outside rustled in the wind and the sea sounded in his ears just as it did in Klaus Störtebeker's all those centuries ago. The sagacity and realistic irony of the aged writer had taken all this away; where there was the fabled bravery of Störtebeker and his men, there was now the prudence of the knowing and detached observer, and the sober magic of the "Fontane tone" had smoothed the waves. Would he succeed in writing the masterpiece—"It does not matter whether it will ever be finished," he said—that would be the synthesis of his youthful enthusiasm for Nordic ballads with the measured rhythms of his present narrative style, between "the old gods," as he wrote, and his mundane skepticism. It was not to be. His last word was not Klaus Störtebeker but Dubslav von Stechlin, an ending hardly to be regretted.

The Woman Taken in Adultery (L'Adultera) and The Poggenpuhl Family (Die Poggenpuhls), the two stories contained in this volume, are in no need of a lengthy introduction or interpretation. The former appeared in 1882 and is one of Fontane's early fictional works (if it is possible to call "early" the work of an author who at the time was sixty-three), whereas the latter, a late work, was published in 1896 when Fontane was seventy-seven. The story of The Woman Taken in Adultery foreshadows, as suggested by the title, Effi Briest, but it is tempting to say that it is not even the theme that it has in common with the later novel. Nor is it merely the exceedingly happy ending of The Woman Taken in Adultery that makes the difference. It is the pervasive lightness of tone, the preponderance of almost playful society sketches that would make any hint at moral gravity inappropriate.

If Fontane himself once said that it was probably the Frenchman in him (the Frenchman that otherwise does not much come to the fore) that made him prefer light and witty conversations to teutonically weighty debates, the cadences of causerie to the accents of earnestness, he might have thought above all of The Woman Taken in Adultery. There came even a point in his negotiations with his publisher at which Fontane rejected the title as too aggressively moralistic, and proposed "Melanie Van der Straaten" instead. It would have been a mistake; but not because the—finally maintained— title makes the most of the play with Tintoretto's painting, a

motif perhaps too lightheartedly and too obviously introduced for the sake of a "rounder rounding-off" of the story.
No, that title would have been wrong because it is not
Melanie who deserves the "title role" but her husband,
Ezechiel van der Straaten, an exquisite portrait of the kind of
man upon whom "society" tended to look down as a parvenu
and who, in his generosity and kindheartedness, was certainly preferable to many of its "legitimate" members. Still,
Fontane's reason for wanting to change the title had nothing
to do with any of that: "It is repugnant to me," he wrote to
the publisher, "rudely to call a woman who is still alive and
is, despite her faults, a lovable and excellent person, 'adul-
tress' to her face."

In other words: the author knew that the public would
recognize the story as a roman à clef; the plot *was* derived
from a society scandal of the day, a scandal with a happy
conclusion. "The *real* story did take this course," he wrote in
a letter, defending himself with a straight face—just as if he
were unaware of the difference between art and fact—against
the reproach of moral laxity, "and the lady in question, much
loved and respected, lives up there in East Prussia, surrounded by her many children."

Happily, the time is no more when the debate about *The
Woman Taken in Adultery* centered upon a possibly offensive
indiscretion. The Mme Ravené in Berlin who found happiness as Frau Simon no longer arouses any public interest. Yet
it is surprising how little the social critic Fontane realized the
weight of the problem. For the role that adultery plays in the
novel of the nineteenth century—not to mention the shatter-
ingly unmedieval, "modern" treatment that *Tristan and Isolde*
received from Wagner—is, to say the least, underestimated
by anyone's discussing it, as Fontane does in his letters, in
terms of what "really" occurred: a satisfactory second marriage, it appears, and not a moral disaster. Still, the uproar
that *Madame Bovary* caused is more in keeping with the *historical* momentum of the theme than the worry about the
embarrassment that Fontane's novel may have caused to the
Simons in Königsberg. For the dominant position of adultery

among the themes of nineteenth-century literature is indi-
cative, through personal-emotional destinies, of revolutions
that certainly have not yet ceased to convulse a civilization
which once upon a time looked upon itself as Christian. With
regard to the novel, it was, after Goethe's *Elective Affinities*,
only Tolstoy who, in *Anna Karenina*, fathomed the tragic
depths of the theme. Yet in *The Woman Taken in Adultery* Fontane has endowed it with as much worldly wisdom, charm
and *bonhomie* as there is room for in the space between
tragedy and comedy.

Recommending *The Poggenpuhl Family* to the benevolent
attention of a critic-friend, Fontane singled out as its two
virtues that it was short and that, unlike some noisier produc-
tions of the time, no shots were fired in it. And a few days
later (the friendly review had appeared on the Sunday) he
thanked the critic for that first public acclaim: "Now there are
bound to follow others who will find its gadabout style"—
Bummelstil is the word that Fontane has coined to describe its
manner—"not lacking in artistic merit and 'realistic' despite
the absence of Jack the Ripper." This was, of course, a little
sarcasm aimed at what he most disliked in the "naturalist"
upheaval: its violence and sensationalism. Yet he seems resigned to readers now having "other ideals," ideals
"younger" than the voice that makes itself heard in *The
Poggenpuhl Family:* "The book is not a novel and has no plot,
the 'How' must compensate for the missing 'What'—I am
delighted when the work is judged like this. Of course, a
body of literature cannot be based on the taste of ancient
gentlemen. But now and then something like it may pass."
Indeed, it may; and may give the kind of pleasure that Fontane's last novel, *Der Stechlin*, gives abundantly, a book to
which every word Fontane said about the much shorter
Poggenpuhl Family may be applied: the pleasure of the colors
and the serenely resigned wisdom of a bright autumn day.
One of the publishers to whom *The Poggenpuhl Family* was
offered refused it because, he feared, it ridiculed the nobility.
"What nonsense," Fontane exclaimed in his diary, "it is a
glorification of it." A glorification? Well, yes, in the "Fontane
tone": the tone of a voice that speaks affectionately, with gen-

tle irony and the hushed knowledge of the vanity of all things. There is a fine residue of "Was soll der Unsinn?"—"What on earth is it all about?"—even in his most determined affirmations.

TRANSLATOR'S NOTE

Germans, however well born or educated, speak with a regional accent. Sometimes it is so slight as to be hardly detectable, and it gets broader as you go down the social scale until in some parts of the country the local dialect is almost a separate language. Educated persons speaking to uneducated ones often use a broader accent and more dialect words than they would when speaking to their equals. Fontane was brilliant at rendering these nuances, and much of the charm of his novels lies in the way he does it. But there seems to be no way of producing English equivalents which do not sound phony, so I have reluctantly abandoned the attempt to do so. My editor has also persuaded me not to use the German forms of address such as "Herr General" or "gnädige Frau" (gracious lady) which punctuate the text, but either to leave them out or to replace them with more general expressions such as "sir" or "ma'am."

In *The Woman Taken in Adultery* I have used two different spellings to translate the German title "Rat" (often a suffix). "Kommerzien*rat*," Commercial Councillor, is an honorific title (like "Privy Councillor" in England, but less exalted); but "Legations*rat*" describes a rank in the foreign service: "Counselor."

Finally, American readers may be surprised at the view which seems to be generally accepted by the characters in *The Woman Taken in Adultery* that Americans are cold and brusque of manner: but this view was quite common in nineteenth-century Germany (at any rate in fiction), when the United States was regarded as the country of streamlined modern efficiency whose inhabitants had no time for *douceur de vivre* or politeness.

The Woman Taken
in Adultery

1

COMMERCIAL COUNCILLOR
van der STRAATEN

Commercial Councillor[1] van der Straaten, of 4 Grosse Petri-strasse, was incontestably one of the most substantial finan-ciers in the capital, a fact scarcely affected by the circumstance that his solid reputation rested more on his business than on his personality. On the stock exchange his position was un-questioned; in society it was not. If you kept your ears open, you soon discovered the reason: he had been too little in the world and had failed to acquire a generally acceptable degree of polish or even a bearing suitable to his position. A few recent trips to Paris and Italy—none of them, by the way, lasting more than a few weeks—had done little to alter this state of affairs and had affected neither his typically Berlin manner nor his fondness for vigorous locutions and local proverbs of a somewhat uncouth nature. As he himself liked to put it, he called a spade a spade; and, born of wealthy parents, he had been accustomed from an early age to do and say exactly as he pleased. Two things he hated: one was to stand on ceremony; the other, to change his ways. Not that, in theory, he considered himself past improvement: far from it. But he denied that, in practice, there was any need for such a thing. He was fond of expounding this view, and he would say that most people were wretched specimens, rotten to the core; by comparison with them his own character bordered on the angelic. Besides, he could see no reason to strive for self-improvement and to make himself uncomfortable. You had only to look at any dissenter—or any divinity student for that matter—any day of the week to see at once that such endeavors never led to any good. It was always the same story: to drive out the devil you had to call on Beelzebub. So he preferred to leave things as they were. When he had finished his speech, he would look around complacently and conclude with satisfaction and a display of culture, "Touch it not, touch it not"[2]—for he liked to throw in a little verse, especially if it allowed him to express his typically Berlin predilection for a cozy kind of sentimentality. It goes without saying that he could laugh at himself for this very trait.

It will now have become obvious that van der Straaten was a man who combined sentiment with a sense of humor; his Berlinisms and cynical remarks were nothing more than the somewhat unruly offspring of his independent spirit and unfailing cheerfulness. In fact, there was nothing in the world for which he was so constantly in the mood as witticisms and repartee—a characteristic immediately apparent when he was introduced to anyone in society. For on these and similar occasions he was invariably asked whether he was related, even distantly, to the Manasse Vanderstraaten who was famous for his performances in Gutzkow's plays;[3] and he never tired of denying any connection with the celebrated actor, promptly and under three headings: (1) his own name was spelled not as one word but as three; (2) in spite of the fact that his first name was Ezechiel, he had not only been baptized but had had the good fortune (by no means shared by every Prussian) of being received into Christ's Holy Church by a Lutheran bishop—old Bishop Ross, as a matter of fact; and (3) for some time now he had had the advantage of having as mistress of his house a lady whose name was not Judith but Melanie; Melanie, moreover, was not his daughter but his spouse. This last word he uttered with a certain solemnity in which seriousness and jest were neatly harmonized.

But the seriousness was dominant, at least in his heart. It could not be otherwise, for the young woman was almost more his pride than his joy. She was the eldest daughter of Jean de Caparoux, a nobleman from French Switzerland who had spent many years as consul-general in the North German capital. She had been brought up as the cherished child of a rich and distinguished family, and all her gifts had been cultivated most felicitously. Her sunny grace was almost greater

than her wit, and her amiability greater even than either.
Every advantage of the Gallic temperament seemed combined in her. Its weaknesses too, perhaps? Nothing had ever
been heard on the subject. Her father died young, and instead of the expected wealth he left nothing but debts. It was
about this time that van der Straaten, then forty-two years
old, asked for the hand of the seventeen-year-old Melanie
and was accepted. Understandably, friends of both families
were not lacking in gloomy prophecies. But it looked as
though they were to be proved wrong. Ten happy years—
happy for both parties—had passed; Melanie lived like a
princess in a fairy tale, and van der Straaten was delighted to
resign himself to the nickname Ezel,[4] which his young wife
had substituted for the cumbersome and slightly suspect
Ezechiel. Nothing was missing. There were even children to
bless the marriage: two daughters, the younger the image of
her father, the elder of her mother—tall and slim and with
long dark locks. But while the mother's eyes were always
smiling, the daughter's were grave and melancholy, as
though they could see into the future.

2

"THE WOMAN TAKEN
IN ADULTERY"

The van der Straatens usually spent the winter months in
their city apartment, which was old-fashioned but not lacking
in comfort. In any case it was more convenient for the social
life of the season than their summer villa on the river Spree,
in the northwest part of the Tiergarten.

It was two days after the first subscription ball.[5] Van der
Straaten and his wife were breakfasting as usual in the pan-
neled study. Almost immediately outside their window,
Saint Peter's was striking nine; a little French mantel clock

chimed in punctually, but in its haste and eagerness it soon outstripped the slow, hollow strokes from outside. Everything breathed comfort, especially the master of the house, leaning back in his rocking chair and simultaneously absorbing his coffee and the account of the subscription ball in the morning paper. Now and then he would lay the paper down and laugh.

"What are you laughing at now, Ezel?" asked Melanie, flirtatiously flapping her left slipper. "What is it this time? I'll wager the evening dress you are going to buy me this very day against that horrid red cravat of yours, which you've tied crooked again just to spite me, that you've managed to find some double meaning."

"He really does write well," said van der Straaten without picking up the challenge. "And what gives me the most pleasure is that she takes it all so seriously."

"Who does?"

"Who? The Maywald woman, of course, your rival. Just listen now. Or read it for yourself."

"No, I don't want to. I don't like those reports all about decolletés and filled with people's initials."

"And you know why you don't? Because they haven't got around to you yet. Yes, Lanni, I'm afraid you are beneath his notice."

"So I should hope! I wouldn't stand for it."

"Stand for it? What do you mean, stand for it? Do you suppose that the daughters of former consuls general go through life as unapproachable as vestal virgins or that they are sacrosanct like envoys and ambassadors? I'll tell you a proverb that you people from Geneva don't know . . ."

"And what may that be?"

"'A cat may look at a king.' And I tell you, Lanni, if you can look at something, you can write about it. Or do you want me to challenge him? Pistols at ten paces?"

Melanie laughed. "No, Ezel, I'd die if you got killed."

"Well, think it over. The best thing that can happen to a young woman like you is widowhood—'le veuvage,' as my landlady in Paris used to keep assuring me. By the way, she's the best of all my travel souvenirs. But you ought to have seen her, a fat, black-haired little creature..."

"I'm not sorry I never had that pleasure. I'd much rather know how old she was."

"Fifty. Love doesn't always fall upon a bed of roses."

"Oh well, then I can forgive her and you too."

And with that, Melanie rose from her high-backed chair, laid down her embroidery canvas, and went to the central window.

Down below was the lively bustle of market day, which the young woman loved to watch. She was intrigued by the contrasts; immediately beside the church door was a small, low table at which a little old lady was selling honey in glass jars of various sizes with scalloped paper covers tied down with red yarn. Next to her was a game stall with six hares hanging upside down, gazing mournfully across at Melanie. In front of them a little girl ran to and fro, her pinched face muffled in a hood; she was selling toy sheep to the passers-by for Christmas gifts. A gray sky hung over all. A few feathery snowflakes fluttered down, and, as they reached the ground, a current of air would whirl them up again.

The sight of the dancing snowflakes filled Melanie with a kind of longing, a longing to rise and fall and rise as they did. She was about to summon up her usual spirit of mocking gaiety and to laugh at herself for this access of yearning; but as she was turning back into the room she noticed one of those long, low-wheeled carts known as drays. It was coming from the Brüderstrasse and was a perfect example of its kind with not one characteristic feature missing. At the back, the double board used for unloading was tilted up at right angles; the driver, with a big beard and leather apron, stood at the front, and in the middle a little mongrel dog, half Pomeranian and half terrier, ran up and down barking at anyone who looked as though he might venture within five paces of the dray. Its exaggerated vigilance was hardly justified, for only one parcel was left on the long board; the driver picked it up in his two gigantic hands as though it were a mere cardboard box and carried it into the hall.

Meanwhile van der Straaten, having finished his paper, had moved to his desk by the corner window.

"What handsome fellows those drivers are," said Melanie. "And so strong. And that marvelous beard. I think Samson must have looked just like that."

"Well, I don't," said van der Straaten drily.

"Or Wayland the Smith."[6]

"That's more like it. And sooner or later that whole business will have to be settled. Because I bet you ten to one the 'master'[7] is holding him under his hammer for some future work. Or let us say on his anvil. It sounds a bit more elegant."

"Ezel, I really must beg you... you know..."

But before she could finish there was a knock at the door. One of the young clerks appeared, and with a bow to Melanie he handed his employer a bill of lading. It was in Italian and said in large letters: "To be delivered personally to the addressee."

Van der Straaten read it and was galvanized.

"Ah, from Salviati! That's nice, that's good. Bring the box up at once. You stay here, Melanie... Well, he's kept his word... I'm delighted, really delighted. And so will you be. Something from Venice. You were so fond of Venice."

And rambling on in short sentences he produced a chisel from his desk drawer. When the box was brought in, he handled the chisel as nimbly and confidently as if it had been a corkscrew or some implement he used daily. He prised off the lid with ease, revealing a picture screwed to the underside. This he placed on a large stand, like an easel, which he had moved from a corner to a position in front of the window. The young clerk had left meanwhile; van der Straaten took Melanie's hand and led her to the picture with a certain solemnity: "Well, Lanni, how do you like it?... Don't worry, I'll help you out: it's a Tintoretto."

"A copy?"

"Of course," he stammered, slightly embarrassed. "They don't sell the originals. Not that I could afford one. But all the same, I should have thought..."

Meanwhile Melanie had studied the main figures in the painting through her lorgnette. Now she said: "Ah, *The*

Woman Taken in Adultery! . . . Now I recognize it. But why did you have to choose that one? It's really quite a dangerous picture, as dangerous as when He said . . . you know the bit I mean?"

"Let him that is without sin among you . . ."

"That's it. And I can never help feeling there's something encouraging in those words. Sly old Tintoretto certainly interpreted it that way. Just look! She's been crying. Of course she has. You know why? Because they've told her over and over again how wicked she's been. And now she believes it, or at least she wants to believe it. But her heart rebels and just won't accept it . . . I must confess, I really find her very touching. There's so much innocence in her guilt. And it's as if it had all been predestined."

As she spoke, Melanie had grown more serious and had stepped back from the painting. Now she asked, "Have you decided where to hang it?"

"Yes, here." And he pointed to a place near his desk.

"I thought you'd put it in the gallery," she continued. "To tell you the truth, it will look a bit odd on that wall over there. People . . ."

"Go on!"

"People will be tempted to make jokes about it and malicious comments. I can just hear Reiff and Duquede passing remarks—perhaps about you, and certainly about me."

Van der Straaten was leaning on his desk and smiling.

"You're smiling . . . and normally you laugh much more and much louder than necessary. You're hiding something. Tell me, what have you got against me? I know very well, you're not as innocent as you pretend. And I know something else too: people who never get upset can be very strange. I once read something about a Russian prince, I think his name was Suboff. No, there were two—two brothers. They were playing cards, and then they went and murdered Czar Paul, and then they went on playing cards. I almost think you could do that. And with a clear conscience and without losing any sleep."

"So that's why I'm King Ezel?"

"Oh no, that's not why. I was still half a child when I called you that. And I didn't really know you then. But now I do know you, and there's something inside you that's either very good or very bad... I can't decide which... But let's get on. Our coffee is getting cold."

She moved away from the window and sat down again on her high-backed chair, took up her needle and canvas, and made a few rapid stitches. But at the same time she did not take her eyes off him, because she wanted to know what was going on in his mind.

Nor did he wish to hide it any longer. In spite of all his friendships, he had no friend, no one in whom he could confide; and so the painting for once drew him out of his shell.

"I've never tormented you with jealousy, Lanni."

"And I've never given you cause."

"No. But... here today and gone tomorrow. I mean, everything in life can change. And you see, last year when we were in Venice and I saw this picture, everything suddenly became quite clear to me. And that's when I asked Salviati to have it copied. I want to have it where I can see it, a sort of memento mori, like the Capuchins, who aren't normally my cup of tea at all. Because you see, Lanni, people are different even in the way they feel fear. Some are like ostriches and bury their heads in the sand and don't want to know. But others would rather keep their fate in full view and get used to living with it. They are fully aware that some day or other they will die, and they have their coffin made and look at it as often as they can. And by constantly imagining their death, they finally rob it of its terror. And you see, Lanni, that's what I want to do too, and this painting is to help me to do it. Because I know it's hereditary in our family. And as sure as the hand on that clock..."

"But Ezel," Melanie interrupted, "whatever is the matter with you? I ask you, what will that kind of talk lead to? If that's how you see things, I can't understand why you don't have me incarcerated."

"I've thought of it. And I admit 'Melanie the nun' doesn't sound bad, and it would make a good ballad. But none of that would make any difference. You wouldn't believe what lovers can do when they have the will. And they always do have the will."

"Oh, I can believe it all right."

"There you are, then," laughed van der Straaten, his good humor restored by her joking reply. "That's how I like to hear you talk. And as a reward I won't hang the picture over there in the corner but in the gallery. That's a promise. And just to keep nothing from you: my thoughts on the whole subject are full of change and contradiction; sometimes I think: I may die before it happens. Gain time, gain all. The most banal sayings are always the truest."

"Well, then, don't forget 'speaking of the devil . . .'"

He nodded. "You're right there. And we won't. Let's put this whole last hour right out of our minds. If I ever remind you of it, it will be in a spirit of peace and as a sign of reconciliation. Don't laugh. What will be, will be. What was that you said? There's so much innocence in her guilt . . ."

"Predestined, I said. It was her destiny. But what's predestined today is that we should go for a drive, and that's the really important thing. Because I need that dress far far more than you need the Tintoretto. And I was really a fool and an idiot to take it all in deadly earnest and to believe every word you said. You wanted the picture, *c'est tout.* And now farewell, my Prince of Denmark, my dreamer. To be or not to be . . . Variations by Ezechiel van der Straaten."

And she rose, laughing, and climbed the little trellicework staircase that led from van der Straaten's room to the bedroom on the second floor.

3

A LIVE-IN GUEST

It has already been said that van der Straaten oscillated between the earthy and the sentimental, between one extreme and the other. Thus it was hardly surprising that the conversation in front of the Tintoretto left no lasting echo in his heart. Nor indeed in that of his wife. It was only while it was going on that Melanie had been really taken aback—not because it was so much more personal than any previous conversation they had ever had. But now it was over. The picture hung in the gallery where no one saw it; and when van der Straaten happened to look at it he would smile with almost cheerful resignation. He had the fatalism of a humorist—a fatalism twice as strong if the humorist also happens to be a man of the world.

It had been a lively season. But although Easter was late, that too was past, and the time had come when they regularly brought up the question, When shall we move to the country?

"Soon," said Melanie who was already counting the days.

"But it's not even the middle of May, and we could still get one of those icy spells."

"They don't last long."

"All right," laughed van der Straaten. "And I'm all the more agreeable as it's the only way *I* can maintain my own rule. Up to a point, at least. But better a weak rule than none at all."

These words had been exchanged over breakfast on one of the last days of April. It was about noon when the commercial councillor sent word from his office asking his wife to postpone her drive for a quarter of an hour as he had something to tell her. Melanie sent back the reply that she would be pleased to see him and would count on his company for her drive.

Over the years the van der Straatens had fallen into the habit of such courtesies, not, however, without occasional lapses. Van der Straaten especially had made an effort because, as he would declare, "he owed the noble house of de Caparoux a degree of chivalry"; and the most important feature of this chivalry was punctuality and not keeping his wife waiting.

And so, soon after the announcement of his arrival, he appeared in her room.

It had the same proportions as his own, but it was much brighter and more cheerful, partly because there was no paneling, but mainly because it was not encumbered with pictures dark with age. There was one picture only: a full-length portrait of Melanie with a background of waving corn; she herself was in the act of fastening some poppies to her hat. The walls were hung with white silk, and the window bays were filled with potted hyacinths. In front of one of these, a graceful little marble-topped table supported a birdcage as clean and neat as a bandbox, containing a gray cockatoo. This was the real tyrant of the household, resented as much as it was envied by the servants. Melanie was talking to the bird when Ezechiel entered in a state of amused excitement. He bowed respectfully to the cockatoo before leading his wife to the sofa. Then he pulled up an armchair and sat down beside her.

He did all this with so much solemnity that Melanie began to laugh.

"You look as though you were preparing to make a very special confession. But I shall make it easy for you. Is it an old sin? Something from your murky past?"

"No, Lanni, it's something here and now."

"Well, in that case I had better wait and not be carried away into giving a general absolution. Tell me, what is it?"

"A mere trifle."

"Hardly, to judge by the fuss you're making."

"But it really is a trifle. We are about to receive a visitor, or rather a guest, or, if I may use the expression, a live-in guest. To cut a long story short, for it's no good beating about the bush: a new member of the household."

Melanie had been crumbling the chocolate cookie on the plate she was holding; now she put her index finger on van der Stratten's hand and said, "And you call that a trifle? You know very well it's a very serious matter. I don't have the advantage of being a native of this city, but I've been long enough in your exquisite midst to know what a live-in guest is. The word alone, which doesn't seem to exist anywhere else, is enough to make one anxious. And what is even a

live-in guest in comparison with a new member of the household . . . is it a lady?"

"No, a gentleman."

"A gentleman! Ezel, I beg of you . . ."

"He is a trainee, coming to learn the business, the eldest
son of a Frankfurt firm with whom I have friendly relations.
He's been in Paris and London—naturally—and he's just
come from New York to set up a new branch here. But first he
wants to learn the local customs, or rather to relearn them,
here in our firm, because he's half forgotten them after being
abroad. It's an act of particular trust. Besides, I'm under an
obligation to his father, and I beg you not to put me in an
embarrassing position. I thought we could give him the two
empty rooms on the lefthand passage."

"And force him to spend the summer looking at the
flagstones in our yard and Christel's potted geraniums?"

"We can't give more than we have. And he's the last
person to expect it. People who have traveled a lot are always
the ones to set the least store by things like that. It's true our
yard hasn't much to offer. But would he be better off at the
front of the house? A bit of church railing with a lilac bush
and the game stall on market days."

"*Eh bien,* Ezel, *faisons le jeu.* I hope there's nothing terrible lurking in the background, no conspiracies, no plans
that you're concealing from me. Because you are a very secre-
tive person. And if it doesn't spoil your secrets, then at least
I'd like to know the name of this new member of our
household."

"Ebenezer Rubehn."

"Ebenezer Rubehn," Melanie repeated, lingering on every
syllable. "I must confess that a Christian, Germanic sort of
name would have been more to my liking. Much more. As
though your being Ezechiel were not quite enough. And now
Ebenezer. Ebenezer Rubehn! I ask you, what is that *accent
grave* supposed to mean, that emphasis on the last syllable?
Suspect, highly suspect."

"I should explain he spells it with an *h.*"

"With an *h!* You don't expect me to believe that the *h* is
original and authentic? It's an interpolation, an attempt to

deny the facts, a deliberate smoke screen. I can see Jacob's twelve sons very clearly behind it. And him on the flank."

"And yet you're wrong, Lanni. What about Rubens? I mean the great Peter Paul? All right, he had an *s*. But an *h* is as good as an *s*. And anyway, he's been christened. Whether by a bishop or not is neither here nor there: I don't know, and I'd rather he hadn't, because I want to have at least one advantage over him. But seriously, you're doing him an injustice. He's not only a Christian, he's a Protestant like you and me. And if you still have doubts, let your eyes convince you."

Van der Straaten started to pull a visiting card with a photograph from a small yellow envelope that he had ready in his hand. But Melanie would not let him and said with increasing merriment, "Did you say New York? Did you say London? I was expecting a gentleman, a man of the world, and there he is sending you his photograph as though he were making an assignation. Krug's Garden Café, with an engagement in the offing."

"And yet he's perfectly innocent. Please believe me. I wanted to be sure, sure for your sake, and so I wrote to old Goeschen of Goeschen, Goldschmidt, and Company. He's a discreet old boy. That's where the photograph comes from. It's my fault, not his, really and truly, and even on my honor, if you will permit the expression."

Melanie took the envelope and glanced at the picture inside. Suddenly her expression changed. "Oh, he's not bad. Distinguished looking. An officer out of uniform or an embassy attaché. And even a little ribbon! Is that the *Légion d'honneur?*"

"No, closer to home. He was with the Fifth Dragoons and was decorated after Chartres and Poupry."

"Is that a battle you invented?"

"No. Anyone can make a mistake, and as a free-born native of Switzerland you ought to know that foreign languages don't always have much regard for one another's pronunciation. You see, Lanni, sometimes I'm better than my reputation."

"And when may we expect our new family friend?"

"New member of the household," corrected van der

Straaten. "Just because of his military status there's no need to rush his promotion. By the way, he's engaged, or as good as."

"What a pity."

"A pity? Why?"

"Because people who are engaged are nearly always bores. When they're together they're affectionate—oppressively so for everyone else; and when they're apart they're always writing letters or composing letters in their minds. And the husband-to-be is worse than the bride. And if one should feel like falling in love with him, one would have to ruin two lives."

"Two?"

"Yes, his and hers."

"I'd have counted three," laughed van der Straaten. I bet you'd forgotten the third altogether. Husbands don't count. And if they show surprise, that only makes them ridiculous. Well, far be it from me to whitewash you blackamoors. By the way, do you know the painting *The Moor's Bath?*"

"Oh Ezel, you know I don't know any paintings, and old ones least of all."

"Sweet simplicitas from the house of de Caparoux," said van der Straaten rejoicing. Nothing pleased him more than Melanie exposing a weakness, which sometimes, wisely, she did on purpose. "Old paintings? It's no older than I am."

"Well, in that case it's exactly the right age."

"Bravissimo. That's the way I like you. Full of fun and malice. And now tell me, what shall we do? Where shall we go gallivanting off to?"

"Please, Ezel, no Berlinisms. Only yesterday you . . ."

"And I'll keep my promise. It's just that when I'm happy it breaks out of me. And now come along, let's go to Haas and look at some carpets . . . 'exactly the right age'—excellent; excellent."

"And now tell me, Papa dear: who is the fairest in the land?"

"Melanie."

"And who's the sweetest, cleverest, best?"

"Melanie, Melanie."

"Right, right . . . and that's that; you're a good judge of people."

4

THE INNER CIRCLE

The notorious cold days in mid-May had been exceptionally severe, but not to the displeasure of the van der Straatens, who took it as a sign that winter had fired the last salvo and was unquestionably and irreversibly on the retreat. Now at last it was possible to go out without a care, without worrying about frosty mornings or, worse still, about being snowed in overnight. They all looked forward to the move, the children as well, but most of all van der Straaten himself, who said that "the only birth at which he liked to be present was the birth of spring." But, before leaving, they were to give a little farewell dinner just for the members of their innermost circle.

First among these—and actually more a relative than a friend—was Major Gryczinski from the Alsenstrasse, a young officer with stiff side whiskers curled à l'anglaise and intelligent blue eyes. Three years ago he had won the hand of the charming Jacobine de Caparoux, Melanie's younger sister—not as beautiful as Melanie, perhaps, but with red-gold hair which, in the opinion of some, restored the balance between the sisters. Gryczinski was a staff officer, and like all his fellows he was firmly convinced that no two colors were less alike than the ordinary Prussian military red on the one hand, and the red of the General Staff on the other. It goes without saying that he was a careerist; but, in deference to history, let it be said that despite his ambition he was capable, when not too sorely tempted, of showing a modest degree of consideration toward his fellow men; and that he did not regard the struggle for existence absolutely as though it were the crossing of the Beresina. Like his great chief,[8] he was a man of few words; but unlike him he wore a perpetual smile of encour-

agement for every speaker, letting it shine equally upon the
just and unjust, thereby sagely avoiding the necessity of taking sides.

Gryczinski, as has already been intimated, was more of a
relative than a friend. Among the latter the most distinguished was Baron Duquede, a retired Legation Counselor.
He was over sixty and had been a regular guest in the days of
van der Straaten's father, when the circle of habitués had
been more extensive. For various reasons, including his age,
he was permitted to give full rein to his most salient characteristic, which was to contradict, belittle, and denigrate.
This had earned him the nickname "Negation Counselor,"
but the nickname had done nothing to ameliorate his queru-
lous behavior. Everything was the object of his indignation,
Bismarck especially; since 1866, the year of his own retirement, he had never stopped declaring that the man "was
overrated." He was almost as indignant at the Berlin habit of
Frenchifying everything. His name—an ancient, aristocratic
Altmark name—had a q in it; just because of that, people
pronounced it analogously with the name of Admiral
Duquesne, and he himself was regarded as a member of the
French Colony, "which he might perfectly well put up with,"
Melanie had once remarked. Since that day a silent enmity
had reigned between them.

Next to the Legation Counselor in age and importance was
Police Councillor Reiff. He was a small, stout man with shiny
red cheekbones, a gourmet and raconteur. Butter would not
melt in his mouth while the ladies were at the table, but the
moment they disappeared, he would shine in the telling of
anecdotes that in number and content only a Police Councillor could muster. Even van der Straaten, with gifts of a similar kind, would applaud loudly, sometimes wildly, and give
his neighbors a wink as full of admiration as it was free from
envy.

The neighbors were usually two painters: Arnold Gabler, a
landscapist who, like Reiff and the Legation Counselor, was a
legacy from the days of van der Straaten's father; and Elimar
Schulze, a genre and portrait painter who had joined the

circle only in the last few years. Schulze's membership was based on the fact that only half of him was a painter; the other half was a musician and an enthusiastic Wagnerian. It was because of his claim to this "title," as van der Straaten put it, that Melanie had promoted and obtained his accession. On that occasion her husband had said that he "had no objection to the candidate if only he would change sides and openly and honestly acknowledge his allegiance to music as the one and only salvation." Elimar, always good-humored, had replied by asking "to be spared this step, simply because it would only lead to the exact opposite of the desired result. As things were, among painters he was generally considered a musician; but if he were to become a musician, he would certainly be thought a painter among musicians, and thereby be raised once more to what the Commercial Councillor considered the higher rank."

All the guests who had been invited for seven o'clock that evening belonged to this circle of friends and relatives. Van der Straaten liked to dine late, and he was given to quite witty remarks about the difference between artificial darkness at four o'clock and natural darkness at seven. Artificial four o'clock darkness was no better than a bottle of young wine that had been hung in the chimney and draped in cobwebs to make it appear old and mellow. But a delicate palate could taste the young wine and a delicate nervous system feel the young darkness. These remarks—especially the final words about the "delicate nervous system"—were always greeted with hearty laughter by Melanie.

Unlike the Tiergarten villa, which was equipped with every comfort, the van der Straaten's town house had no proper dining room. The two large and four small dinner parties they gave during the winter months took place in the anteroom of their large picture gallery. This part of the gallery overlapped from the right wing into the front part of the house. It lay directly behind Melanie's room; from which, as soon as the wide double doors were opened, the guests made their entrance.

Today, as always, van der Straaten took in his blonde

sister-in-law, Melanie followed on Duquede's arm, and the other four gentlemen followed in pairs. It was their traditional order, and the Major was as skillful in alternating between the two painters as he was at avoiding the Police Councillor. Although he was resigned and willing to submit night and day to Reiff's stories, he could not bring himself to offer his arm to him as to an equal. He was in full accord with the views of his profession and, with an emphasis strengthened by his personal feelings, held firmly to the old distinction between army and police.

All the guests were familiar with their surroundings and had no cause for astonishment or admiration. Anyone arriving for the first time, however, would certainly have been struck by the fact that the room in which they were dining was not really a dining room, and thus had a unique charm. An elaborate French bronze chandelier cast its light on a copy of Veronese's *Wedding Feast at Canaan* in a magnificent frame. The copy was by a good Italian hand, and anyone but a connoisseur might well take it for the original. It was flanked by two still lifes with even larger and more splendid baroque frames. Along with fruit and vegetables, the still lifes depicted lobsters, salmon, and blue mackerel. Their absolute truth to nature was vouched for by van der Straaten's definitive formula of admiration: "They make me feel as though I were crossing the Cölln fish market without my handkerchief."

The sideboard stood against the far wall, and a door beside it connected conveniently with the basement kitchen.

5

AT TABLE

"Let us sit down," said van der Straaten. "My wife has saved me the bother of seating you by writing out place cards."

And so saying, he picked up one of the cards and ran his

eye over it—a naturally good eye which had been improved by much looking at art. "Ah, very good. You've hit the nail on the head, Elimar. Charming, charming. Of course, it has to be Cupid with his bow. It is extraordinary the way you painters never get that eternal archer out of your systems."

"If you suppressed him or dismissed him from his post, we should have to make a solemn protest," said the reddish-blonde sister.

Meanwhile everyone had sat down, and it turned out that Melanie had deviated from the usual seating order. Van der Straaten sat between his wife and his sister-in-law, opposite him was the major flanked by Gabler and Elimar, and the ends of the table were occupied by Police Councillor Reiff and Legation Counselor Duquede.

The soup had just been served, and now it was time for the Montefiascone for which the house had long been famous. Van der Straaten addressed his brother-in-law across the table.

"Gryczinski, major and brother-in-law," he began lightly and with condescending familiarity, "three months from now we shall be at war. I beg of you, don't say no, don't contradict me. It's well known that you people who have to fight it are always the last to hear of it. In June the fat will be in the fire, or very nearly. It's one of the so-called legitimate peculiarities of Prussian policy to spoil the summer vacation for all Privy Councillors, and as far as the cure at Karlsbad and Teplitz is concerned, that includes Commercial Councillors as well. I repeat: in two months we shall have brought matters to the boil, and in three we shall have war. They'll end up by finding some sort of Benedetti, and an Ems can be found anywhere in the world."

Twirling the thickest part of his whiskers with his left hand Gryczinski said, "Brother-in-law, you are too much influenced by stock exchange gossip, not to say stock exchange speculation. I assure you that there is not the smallest cloud on the horizon, and if it's true that we are working on a war plan at this moment, then it's only to determine the hypothetical spot where Russia and England will clash and fight it out."

Both ladies were firm supporters of the peace party, the dark one because she did not want to lose her fortune, the fair one because she did not want to lose her husband. So they both cheered the speaker while the Police Councillor, growing humble, remarked: "I should like to express my loyal agreement with the major, with all my heart and soul." Here it must be said that he was fond of speaking of his soul. "Altogether," he continued, "nothing could be further from the truth than to represent His Highness, the Prince, a most peaceloving man, as a bombardier with his fuse permanently ablaze, ready to blast off a European war as though it were one of Krupp's giant guns. I repeat, nothing could be further from the truth. Gambling is for people who have nothing to lose, neither money nor reputation. The prince has both. I'll wager he doesn't feel like staking his pile of double winnings on the war card. He won in 1864 (only a negligible amount), doubled his winnings in 1866, and trebled them in 1870; but he will be careful not to get involved in a six-le-va. He is a well-read man and must know the story of the fisherman and his wife..."[9]

"...the spicy end of which I am sure our friend the Police Councillor will not withhold from us" remarked van der Straaten, whose own hospitality was beginning to go to his head.

But bowing to the ladies in guarantee of their safety, the Police Councillor dropped the fairy tale and its notorious final sentence and merely said, "Win all, lose all. And fortune is even more capricious than ladies. Yes, ladies: than ladies. For caprice—and I speak as a happily married man—is the privilege and charm of the fair sex. The prince has been lucky, but precisely because he has been lucky..."

"He'll take care not to push his luck," the Legation Counselor concluded ironically. "But supposing he did push it? What then? The prince has had some luck, so our friend assures us with the innocent demeanor of a Police Councillor. Luck indeed! I should say so! And not just plain ordinary luck, no, stupendous luck, luck such as has never been seen before. His luck is on such a colossal scale that it's likely to gobble up the man himself and swallow him. Not that I grudge him his luck: envy is foreign to my nature. All the same, it annoys me to see him worshiped as a hero just because of his luck. He's overrated, I say. Believe me, he's something of a plagiarist. There may be explanations, even excuses; but one thing remains certain: he's overrated. Yes, my friends, now he is worshiped as a hero, and soon he will be worshiped as a god. We already have statues and monuments to him, and soon it will be temples. And in every temple there'll be an effigy of him with the Goddess Fortuna at his feet. But they won't call it the temple of Fortuna. They'll call it the temple of Lady Luck, because it will be a gambling den, and our friend Reiff with his six-le-va has spoken truer than he knows, because that is what it will come to sooner or later. Everything's chance and luck, I say—no intellect, and above all no great creative ideas."

"But my dear Legation Counselor," interrupted van der Straaten, "there are just a few little details to take into account: the expulsion of Austria, the creation of the German State..."

"...the *écrasement* of France and the dethroning of the Pope. Pooh, van der Straaten, I know the whole litany. And whom do we have to thank for it, if indeed we have anything to be thankful for? *Whom?* A party that's hostile to him and to me—and he even stole their battle cry. He is a plagiarist, I say, he has simply appropriated other people's ideas, good and bad alike, and then, with the lavish means at his disposal, he has put them into practice. Any one of us could have done it, anyone—Gabler, Elimar, you, I. Reiff..."

"I really must protest..."

"Put them into practice," repeated Duquede. "It's a form of exchange, of barter. I detest it when the underlying ideas are not a man's own. But action without any underlying idea, or with hypocritical or borrowed ideas—that sort of action has something crude and brutal about it, no better than Genghis Khan. And I repeat, I detest it. But what I hate even more is when they muddle up their concepts and mix opposites together; and we have to stand by and watch the venerable conventions of our conservative principles used as a mask to hide revolutionary radicalism. I tell you, van der Straaten, he's sailing under a false flag. And one of his most effective maneuvers is to keep changing flags. But I can see through him, and I know what his real flag is . . ."

"All right, then, name it!"

"The black flag!"

"The pirate flag?"

"Yes. And sooner or later you will all realize it. I tell you, van der Straaten, and you, Elimar; and you, Reiff, you can put it down in your black book tomorrow if you like. Because I'm a gentleman from the Altmark, and I gave up serving that repulsive egotist many years ago, and I tell everyone, young and old: watch out! I'm warning you! You are being deceived, and above all I warn you not to overrate that false knight, that templar of Lady Luck. The idiot populace believe in him because he's driven out the Jesuits. So what? We may be rid of those devils, but the Devil himself remains."

Gryczinski had listened with a well-bred smile. As for van der Straaten, though really an ardent admirer of Bismarck, he was a typical Berliner with a passion for finding fault and he knew no greater pleasure than to see the mighty fallen and a general leveling all around, provided he himself was left standing like a lone mountain. So he nodded to Duquede and called on the servant to offer the Legation Counselor a second helping of the last dish because he had just been sacrificing himself.

"A Spanish onion, Duquede. Please have one. It's just the thing for you. Sharp and pungent. I'm not very keen on Spain. But there are two things I do envy them: their onions and their Murillo."

"I'm surprised," said Gabler. "And what surprises me most is what you just let slip about admiring Murillo—which must mean admiring the Madonna."

"I didn't let that slip, Arnold, not at all. You know, or you ought to know, that I make a distinction between cold and warm Madonnas. It's true I detest cold ones, but that only makes me like the warm ones all the more: *A la bonne heure:* they intoxicate me, like 1811 hock. And along with all those glowing and sparkling Madonnas I include all the Spanish Immaculatas and Concepciones where the Virgin stands on a

half moon in a dark cloak with golden clouds and angels' heads
shining all around her. Yes, Reiff, such things exist. And
there she is, passionately—or perhaps we'd better say
fervently—gazing toward heaven as though her soul were
hatching in an incubator of sanctity."

"An incubator of sanctity," said the Police Councillor, his
eyes secretly beginning to twinkle. "An incubator. Oh, that's
really *magnifique*, superb, an idea we can all interpret and pur-
sue, each according to his degree of enlightenment."

Both young women were somewhat surprised to see their
normally reticent friend balancing on this knife's edge. Their
eyes met, and Melanie quickly realized that at any moment
they might face one of those catastrophes not altogether un-
common at the Commercial Councillor's dinners. The important thing was to get away from the ticklish subject of Murillo,
and, given van der Straaten's obstinacy, this could only be
accomplished by a skillful diversion. She managed to create
one, for the moment at any rate, by remarking with apparent
innocence: "Van der Straaten will laugh at me for presuming
to have an opinion about paintings and painters. But I must
be frank with him: if his daring definition of Madonnas is
acceptable at all, I myself should opt for the middle group of
temperate Madonnas, which he has completely disregarded.
Titian's Madonnas seem to me to have an agreeable, moderate temperature. Altogether, Titian is the painter for me."

"Me too, Melanie. Well said, well said. I've always said I'll
make an art historian of you yet. Haven't I, Arnold? Go on,
confirm it. We haven't got a Bible to swear on, but we've got
Reiff, and a Police Councillor is as good as a gospel. You're
laughing, brother-in-law. Naturally. You would. You don't
notice the police, but we do. By the way, Reiff's glass is
empty. And so is Elimar's. Friedrich, you old dunderhead,
don't just stand there lost in thoughts of love. *Allons enfants.*
What's happened to the Moët? Come on, come on. I don't
like to have my champagne postponed until the last five
minutes. That's a wretched way of showing off one's hospitality. And especially in these damned tapering glasses. One of
these days they're going to get short shrift from me. Glasses
like that are for accountants, not commercial councillors.

You're wrong about Titian, by the way. Or half wrong anyway. He's good at lots of things, but not Madonnas. Venus is
what he's good at. That's his cup of tea. Flesh, flesh. And
there's always a dear little archer hiding somewhere. You
must forgive me, Elimar, I'm not keen on Cupids en masse
on place cards; but a single Cupid is another matter, especially the one in Titian with the red couch and the green
damask curtain drawn back. Yes, ladies and gentlemen,
that's where he belongs, and wherever he sits he's enchanting—at her head or her feet, peering from behind the bed
or the curtain, drawing his bow or just after he's shot his
arrow. Which is the best pose for him? An interesting question, Reiff. I think when he's drawing his bow. And that left
hand in repose, holding the everlasting lace handkerchief.
Oh, superb. Yes, Melanie, we'll celebrate your conversion to
art on the day you admit: *suum cuique*, to Titian his Venus and
to Murillo his Madonna."

"Then I'm afraid you'll have to wait a long time, van der
Straaten, especially for my conversion to Murillo. Because I
think it's creepy, that yellow vapor with all that fervent faith
floating up through it in a state of physical and spiritual
ecstasy. It's not magic, it's witchcraft."

Gryczinski discreetly nodded to his sister-in-law, while
Elimar raised his glass and asked permission to toast the
lovely and amiable lady of the house who had just spoken as
a true sample of German womanhood (French womanhood,
van der Straaten shouted). And they all clinked glasses. But a
sharp ear could have detected a certain tremor and discord in
that harmony, and before the smile had faded from every face
(it lasted longest on the Police Councillor's) van der Straaten
once more broke through all the carefully erected barriers and
started up again in his own particular manner. He was not, he
said, in a position to join his friend Elimar Schulze (he laid ironic
emphasis on both Christian name and surname) in agreeing
with his wife, precious though his friend's agreement might
be to the lady. There was, of course, a difference between
magic and witchcraft, but there was much magic in the world
that was held to be witchcraft, and even more witchcraft that
was held to be magic. And he begged leave to say that he for

his part always stuck to his guns and stood up for his opinions, not saying one thing one day and another the next. What he couldn't endure were double standards.

He paused for a moment, and indeed might have been content to leave it at those generalities. But young Gryczinska, presuming on the latitude allowed to sisters-in-law, found her courage reawakening. She looked at van der Straaten with pert assurance and invited him to pass from his oracular utterances to something more explicit.

"Oh, certainly," said van der Straaten with mounting warmth. "Oh, certainly, my dearly beloved redhead. I am at your orders, and I shall leave the sphere of the oracular and miraculous and blow my trumpet so loud that you will all awaken from your twilight—your twilight of the gods, if you like—as if a fire engine were passing."

"Aha," said Melanie, growing heated in her turn, "so that's what's coming."

"Yes, my sweet angel, that's what's coming, just that. You're proud and complacent and you set yourselves up on the summit of all the arts and move through the skies like a pure *casta diva*, as though you lived on ozone and chastity. And *who* is your idol? That knight of Bayreuth,[10] that sorcerer of sorcerers. And you stake the salvation of your souls on that Tannhäuser and Venusberg fellow as though you were all Voggenhubers at the very least,[11] and you sing and play the stuff morning, noon, and night. Or three times a day as it says on your pill boxes. And your Elimar is in the thick of it. And his everlasting velvet jacket won't save him either. Neither him nor you. Or are you going to dish that stuff up to me as heavenly magic? It's rotten magic, I tell you. And that's why I talked of double standards. You'd label Murillo's magic witchcraft, and Wagner's witchcraft you'd turn into magic. But I tell you, its the other way round, and if it's *not* the other way round, at least I won't have you making distinctions. For after all, it's really all the same and—begging your pardon—there's nothing to choose between a jacket and a pair of . . ."

He actually pronounced the last word of this typically Berlin sartorial comparison, but it was submerged in the noise of a skillful attack by the major, who managed to clink his glass and scrape his chair. At the same time he began: "My dear friends, we have heard the word sorcerer. An excellent word. So let's drink to them all, all these Tannhäusers, and what we think of them is our own business. I drink the health of all sorcerers. All art is sorcery. Don't let's quibble about the word. What are words? Sound and fury. Let's touch glasses. To sorcerers!"

Everyone joined in with a conscious, well-intentioned effort, this time without the slightest tremor; the two painters showed particular enthusiasm, and there was almost no one who did not believe that the danger had been successfully averted. But they were mistaken. Van der Straaten was a man without education, and perhaps it was because he was well aware of his deficiencies that he could not bear to have attention drawn to his bad behavior. He would completely forget himself, and the arrogance of a rich man—a rich man who was always helping others—would go to his head and engulf him. And that is what happened on this occasion. He rose and said: "Cutting down to size is a wonderful thing. I, for instance, cut out coupons. An inferior business, perhaps, but nevertheless under certain circumstances it gives a man the right not to have his words and remarks cut out, especially by people whose intention is to reprimand and educate. I am quite sufficiently educated.

His voice trembled as he spoke, but he continued to look hard at the major through narrowed eyes. The major, a man of the world, smiled to himself and cast a discreet glance at the ladies to indicate that they might now calm down. Then he raised his glass a second time and, effortlessly assuming a cheerful expression, said to van der Straaten, "There's been a lot of talk about cutting. Let's cut that too. I live in the firm conviction that . . ."

At that very moment a cork popped out of a bottle in the wine cooler; Gryczinski quickly saw the advantage he could draw from this circumstance. He broke off in the middle of his sentence and, bowing slightly as he filled his brother-in-law's glass, he said: "Peace, good pint-pot."

Van der Straaten was the last person to resist such an

appeal. "My dear Gryczinski," he said with suddenly awakening sentimentality, "we understand one another, we always have. Lacrimae Christi, Friedrich, quickly. The best thing about it is the name, I'm afraid. Still, that's the name it's got. To each his own; some have this and others have that."

"Too true," Gabler laughed.

"Oh Arnold, you overrate that. Believe me, our Lord was right. Gold is only a chimera.[12] And Elimar would agree with me if it didn't happen to be a line from an unfashionable opera. I must say, I'm sorry it's out of fashion. I'm fond of dancing nuns. But here comes the bottle. Never mind about the dust and the cobwebs. Just leave it in all its unscrubbed holiness. Lacrimae Christi. What a name!"

And their former cheerfulness returned, or at least appeared to return. Van der Straaten continued his monstrous talk about Christ's tears, the blood of the Redeemer, the wine of forgiveness, until at last Melanie was emboldened to say: "You forget, Ezel, the Police Councillor is a Catholic."

"Oh, please," said Reiff, as though he had been caught in some forbidden act.

But van der Straaten swore by all that was holiest that forty years of faithful service in the interests of public security outweighed any advantages or disadvantages of religious persuasion and would certainly be taken into account before the Judgment Seat. The glasses were refilled and emptied, and soon Melanie pushed back her chair and they rose to take coffee in the next room.

6

ON THE WAY HOME

Coffee was taken without any incident, and it was almost ten o'clock when the servant announced the carriage. The announcement was for the benefit of the Gryczinskis; on dinner party nights they regularly had the use of the Commercial

Councillor's horses. Coats and hats were brought in, and the
lovely Jacobine, her head and neck swathed in a white lace
shawl, stood smiling in the midst of the circle, patiently
waiting for the two painters to whom at the very last moment
Gryczinski had offered a lift. The arguments about this
seemed never-ending, and it was not until they were standing by the carriage that a decision was reached. Without
further argument Gabler took the backward-facing seat, while
Elimar hoisted himself up onto the box with an athletic swing;
he affected to choose this place out of consideration for the
passengers inside, but it was really for the sake of his own
convenience and curiosity. The truth was, he longed for a
conversation with the coachman.

He too was a legacy from the days of old van der Straaten,
and he bore the uncoachmanlike name of Emil. But that had
long since been adapted to his circumstances and shortened
to the Low German Ehm. There was the more reason for this
as he had first seen the light of day in the Fritz Reuter[13]
country and had conserved some of his native dialect
alongside his Berlin patois. Elimar was one his favorites, and,
even as he settled into his place, the painter took out a leather
case with several compartments and slipped one of the
uppermost cigars to the old man. "For the return journey,
Ehm," he said confidentially.

Ehm raised his right hand to his coachman's hat in token of
gratitude, and that concluded the preliminaries.

They soon passed the clock on the Spittelmarkt and turned
off into one of the badly paved side streets. Elimar, judging
the time to be ripe, at last asked,

"Well, has the new gentleman arrived?"

"The one from Frankfurt? Not yet, Herr Schulze."

"Well, it won't be long."

"Sure won't. Some time next week, I guess. An' they've
done up all the rooms too. Heavens, they're carrying on as if
he was a prince, first him and now her too. And Christel
thinks he's one of them Jewish ones."

"But a rich one. And an officer. With the Reserve or something."

"Well, I never."

"And they say he can sing."

"Yeah, I'm sure he can do that."

Elimar was sufficiently vain to take exception to this last remark. As it happened, the carriage now turned through the Wallstrasse Gate and into the Opera Square, which lay quiet in the late evening; so he stopped the conversation all the more readily as he did not want the passengers inside the carriage to overhear it.

They, meanwhile, had not yet exchanged a single word—not from ill humor, but out of consideration for the young woman. Glad that more than half the backward-facing seat had remained empty, she had planted her little feet on the upholstery and was leaning back comfortably in the depths of the carriage. She had appeared tired from the moment they got in, and had seemed to excuse herself by mentioning champagne and a headache, pulling her lace shawl around her and closing her eyes. She did not sit up again until they were passing between the palace and the statue of Frederick the Great; she was one of those ultraroyalists who are happy if they see so much as a shadow silhouetted against the curtains of the corner window. That is what she saw now, and she expressed her delight in her own charming, half childlike and half coquettish manner.

She was still prattling on when the carriage stopped at the Brandenburg Gate. This was where the two painters' route diverged; they were down from their seats in a flash and thanked the amiable couple, who now continued their journey along the wide boulevard that cut diagonally through the park toward the Victory Column and the Alsenstrasse behind it.

When they were in the middle of the brightly lit square, the lovely young woman nestled fondly against her husband and said, "What a day that was, Otto. I did admire you."

"It wasn't as hard for me as you think. I just play with him. He's just an old child."

"And Melanie! She feels it, you know. And I'm sorry for her. You're smiling? Aren't you sorry for her?"

"Yes and no, *ma chère*. Nothing in the world comes free. She has her summer villa and her picture gallery..."

"Which she doesn't care for. You know how little it means to her."

"And she has two charming children..."

"For which I almost envy her."

"There you are," laughed the major. "We all have to learn the art of making do with what we have. If I were my brother-in-law, I should say..."

But she closed his mouth with a kiss, and the next moment the carriage drew to a halt.

The two dignitaries—Police Councillor and Legation Counselor—had taken a cab from the corner of the Petristrasse to the Potsdam Gate. From there they intended to walk the rest of the way for the sake of the fresh evening air. But the truth was that they both believed in the maxim that one must make small economies in order to be able to live up to great occasions; the trouble was that, in their case, either the great occasions had never come or they had missed them.

Not a single word had been exchanged during the journey; but now it became necessary to divide six by two: the ensuing conversation appeared to satisfy all parties except the cab-driver. Both councillors therefore took care not to look back, especially Duquede, who was, in any case, the sworn enemy of all busy crossings with railway lines and horse tram bells; and he only relaxed when they reached the Bellevuestrasse, where all the trees were already in bud.

Reiff followed him and then politely and respectfully intercalated himself on the Legation Counselor's left. Suddenly he said, quite out of the blue:

"That was quite an unpleasant affair again today. Don't you agree? And quite honestly, I don't understand him. He's over fifty now, and the edges ought to have rubbed off him. But he's a maverick and always will be."

"Yes," said Duquede, stopping for a moment to catch his breath. "He is a bit of a maverick. But, my dear friend, why shouldn't he be? I reckon he's worth a million, not counting his pictures, and I don't see why a man in his own house and at his own table shouldn't speak as he feels. I confess, Reiff, I'm always delighted when he lets fly like that. The old man was just the same, only worse, and forty years ago people used to say, 'It's a strange sort of house, and it's really impossible to go there.' But impossible or not, everyone did go. That's how it was and still is."

"But he really is a bit short on culture and education."

"For goodness' sake, Reiff, don't start in about culture and education. Those are two completely new-fangled words. The 'great man'[14] himself might have invented them, I detest them so. First of all, there's usually nothing much to them, and even if there is—well, what then? Believe me, they're overrated. But only by people like us. You know why? Because we've nothing better. People who don't have anything else have to be cultured. But if you've got what van der Straaten has, then you don't need all that nonsense. He has a good head and good wits and, what's more, his credit's good. Culture, culture. It's ridiculous."

"I'm not so sure you're right, Duquede. If everything were still as it used to be, fine. A bachelor establishment. But now he's married this young woman—young, and beautiful, and intelligent . . ."

"Come, come, Reiff. Let's not exaggerate. She's not as special as all that. She's a foreigner, from French Switzerland, and Berliners always go crazy about anything foreign. That goes without saying. She's got a bit of Geneva chic. But what does it all add up to? Everything from Geneva is secondhand for a start. And you say she's intelligent. I ask you, what do you mean by intelligent? He's far more intelligent. Or do you suppose it's a matter of the odd French word? Or knowing the *Erlkönig?*[15] I admit she's got some pretty ways, and under certain conditions she can create quite an impression. But there's nothing much to it; all fiddle faddle. Enormously overrated."

"I'm still not sure that you're right," repeated the Police Councillor. "After all, she's from a good family."

Duquede laughed. "No, Reiff, that's just what she's not.

And I can tell you, it's no joking matter with me. Caparoux. It *sounds* all right. Granted. But after all, what does it mean? Red cap or Little Red Riding Hood. It's a name out of a fairy tale—not an aristocratic name. I've taken the trouble to look it up. Just between you and me, Reiff, there is no such thing as Caparoux."

"But what about the major? He has every sort of pride, and surely he's not a man to let people say he's made a misalliance?"

"I know him better. He's a climber. Or let's just say he's a General Staff man. I hate the whole lot of them, and, believe me, Reiff, I have my reasons. Our General Staff is overrated, enormously overrated."

"I'm still not sure you're right," the Police Councillor ventured for the third time. "Just remember what Stoffel said.[16] And he turned out to be right. But let's get back to Gryczinski. How charmingly he behaved tonight. Charming and well-bred."

"Pooh, well-bred. I imagine I too can recognize good breeding when I see it. And I tell you, Reiff, good breeding is quite different. Well-bred. He's cunning, that's all. Or do you suppose he married that little redhead with her swoony eyes because she was called Caparoux—or even de Caparoux, if you insist? He married her because she is her sister's sister. Good heavens—I'm surprised I should have to explain such things to a Police Councillor."

The Police Councillor, whose weaknesses tended to be of an erotic nature, took Duquede's words to imply an amatory relationship between Melanie and the major, and he threw a startled sidelong glance at his tall, lean companion.

But Duquede laughed and said, "No, Reiff, not that, not that. But careerism and flirtation always go hand in hand. That's all. There are people nowadays—and that's another thing we owe to that great architect of the state who casts decent, solid workmen aside—there are people nowadays, I say, who regard everything as a means to an end. Even love. That's the kind of person our friend the major is. I should have said that he married that little thing not because she's her sister's sister but because she's her brother-in-law's sister-in-law. He needs that brother-in-law, and I tell you, Reiff—because I know the climate and the current trends in high places—there are few better recommendations up there. A brother-in-law who's a commercial councillor rates almost as high as a father-in-law who's a commercial councillor. And whatever they say, commercial councillors are gilt-edged; you can always draw on them. You're never without cover."

"So you mean to say..."

"I don't mean to say anything, Reiff. I merely think my thoughts."

With that, however, they had reached the Bendlerstrasse, where they parted. Reiff walked toward the von der Heydt Bridge, while Duquede continued straight on.

Duquede lived near the Hofjägerallee, on a high floor, but it was a first-class address.

7

EBENEZER RUBEHN

A few days later Melanie left the house in the city and moved into the Tiergarten villa. Van der Straaten did not accompany her. Much as he loved the villa, he never moved in permanently until September. Even then it was only because his passion for the orchard exceeded even his passion for collecting paintings. Until September he paid a visit every third day only, assuring anyone who would listen that this was his way of recouping his honeymoon on an hourly basis. Melanie was careful not to contradict; on the contrary, she was all amiability, and on the intervening days she relished the joy of liberty. This joy was much greater than might have been supposed from her position, which appeared to be so dominant and so free. For her supremacy depended on self-control, and to be free of this restraint was her constant secret desire. That desire was fulfilled during the summer days. Then she was free from her husband's demonstrations of affection as well as from his unbridled conversation: and the knowledge of it filled her with a sense of infinite well-being.

Her well-being was increased by the enchanting and almost uninterrupted peacefulness of her life. It is true she loved the city and society and the great world. But when the swallows began to twitter, and the lilac to come into bud, she longed for the solitude of the park; although it was not really solitude, because besides nature—whose language she understood—she had books and music, and, best of all, she had the children. During the season she sometimes never saw them for days at a time, but at the villa she took the keenest interest in their development and their studies. She herself helped them with their languages, especially French, and went through their atlas and history books with them. And she managed to attach a story to every fact and to make it stick in the children's memory. For she was intelligent and possessed the gift of making everything she spoke of clear and vivid for her listeners.

They were quiet days of happiness.

Still the days might have been too quiet if the deepest need of the feminine character—the need for conversation—had remained unfulfilled. But even that need was catered to. Like all wealthy families, the van der Straatens had a retinue of very old and not quite so old ladies who received presents at Christmas and invitations to coffee parties and country outings throughout the year. There were seven or eight of them, but two enjoyed a particularly intimate position: Fräulein Friederike von Sawatzki, tiny and slightly misshapen; and a piano and singing teacher, Anastasia Schmidt, who was a fine tall figure of a woman. On account of their especially privileged position, every Easter Monday van der Straaten himself would ask them whether they felt able to make up their minds to keep his wife company at the villa during the summer months: a question which was always answered with a bow and a cordial yes. But not too cordial, because it would not have done to reveal that the question had been expected.

So this year as always the two ladies had once again been installed as *dames d'honneur:* they appeared on the veranda

every morning toward nine o'clock to breakfast with the children, and at twelve to lunch with Melanie.

Today was no exception.

It must have been nearly one o'clock, and luncheon was
over. But the table had not yet been cleared. All the doors and
windows stood open, intensifying the light breeze, which
stirred the red patterned tablecloth. From the far end of the
passage came the sound of a piece from Cramer's piano
studies: Fräulein Anastasia was endeavoring to correct the
faulty beat: "One, two; one, two." But no one paid any attention to her efforts, least of all Melanie, who was sitting in a
garden chair beside Fräulein Riekchen, as she was usually
called. From time to time she would look up from her
needlework in order to enjoy the full effect of the charming
park landscape immediately about her, familiar though she
was with every detail of it.

It was surely the prettiest spot in the whole park, for
ninety-nine out of every hundred visitors who came to the
place were content to judge the park from this position. At
the end of the main avenue, between the trees just coming
into leaf, the river glinted and shimmered. Lawns were scattered all about, each with an aloe, or a small clump of bushes,
or a glass ball or stone basin in the center. In one of the
smaller basins a little fountain splashed, while a peacock sat
on the rim of the largest, soaking up the midday sun in its
feathers. Doves and peahens had come right up to the veranda, where Riekchen was scattering crumbs for them.

"You will get them too used to this place," said Melanie,
"and we shall have a war with van der Straaten on our
hands."

"I'll take him on," said the little creature.

"Yes, at least you are the only one who could risk it. And
really, Riekchen, I shall be getting quite jealous, he favors you
so much. I believe you are the only person who can say what
they like to him, and so far as I know he's never lost his
temper with you. Do you think it's because he's impressed
with your ancient lineage? Just tell me your full name· and
title. I love to hear it but I always forget it again."

"Aloysia Friederike Sawat von Sawatzki, known as Sattler

von der Hölle,[17] Candidate Canoness of the Convent of Himmelpfort[18] in the Uckermark."

"Beautiful," said Melanie. "How I wish I had a name like that. Believe me, Riekchen, that's what impresses him."

All this was said with affectionate gaiety, and taken in the same spirit by Riekchen. But now she moved her chair closer to Melanie's and took the young woman's hand: "I ought to be cross with you for making fun of me. But who could be cross with you?"

"I'm not making fun of you," said Melanie. "You must have seen for yourself that he treats you more politely and considerately than anyone else."

"Yes," the poor Fräulein said, her voice trembling with emotion. "He treats me well because he has a kind heart, much kinder than many people think, even you, perhaps, Melanie. And he's not so inconsiderate. It's just that he can't bear being put out or provoked—at least by people who really ought not to do it and have no right to. You see, child, that's when he doesn't control himself—not because he can't but because he doesn't want to. And why should he want to? He's rich, and rich people get to know the worst side of other people. Everyone comes rushing up to them, first to kowtow and then to be ungrateful. And being at the receiving end of ingratitude is a bad school for tenderness and love. And that's why the rich lose their faith in noble-mindedness and honesty. But I tell you, and I must keep telling you, your van der Straaten is better than many people think, even than you think yourself."

There was a short pause, not entirely without embarrassment. Then Melanie nodded encouragingly to the old Fräulein and said, "Please go on talking. I love listening when you talk like that."

"Yes, and so I shall. You see, I've already told you, he treats me well because he has a kind heart. But that's not all. He is so gentle to me because he is compassionate. And compassion is far more than mere kindness—it's really the greatest quality a human being can have. And *he* laughs too when he hears my long name, just as you do; but I like it when he laughs like that, because I can hear perfectly well what he's thinking and feeling when he does it."

"And what is he feeling?"

"He feels the contrast between the claims of my name and what I am: poor and old and lonely, and really just a little pocket-sized toy object. And when I say toy object, I'm really being euphemistic and flattering myself."

Melanie had put her cambric handkerchief to her eyes. "You are right," she said. "You are always right. But where can Anastasia be? The lesson seems to have no end. She goes on too much at Liddy, and she will finish by turning the child against it. And that'll be the end. Because nothing in the world is any good unless your heart's in it. Not even music . . . But there's Teichgräber coming to announce a visitor. How irritating. I should much rather have gone on chatting with you."

The old park keeper, after looking about in vain for a member of the household staff, had come up to the veranda and handed over a card.

Melanie read, "'Ebenezer Rubehn (representing Jacob Rubehn and Sons), Lieutenant of the Reserve in the Fifth Dragoons . . .' Oh yes, of course. Ask him to come in." As the old man walked away, Melanie turned to Riekchen in high good humor: "Another one! And in the Reserve, too. I can't stand them, these everlasting lieutenants. There simply aren't any plain human beings left."

These observations would doubtless have continued had it not been for the crunch of steps on the gravel path, which left no doubt about the rapid approach of the visitor. The next moment the new arrival was standing before the veranda and bowing to the two ladies.

Melanie had risen and taken a step toward him. "I am glad to see you. First of all, allow me to introduce my dear friend and companion . . . Herr Ebenezer Rubehn, Fräulein Friederike von Sawatzki."

A look of surprise flitted across Rubehn's face, more, if Melanie's interpretation was correct, on account of Riekchen than on her own. But Ebenezer was man of the world enough quickly to master his surprise. With a second bow to Melanie's friend, he apologized for having put off his visit to the villa until today.

Melanie passed lightly over the apology and countered by asking her visitor to forgive his rural reception and to overlook the uncleared table. "*Mais à la guerre comme à la guerre*—a warlike expression, but I've no intention of starting a serious conversation about war."

"In fact you're trying to make sure there won't be any such conversation under any circumstances whatever," laughed Rubehn. "But never fear. I know ladies have no enthusiasm for the subject unless it's a question of nursing the wounded. The moment the last patient has left the military hospital, all their warlike feelings evaporate. And as women are always right about everything, so they are about that. There is nothing sadder than to have to keep listening to stories of dubious interest and even more dubious veracity on the subject of thoroughly mediocre acts of heroism; but on the other hand nothing in the world is more worthwhile than helping and healing."

As he spoke, Melanie had put down her needlework and looked at him with frank encouragement. "Oh, how right you are. But someone who speaks so warmly about hospital service and helping and healing, and how well it all suits us women—well, he must have experienced the benefits of it himself. And so there you are, telling me your secrets in the first five minutes in spite of yourself. Don't try to contradict me; you won't succeed. And since you seem to know so much about the female heart, you must know our two strongest suits: obstinacy and guessing. We can guess anything..."

"And do you always guess right?"

"Not always, but more often than not. And now tell me how you like our fair city, and our house, and whether you have enough self-confidence to think you can live in your backyard dungeon—which really only lacks bars over the window—without falling into melancholia. But it was all we had. And you can't make a silk purse, as the saying goes..."

"Oh, you shame me, dear lady. And it's only now that I'm here that I realize what a sacrifice you've made for my sake. And I really feel entitled to say, now that I know . . ."

But he did not finish the sentence and suddenly listened in the direction of the house. The music lesson had stopped some time earlier, and now there came the sound of accomplished playing, with every nuance clearly audible. It was *Wotan's Farewell*, and Rubehn appeared so enchanted that he found it difficult to tear himself away and resume the conversation. At last, however, he pulled himself together, and with another bow to Riekchen he said: "I beg your pardon, ma'am. Did I catch the name properly? Fräulein von Sawatzki?"

The Fräulein nodded.

"I spent a summer in Wildbad-Gastein with a young officer of that name. Immediately after the war. A very charming young man. Could he be a relative . . . ?"

"A cousin," said Fräulein Riekchen. "There are only a few people of that name, and we're all related. I am glad to hear of him through you. He was wounded right at the end of the war, on the last day. And very seriously. I have not heard from him for a long time. Is he recovered?"

"I think I may say: completely. He is back with his regiment—a fact which by a happy coincidence I can confirm from my own recent experience . . . But we shall have to drop the subject, Fräulein von Sawatzki. Frau van der Straaten is already smiling and admiring the skill with which I have used your cousin to try and get back to the topic of war and its consequences. So I suggest we listen to that wonderful playing . . . oh, what a pity it's stopping."

He fell silent. But when no further sound came from the house, he continued with an emphasis normally foreign to him but now completely sincere: "Oh, Frau van der Straaten, what an enchanted garden you live in! A peacock sunning itself, and so many doves and so tame . . . as though this veranda were Saint Mark's Square or the island of Cyprus itself! And the fountain playing, and now that aria . . . truly, if it were not that even the sincerest admiration can be out of place and importunate . . ."

He interrupted himself, for just then there was a sound of footsteps from the passage. Half turning, Melanie said: "Ah, Anastasia! You've come at exactly the right moment! Our dear new house guest has just been expressing his gratitude and admiration, and now you can receive his compliments in person. Allow me to introduce you: Herr Ebenezer Rubehn, Fräulein Anastasia Schmidt... And this is my daughter Lydia," Melanie added, pointing to the beautiful child who had paused in the doorway beside the music teacher and was examining the stranger with a solemn, almost hostile expression.

Rubehn noticed the look. But she was a child, and so he turned without further ado to Anastasia and began to say flattering things to her about her playing and the direction of her musical taste.

Anastasia bowed, and Melanie, who had not missed a word, continued with great vivacity, "Well, if I have understood you, we may count you as one of ourselves? Anastasia, what a piece of luck! You must realize, Herr Rubehn, that we occupy two camps here, and that the house of van der Straaten, which will now be your house too, is divided into picture-loving Montecchi and music-worshiping Capuletti. As for me, I'm *tout à fait* Capulet and Juliet. But without the tragic ending. And I must add, for good measure, that we— Anastasia and I—belong to that little community whose name and focus I don't even need to mention. There is just one thing I want to know straight away; and I consider curiosity to be one of my feminine privileges: to which of his works do you award the crown? Which shows him at his most remarkable or, at heart, at his most individual?"

"The *Meistersinger*."

"Granted. And now we are agreed, and at the next opportunity we can blow van der Straaten and Gabler and especially that long and long-winded Legation Counselor right up into the air. That lanky Duquede. Oh, he'll go up like a rocket. Won't he, Anastasia?"

Rubehn had picked up his hat. But Melanie was unusually delighted and stimulated by the whole meeting, and she continued with growing enthusiasm, "They are all just names to you now. But in another week or two you will have got to know the whole of our little world. I should not like you to put off the opportunity. For today the veranda has had to do the honors of the house. But remember, we have a grand piano. Soon—and often—you must try it out. Au revoir."

He kissed the beautiful lady's hand, bowed gravely to Riekchen and Anastasia, and left. Lydia he did not notice.

But she noticed him.

"You're looking after him," said Melanie. "Did you like him?"

"No."

Everyone laughed. But Lydia went back into the house, and there were tears in her large eyes.

8

ON THE STRALOW MEADOW

Weeks had passed since Rubehn's first visit, and the favorable impression he had made remained on a rising course, like the barometer. Every second or third day he would appear with van der Straaten, and van der Straaten himself shared the general liking for the new member of the household and never forgot to offer him a place in his high-wheeled gig when he was driving out of town. All through those weeks a cloudless sky hung over the villa, which was filled with more laughter and conversation, more gossip and music than for many a long time. Van der Straaten himself, of course, could not reconcile himself to all the music making even now, and was given to wishing "they would all join the Flying Dutchman's crew"; but in his heart of hearts he was more pleased with the "pretentious noise" than he cared to admit, because the Wagner cult gave him an inexhaustible supply of fresh material for his favorite form of conversation. Siegfried and

Brünnhilde, Tristan and Isolde—what a profitable arena! And sometimes when he set his charger full tilt at these targets it was doubtful who derived more pleasure from the music—the group around the piano or van der Straaten in his exhilaration.

Summer was almost past its height when, one splendid August afternoon, van der Straaten proposed that they should make an excursion by land and river. "Rubehn has been roughly three months in our city now, and he has only seen what lies between the counting house and the villa. It's time he got to know our lakes and shores, marvels of nature that put all the inflated splendors of the Rhine and Main to shame. Treptow and Stralow, then, and quickly too. For in a week we shall have the Stralow run of fishes, which in itself, of course, is a bonny feast of Maying, but a bit rough and not particularly good for meadows and lawns. And so I suggest an outing tomorrow afternoon. Agreed?"

His speech was greeted joyfully. Melanie jumped up to give him a kiss, and Fräulein Riekchen related how it was exactly thirty-three years since she had last been to Treptow, to one of the Dobremonts' big fireworks parties—the very same Dobremont who later blew himself up along with his whole laboratory. "And why did he blow himself up? Because people who play with fire always feel too safe and don't think of the danger. Yes, Melanie, you may laugh. But it is so: they don't think of the danger."

They proceeded at once to make all necessary arrangements. It was agreed to drive to town about noon the next day, take a light luncheon there, and start on the excursion immediately afterward—the three ladies in the carriage, van der Straaten and Rubehn either on foot or by steamer. It was all quickly settled, and only the question of who else might be included seemed to present a few difficulties.

"The Gryczinskis?" asked van der Straaten and was satisfied when there was a general silence. For much as he loved his red-gold sister-in-law, who, with her affectionate and docile nature, embodied one of his little feminine ideals, he did not care for the major, whose superior manner oppressed him.

"Well then, what about Duquede?" he continued, touching his lip with the pencil he held ready to write down the name.

"No," said Melanie, "not Duquede. And though I can't bear the 'wet blanket' cliché, it's the only metaphor that fits him. At Stralow he'd prove to us that Treptow was overrated, and at Treptow it would be the other way round. We don't need a retired Legation Counselor to convince us of the truth of this proposition, not even a nobleman from the Altmark."

"All right, I agree," said van der Straaten. "How about Reiff?"

"Reiff, yes," came the delighted reply. All three ladies clapped their hands and Melanie added, "He's polite and well-mannered and not a spoilsport, and he always carries your things for you. And then, because he's known everywhere, it's like traveling with an escort, and everyone greets him so civilly, and sometimes I've almost expected the guard at the Brandenburg Gate to present arms."

"Oh, but that's not because of old Reiff," said Anastasia, who never missed an opportunity of ingratiating herself by some little show of flattery. "That's because of *you*. They thought you were a princess."

"No digressions, please," interrupted van der Straaten, "especially in the service of feminine vanity. On the principle of turn and turn about, that sort of thing can escalate enormously. I have written down Reiff, and Arnold and Elimar go without saying. A boating party with no singing is a monstrosity. Even I will concede that. And now, any more suggestions? None? Good. So it's Reiff and Arnold and Elimar, and I shall let them know by pneumatic dispatch. Five o'clock. And we'll wait for them out at Löbbeke's."

The next day the villa was full of excitement and bustle, far more than if they had been planning a journey to Teplitz or Karlsbad. Naturally, because a trip to Stralow was more unusual. The children were to be included, there was room enough in the carriage, but Lydia would not be persuaded and declared firmly that she did not *want* to go. To avoid a scene, they yielded to her, and the younger sister too stayed at home, because it was her habit to follow the elder in all things.

As arranged, they had a fork luncheon in town in van der Straaten's own room. He wanted it to be as much like a voyage or hunting party as possible, and was in the best of humor. It was not spoiled even by the last-minute arrival—after they had already sat down—of a refusal from Reiff. The Police Councillor wrote: "Chief just spoke to me confidentially. Leaving today. Eleven fifty. Cannot reveal reason. Reiff. P.S. Please kiss the lovely lady's hand for me and tell her I am inconsolable."

Van der Straaten was overcome by a violent fit of coughing because he had unwisely taken a sip of sherry as he read. He carried on nevertheless through his coughing and uncontrollable laughter, and let his imagination run riot on the subject of Reiff's heroic exploits. "A political mission. Marvellous. 'Fear not, my country!'[19] But there's someone who does have plenty to be afraid of, and that's the poor wretch he's after. Or I might as well say it straight out: the conspirator whose steps he's dogging. Because it must be a crime against the state or high treason if they put a man like Reiff personally in the saddle. True or not, little saddler of hell?[20] And this very night. It's pure balladry. 'We saddle at midnight.'[21] Oh, Leonore! Oh, Reiff, Reiff." And he went on laughing convulsively.

Nor did he spare Arnold and Elimar. It had been arranged that they should join the party out at Stralow. The mantle clock struck four and reminded them that they must hurry. The coach was waiting and the ladies got in and took their places—Fräulein Riekchen beside Melanie, Anastasia with her back to the horses. Waving their fans and parasols they set off through the square and the streets, first toward the Frankfurter Linden, and then toward the Stralow Gate.

Van der Straaten and Rubehn followed a quarter of an hour later in a second-class cab which they had chosen for its "authenticity"; but as soon as they were outside the town they got out and continued their way on foot through the water meadows.

The clock was striking five as our pedestrians reached the village and beheld Ehm in the middle of it. He had driven onto the lefthand verge and had just placed a full bag of fodder on the manger for his Trakehnen horses,[22] which already looked very well fed. On the other side of the road stood a small house, like the gingerbread house in the fairy tale, brownish in color and appetizing to the eye, and so low that one could easily put one's hand in the roof gutter. The door was correspondingly low, barely high enough for a man; above it was a faded blue sign with the words "Löbbeke's Coffee House." Three or four pollard limes in front of the building separated the sidewalk from the road, where hundreds of sparrows were hopping about chirping and picking up the grain that the horses had scattered.

"That is the Stralow Ship Hotel" (using the English term), said van der Straaten in the tone of a Cicerone; he was just about to enter the coffee house when Ehm crossed the road in order to report, in a manner both official and confidential, that "the ladies had gone ahead toward the meadow, and the painter gentlemen too. And the gentlemen had been waiting for the carriage and had let down the step and everything. First Herr Gabler and then Herr Schulze. And then they'd bought balloons and rubber balls at the stall where you played dice. And hoops too and a little drum and all sorts of things. And they'd taken a boy along to carry the hoops and sticks. And Herr Elimar out in front all the time with a harmonica."

"For heaven's sake," cried van der Straaten, "A squeeze-box?"

"No, sir. More like a mouth organ."

"Thank God ... And now come along, Rubehn. And you Ehm, you're not to wait for us. Get yourself something to eat ... Do you hear?"

Ehm had taken off his hat. But his expression showed clearly that he would wait.

On the other side of the village was a splendid expanse of meadow stretching all the way to the churchyard wall. The ladies had settled down nearby and were chatting to Gabler, while Elimar was doing a Monsieur Hercules act and rolling one of the large rubber balls along his arm and shoulder.

Van der Straaten and Rubehn could hear clapping and cries

of bravo from afar, and they joined in the applause enthusiastically. Only then did the others see them, and Melanie
jumped up and threw one of the large balls toward her husband by way of greeting. But she had not aimed well; the ball
went to the side, and Rubehn caught it. A moment later they
all exchanged greetings, and the young woman said, "You
are skillful. You really know how to catch a ball in flight."

"I wish I could catch Lady Luck."

"Perhaps it was Lady Luck."

Van der Straaten, hearing them, said that this elaborate
word play must stop; otherwise he would have to send a wire
to the fiancée or even dispatch Reiff on a confidential mission.
Whereupon Rubehn implored him for the hundreth time to
stop going on about the "everlasting fiancée"; for the present,
such a person existed only the realm of dreams. But van der
Straaten put on his crafty expression and said that he knew
better.

Then they returned to their encampment, which quickly
turned into a playground. Hoops and balls flew through the
air, and as the ladies were fond of changing from game to
game, they managed in an hour and a half to run through
blind man's buff, grandmother's footsteps, and puss in the
corner. The last was the most popular, especially with van
der Straaten, who liked to see Riekchen's sharp profile with
her kindly but somewhat piercing eyes looking out from behind a tree. For like most people with deformities, she had an
owlish look.

And so it went on, until the sun warned them that it was
time to return. Schulze, with his mouth organ, led on as
before, and Gabler marched beside him playing the little
drum like a tambourine. He would strike it with his knuckles,
throw it into the air and catch it again. Then came the two van
der Straatens, followed by Rubehn and Fräulein Riekchen,
while Anastasia, dreamily picking flowers, brought up the
rear. She was lost in sweet questions and imaginings, because when they were playing blind man's buff and Elimar
had caught her he had uttered words that could not be mis-
construed. Unless he were an infamous and double-tongued

liar. And that he was not... A man who could walk at the head of their group and play his harmonica with such childlike innocence could not be a deceiver.

And she bent down once more (how many times had she done it?) to count the petals of a buttercup and her chances of happiness.

9

LÖBBEKE'S COFFEE HOUSE

During those two hours nothing had changed outside Löbbeke's coffee house except that the sparrows were now chirping in the pollard limes instead of in the road. But no one paid any attention to this music, least of all van der Straaten, who had just given Melanie's arm to Elimar and taken the head of the procession himself. "Look out!" he cried and stooped in order to negotiate the low door with safety.

And they all followed his advice and example.

Inside there were a few steps down, because the floor was a good deal lower than the road outside; they were greeted by a musty cellar atmosphere and it was hard to say whether this was improved or not by a bitter, beery element in it. Halfway along the righthand side of the room was a small recess with a stove and chimney, not unlike a ship's galley, while on the left a bar projected by several feet. Behind this was a dresser with plates and cups above and liqueur bottles of various sizes bulging out below. Between the bar and the dresser the mistress of this domain sat enthroned, a tall, well-built blonde in her middle thirties who could certainly have claimed to be a beauty but for her eyes. Physically her eyes were beautiful too, and there was no fault to be found with them except that they had become accustomed to dividing all men into two classes: those they winked at, "See you later"; and those they mocked, "We know your sort." Whatever did not fit into these two categories was an object of pity and shrugging off.

It must unfortunately be said that van der Straaten was among the shrugged off. Not because of his age; on the contrary, age was something she knew how to value. It was because he had always had the weakness of wanting to be popular at all costs. And as far as the blonde was concerned, that was the most contemptible thing of all.

At the back of the hall an even lower door led into a garden, where a dozen green painted tables with matching chairs propped up against them stood among some puny trees. On the right was a bowling alley, the front end of which was out of sight and probably reached out into the road. Van der Straaten ironically pointed out all these splendors and discoursed upon the merits of nations that had maintained their unpretentiousness; then he walked down a little slope leading from the garden onto a glass-covered veranda, rather like a greenhouse, beside the Spree. Choosing one of the open sections, the company pushed two or three tables together; they now had a view of a narrow, rickety gang plank with a raft permanently anchored beyond it on the left. This belonged to the house next door and was the landing stage for the little Spree steamers.

Rubehn was forced to accept the best place because, being a stranger, he was to have an unimpeded view downstream where the city shimmered red and gold in the haze of the hot summer's day. Elimar and Gabler had walked out onto the gang plank. Everyone enjoyed the spectacle, and van der Straaten said: "Look, Melanie. The palace dome. Doesn't it look like Santa Maria Saluta?"

"Saluté," Melanie corrected, putting the accent on the last syllable.

"All right, all right, Saluté, then," repeated van der Straaten, likewise emphasizing the e. "Have it your own way. I don't pretend to be the doyen of ancient languages—I forget his name. Salus, salutis, fourth declension, or third, that's all I need. And Saluta or Saluté, it's all the same to me. But I must say, those dear Italians are pretty unreliable about everything, even their end syllables: sometimes e and sometimes *a*. But let's stop studying languages and study the menu instead. Of course the menu here is transmitted from mouth to mouth, a fact which enables me to banish memories of a blonde apparition. Isn't that so, Anastasia?"

"The Commercial Councillor is pleased to jest," replied Anastasia, ruffled. "I do not believe a menu can be transmitted from mouth to mouth."

"That would have to be a matter for experiment, and I for my part would guarantee success. But not until Luna has risen and then modestly hidden her face behind a veil of clouds. It must wait until then, and until then let there be peace between us. And now, Arnold, in your capacity as Gabler[23] I nominate you hereditary master of the kitchens and trustfully lay our bodily welfare in your hands."

"I accept the charge," said Gabler, "provided that, in the words of our unfortunately absent friend Gryczinski, you will issue a few directives."

"Certainly, certainly," said van der Straaten.

"Well then, begin."

"Right. Then I propose eel with cucumber salad ... Agreed?"

"Yes," chimed the chorus.

"And then poussin and new potatoes ... Agreed?"

"Yes."

"Then there only remains the problem of drink. I could have solved it beforehand with the help of Ehm and the carriage boot, but I hate dragging a wine cellar along on country outings. First of all it hurts the feelings of the people who are, after all, one's hosts; and secondly it means sticking in a rut, which is what one wants to get out of. Why do we go on excursions? Why, I ask you? Not to live better, but to live differently, to experience the customs and ways of other people, which includes the local resources of their villages and provinces. And as we do not dwell in the land of Canaan whence Caleb plucked grapes, I vote for the traditional product of these parts, for a cool blonde ale. There's no Swiss without money and no Stralow without light ale. I bet even Gryczinski has never issued better directives. And now off you go, Arnold ... A cool blonde. I wonder whether our blonde in there between the bar and the dresser falls into the same category?"

Elimar, meanwhile, had been watching the setting sun from the shaky landing stage, where, automatically and quite unconsciously, he was bending and stretching his knee like a gymnast preparing to jump. Then suddenly, as he was still bouncing up and down, the plank snapped and broke; only his presence of mind in grabbing one of the piles prevented his falling into the water, which was particularly deep by the steamer landing. The ladies cried out, and Anastasia was still trembling when he appeared wearing a victorious smile at his own self-rescue—a smile that only increased under a volley of reproaches for "foolhardiness" and "lack of consideration for other people's feelings."

Naturally an incident like this could not take place without a wealth of commentary and hypothesis, with "ifs" and "whats" playing a principal part and recurring endlessly. *What* would have happened if Elimar had not seized the pole in time? *What* if he had seized it but still fallen in? And finally, *what* if he had not happened to be a good swimmer?

Melanie quickly regained her equanimity and declared that it would have been imperative for van der Straaten to jump in after Elimar, first because he was the originator of the excursion, second as a man of stern resolve, and third as a Commercial Councillor, because historical records showed that no Commercial Councillor had ever drowned, not even in the Flood.

Van der Straaten liked nothing better than to be teased like this by his wife, but while he thanked the company for crediting him with so much heroism, he begged them not to presume upon it.

He belonged neither to the old firm of Leander, nor to the new one of Captain Boyton; on the contrary, in the matter of heroics he belonged to the school of his friend Heine, who had never missed an opportunity of expressing, honestly and directly, his extreme distaste for the tragical manner.

"But," said Melanie, "the tragical manner is exactly what we women expect of you!"

"Tragical manner indeed!" said van der Straaten. "A cheerful manner is what you demand, and a young dandy to hold the skein for you when you wind your wool. And he has to kneel on a footstool, which curiously enough always has a little dog embroidered on it. Presumably a symbol of faithfulness. And the admirer sighs like the young man at prayer, and gazes at you, languishing, and assures you of his deepest sympathy. Because of course you must be unhappy. And then more sighs and a pause. Of course, of course, your husband is a good man (all husbands are good men), but, *enfin*, goodness is not enough, a woman needs to be *understood*. That's what counts, otherwise marriage is a base condition, very base, the basest condition of all. And then he sighs for the third time. And by the time you have finished winding your wool (which naturally takes as long as possible) you believe it all. For every one of you is born to be the bride of an Indian prince or the Shah of Persia, at the very least. For the carpets if nothing else."

During this characteristic van der Straaten outburst, Melanie had shaken her head. Now she answered flippantly and with a shade of haughtiness, "I don't know, Ezel, why you keep going on about wool. I wind silk."

This remark would probably have drawn a pointed reply. But at that moment a plump maid in short sleeves appeared, who immediately became the center of everyone's attention, if only for the panache with which she snapped open her tablecloth as though to announce the start of the proceedings. And sure enough, the steaming dishes quickly made their appearance, and the tall glasses of pale ale; even the anisette for Anastasia had not been forgotten. There were several anisettes, in fact, for Gabler was a man of the world and had borne in mind the attitude of ladies in general to anisette. Indeed, he could not help smiling (and van der Straaten with him), for no sooner had the tray appeared than he saw Riekchen begin to sip, her owlish eyes growing larger and more genial all the time.

Meanwhile dusk had fallen, and it was beginning to grow cool. Gabler and Elimar went to fetch a pile of shawls and rugs from the carriage. Melanie threw a black and white striped burnoose around her, pulling up the hood coquettishly, and she looked more charming than ever. One of the silken tassels hung over her forehead and moved to and fro when she spoke or listened animatedly to the others. Up to now the conversation had been mainly gossip about the Gryczinskis, and especially about the Police Councillor and his new Catiline conspiracy; now at last it turned to more appropriate and at the same time more harmless topics such as, for instance, the exceptional brightness of the Big Dipper.

"Almost as bright as Charles's Wain," Riekchen chimed in. She was not very strong on astronomy. And then they remembered that it was exactly the right time of year for shooting stars, upon which van der Straaten not only began to count the falling stars but went so far as to claim that "really everything in the world existed only for the purpose of falling: stars, angels—only women were exempt."

Melanie started, but no one saw it, least of all van der Straaten, and after they had gone on counting and disputing a while and the evening had grown colder and colder, they agreed that there was only one way of dealing with these arctic conditions: a bowl of mulled wine. It was van der Straaten himself who made the suggestion as well as the following definition: "mulled wine is that form of wine in which the wine itself signifies nothing, and the cloves everything." Upon that definition they decided to risk it and placed the order. Lo and behold, after a comparatively short time the blonde hostess appeared in person and carefully set down a bowl in the middle of the table.

She raised the lid and laughed with pleasure at the genuinely grateful "ah's" of her guests as they breathed in the warm and reviving steam. A charming, fair-haired boy had come with her and clung to his mother's skirts.

"Yours?" asked van der Straaten with a friendly gesture of the hand.

"Who else's?" answered the blonde drily as she tried to exchange a few looks with Rubehn across the table. But when this maneuver failed, she buried her hand in the child's fair curls and said, "Come on, Pauleken. The ladies and gentlemen would rather be alone."

Elimar looked after her in puzzlement and rubbed his forehead. At last he said, "Thank God, now I've got it. I knew I'd seen her somewhere. Somewhere or other. The *Triumph of Germanicus*: Thusnelda to the life."

"I can't see it," replied van der Straaten, who was an admirer of Piloty's. "The proportions and measurements aren't right, always supposing that one can discuss such things with our ladies present. But Anastasia will forgive me if I just point out the main difference: Piloty shows Tumelicus in the pod, whereas this child can already hang on to his mother's apron. The whitest apron I've ever seen. But be it whiter than snow and brighter than day, calumny will still have her say."

These two lines were spoken in a deliberately sarcastic singsong. Rubehn did not care for van der Straaten's manner; he turned aside and gazed to the left where the stars danced on the river. Melanie saw him and the blood rushed to her head as never before. All these years her husband's manner and speech had embarrassed her hundreds of times, sometimes deeply, but that was all. Today, for the first time, she felt ashamed of him.

Van der Straaten, however, remained unaware of her malaise and clung faster than ever to his Thusnelda theme, thinking—quite correctly, as far as that went—that he would never find a better one for his own special purpose.

"Now I ask you all, is this a Thusnelda? You must elevate your thoughts to a higher sphere, my friends. The goddess Aphrodite, the Venus of these parts, Venus Spreavensis, risen straight from the waves that nearly finished off our faithful Elimar. But if I am not mistaken, my friends, we are dealing with a little more than that. What we see, if my observation is correct, or, let's say, if my hunch is correct, is a marriage of ancient and modern: Venus Spreavensis and Venus Kallipygos. A bold assertion, I agree. But in Greek and in music there's nothing you can't say. Am I right, Anastasia? Am I right, Elimar? And to prove I'm right, I've remembered a marvelous kallipygos epigram...No, not an epigram...what's it called when you get two lines without a rhyme?"

"Distich."

"That's right. Well then, I remember a distich . . . oh, there, now I've forgotten it . . . Melanie, how did it go? You used to recite it so nicely and it always made you laugh. And now you've forgotten it too. Or have you forgotten it on purpose? . . . Please . . . I hate that kind of nonsense. Do remember. It was something about the bloom on peaches, and I said you could really feel it. And you thought so too and you agreed with me . . . But the glasses are empty."

"And I think we'll leave them empty," said Melanie sharply. Changing color, she opened and closed her parasol mechanically. "I think we'll leave them empty. It's only mulled wine, after all. And if we want to go to the other side, then its time, *high* time," and she emphasized the word.

"That's all right with me," said van der Straaten, but it was all too clear from his tone that his good humor was beginning to change into the opposite. "That's all right with me, and I am only sorry that once again I appear to have given offense and snubbed the higher aspirations of the noble house of de Caparoux. It's always the same old song, and I'm sick of hearing it. And if I ever do want to hear it, then I can invite my brother-in-law the major to dinner; he's lord high chamberlain at the court of propriety and boredom. He's not here today, and I'd just as soon his sister-in-law had not seen fit to stand in for him. I hate prudery and all those pretensions to higher forms of morality—they mean nothing at all. Or at least one can only hope they mean nothing at all. I've a right to say so, and anyway, I *will* say so, and what I say, I say."

No one replied. A feeble attempt of Gabler's to change the conversation met with no success. So they made all the necessary preparations for the crossing to Treptow in a fairly businesslike though much quieter tone; they were to take two small boats, and Ehm was to drive across the nearest bridge and wait for them on the opposite bank. Everyone agreed except for Fräulein Riekchen, who shyly declared that "rocking about in a boat had always been death to her." Whereupon van der Straaten was seized by a fit of chivalry, and offered to remain with her on the glass-covered veranda and wait for the next steamer.

10

WHERE ARE WE DRIFTING?

It was not long before two rowboats emerged from the darkness of the opposite bank and steered downstream toward the raft. A lantern pole hung from each bow. The same boy who had carried the hoops to the churchyard meadow in the afternoon sat in the smaller boat towing the empty, larger boat behind him on a chain. It was a pretty picture, and the two boats had scarcely pulled in to the raft before the impatient travelers climbed aboard. Rubehn and Melanie took the smaller boat, Anastasia and the two painters the larger. This arrangement had come about of its own accord because Elimar and Gabler were experienced oarsmen and needed no guidance. They led on ahead, and the boy followed with the smaller boat.

After watching them for a while, van der Straaten said to his companion, "I'm quite glad, Riekchen, that we are staying behind and waiting for the steamer. I've been wanting to ask you how you like our new house guest. You don't talk much, and people who don't talk are good observers."

"Oh, I like him."

"And I'm glad you do, Riekchen. Only I'm sorry about the 'oh,' because it cancels out a good deal of the praise; and 'oh, I like him,' is not really much better than 'oh, I don't like him.' You see, I'm not going to let you off. Now come on, speak up. Why only 'oh'? What is it? What's wrong? Is it the airs and graces of the Reserve lieutenant that you distrust? Is he too much the gentleman or not enough? Do you think he's too boisterous or too quiet, too modest or too proud, too warm or too cold?"

"Now you've got it."

"Got what?"

"Too cold. Yes, he's too cold. The first time I saw him, he made a good impression on me, though not as good as on Anastasia. Anastasia sings, and she's an eccentric, and she wants a man."

"Every woman wants a man."

"Me too?" laughed Riekchen.

"Who knows?"

"Well, at first I liked him. That was on the veranda, right after lunch. We had just pushed the blue dishes aside, and it seems as though it had been yesterday. Then old Teichgräber came and brought his card. And then he came himself. Well, he does have a certain distinction, you can tell at first glance that he's never known life's petty cares. And that's nice, I don't want to belittle it. But he has a certain reserve too. And when I say reserve, that's not really the whole story. Because reserve is right and proper. But he goes too far. At first I thought it was a slight shyness, which is attractive, even in a man of the world, and I thought he would get over it. But I could soon see that it wasn't shyness. No, on the contrary. It's self-confidence. He has the sort of assurance Americans have. And he's as cold as he's sure of himself."

"Ah, Riekchen, he was out there too long, and it's no place to learn modesty and warmth."

"Those things can't be learned. I'm afraid they can be un-learned, though."

"Unlearned? But I ask you, Riekchen, he's from Frankfurt!"

While this conversation was going on in the glass veranda the two boats were steering toward the middle of the stream. The larger was full of jokes and laughter, but the smaller followed in complete silence. Melanie leaned over the side and let the water trickle through her fingers.

"Is only the water allowed to touch your hand?"

"It's cooling and I feel so hot."

"Then take off your burnoose . . .," and he rose to help her.

"No," she said vehemently, warding him off. "I'm cold." And now he saw that she really was shivering as though she were.

They followed the other boat in silence again and listened to the songs coming across the water. At first it was "Long, long ago" (in English), and every time they came to the refrain, Melanie hummed it with them. And now they were laughing in the other boat, starting one song after another and rejecting them all just as rapidly, until finally they seemed to have agreed on "Oh, could I but see on yonder heath."[24] They actually persevered and sang through all the verses. But Melanie no longer sang softly with them, for she did not want the trembling in her voice to betray her emotion.

They were in the middle of the stream, out of earshot of the boat in front, and the boy who was rowing them pulled in his oars with a jerk and lay back comfortably, leaving the boat to drift.

"He's looking at the stars too," said Rubehn.

"And counting the ones that fall," said Melanie with a bitter laugh. "But you mustn't look at me in surprise like that, dear friend, as though I had said something unusual. As you know, or at least as you ought to know after today, that's the tone of our house. A little sharp, a little ambiguous, and always inappropriate. I'm trying to adopt my husband's mode of expression. But of course I can't compete with him. He is simply inimitable, and brilliant at finding words to wound and expose and shame a person."

"You must not let it embitter you."

"I don't *let* it. But I am embittered, and I want to get it off my chest, and that's why I'm speaking like this. Van der Straaten . . ."

" . . . is different from other people. But he loves you and I believe . . . And he's a good man."

"And he's a good man," Melanie repeated fiercely and with an almost convulsive gaiety. "All husbands are good men. And now all we need is a skein of wool and a footstool with the symbol of fidelity, and there we are again. Oh, how could you say *that*? How could you try to justify him by talking just the way he does?"

"Whatever way I talked would have been offensive."

"Perhaps . . . or perhaps we'd better say certainly. Because it was simply too much, that everlasting harping on things which should only be mentioned between two people alone, and hardly even then. But he knows no secrets because nothing seems worth keeping secret to him. Because he holds nothing sacred. And anyone who doesn't agree with him is a hypocrite, or merely ridiculous. And all that in front of you . . ."

He took her hand and felt that she was feverish.

But the stars glittered, and their reflections danced on the water around them, and the boat rocked gently and drifted on the stream, and the question grew louder and louder in Melanie's heart: where are we drifting?

And lo and behold, it seemed as though the boy had been disturbed by the same question, for he suddenly sprang up and looked about him. Seeing that they had gone far beyond the place where they were to land, he seized both oars and swung the boat around to the left, to get out of the current and back toward the other shore as fast as possible. He succeeded, and in less than five minutes they saw the trees in Treptow Park illuminated by flares, and Rubehn and Melanie heard Anastasia's laughter in the boat ahead. Then the laughter ceased and the singing began again. But it was another song, and "Rotraud, fair Rotraud" sounded across the water: first loud and joyful, and then melancholy as it died away on the words, "Be silent, my heart."[25]

"Be silent, my heart," Rubehn repeated. "Is that what you want?"

Melanie did not reply. But the boat drew into the shore, where Elimar and Arnold stood waiting attentively. A moment later the steamer arrived, and Riekchen and van der Straaten got out. He was gay and talkative.

He took Melanie's arm and seemed to have completely forgotten the scene that had disturbed the evening.

11

TO THE MINISTER

"Where are we drifting?" had been the question in Melanie's heart, and she could not forget it. But she got over the feverish excitement of that hour, and, in the days that followed, her self-command returned.

She was able to maintain it, and quivered only for a moment when, a week later, she saw Rubehn stop outside the gate and then make straight for the veranda. She stepped out to meet him, as was her custom, and said, "I'm so pleased to see you again. We used to see you every three days, and now you've neglected us for almost a week. But you will be punished forthwith. You'll find only Anastasia and me here. Our Riekchen, for whom I know you have a high regard (not high enough, of course), has left us for a whole month to look after seven little cousins in the country. All boys and all Sawatzkis, and in their wilder moments they're probably all little saddlers of hell!"

"Probably! Certainly, I should say. And Riekchen as tutor and regent! What a regime!"

"Oh, you misjudge her. She knows how to assert her authority."

"All the same, I should hate to see the gardener's despair at his trampled flower beds or the forester's at the depredation to his game! A little Junker shoots everything furred or feathered in sight. And seven of them! But I forget: I have a message. Van der Straaten . . . your husband . . . says you are not to expect him for dinner. He has been sent for by the Minister about some kind of commission of inquiry. It doesn't begin until tomorrow, actually. But today there's a prelude —a dinner. You know, ma'am, nowadays we have nothing but commissions of inquiry."

"Nothing but commissions of inquiry, perhaps, but no more ma'ams. At least not here and not between us. I'm really only 'ma'am' at the Gryczinskis. With you, I'm your good friend and nothing else. All right?" And she gave him her hand, which he took and kissed. "And I don't want us to have lived through these last six days only just to set our friendship back by as many weeks. So no more ma'am." And she forced herself to look at him. But her heart beat fast and her voice shook at the memory of that evening, all too clear in her mind.

"Yes, my friend," she resumed after a short pause, "we must get that clear between us. And while we're getting things clear, there is something else on my mind, something very personal and tricky. Because it's high time I gave you a name. Because you haven't really got one, at least, not a name one can use . . ."

"I should have thought I had," said Rubehn with a touch of embarrassment and displeasure.

"I should have thought I had," Melanie repeated, laughing. "Extraordinary how even intelligent, even the most intelligent people are always sensitive on that one point. But I beg you, please don't feel you have to be sensitive about anything. You yourself shall decide. Now answer me on your honor as a man: is Ebenezer a name? I mean a name for every day, for conversation, for talk—which, after all, is our favorite occupation. Ebenezer! Oh, you mustn't look so cross. Ebenezer's a name for a high priest or for someone training to be one, and I can just see him brandishing the sacrificial knife. And you see, that makes me shudder. *Au fond*, Ebenezer is no better than Aaron. And there's nothing to be done with it. I managed to condense Ezechiel down to Ezel. But Ebenezer!"

Anastasia enjoyed Rubehn's discomfiture; then she said, "I can think of a way out!"

"Oh, so can I. And I could formulate it all in one sentence which would sound positively grammatical: reform and restore the abstruse family name of Rubehn into the ancient name of Reuben, which has always been one of my favorites."

"That's just what I was going to say," Anastasia hastened to put in.

"But I said it!"

And in this light-hearted battle for precedence, Melanie joked herself back into her old carefree state of mind; finally she turned to Rubehn and went on, "And do you know, dear friend, choosing a name like this really means something to me? Reuben—I must say it again—has always been my favorite among the twelve. He had the generosity of the eldest—the eldest has it simply because he *is* the eldest. Just consider whether I'm not right. The firstborn is naturally in a dominant position, and that saves him from pettiness and intrigue."

"Every firstborn will be in your debt for glorifying him like that, particularly every Reuben. And yet I must be open with you: I should have chosen a different one among the twelve."

"Not a better one, though. And I hope I can prove it to you. There's no need to waste time over the six half-legitimates. You're nodding—so you agree. So let's proceed to the first exhibit, the babies of the family, mother's little darlings. Much has been made of them, but you must agree that the future Egyptian excellency was not put down the well quite without reason. He was simply an *enfant terrible*. And then the youngest of all! Spoiled and badly brought up. I have a youngest myself, so I know what I'm talking about... So we're really only left with those four old veterans of Leah's. All right, all four have their merits. But still, there's a difference. You can see the future priest lurking in Levi, and the future king in Judah—you will have to forgive my disloyalty to the Crown; after all, I am a free Swiss. And so we are left with the remainder—the last two, though of course they're really the first two. *Eh bien,* I don't want to niggle or find fault, and I'll give Simeon his due. He was a character, and that's why he wanted to finish the boy off—characters never go for half measures. But then Reuben stepped in, *my* Reuben, and saved the boy because he remembered their old father. Because he had a heart and compassion and generosity. And if some of it was weakness, I'm not saying so. He had the vices of his own virtues like the rest of us. That's all it was—nothing else. And that's why it's got to be Reuben—Reuben, Reuben. And there'll be no appeal and no refusal.

Anastasia, you can pick a branch for the christening and the coronation—there—from that ash tree over there. Then we can call it the Reuben ash."

And this playful chatter would doubtless have continued if at that very moment the familiar two-wheeled gig had not come into sight. Van der Straaten was sitting on the towering seat and saluted them across the fence with his whip. And now the vehicle drew up, and the Commercial Councillor and member of the Commission of Inquiry appeared on the veranda beaming with happiness and pleasurable excitement. He kissed Melanie on the forehead and declared over and over again that he had been unable to resist spending half an hour *au sein de sa famille* before leaving for the ministerial dinner.

He sat down and called into the house, "Liddy, Liddy! Hurry! Look sharp now. Quickly, quickly. And Heth too, our stepchild, poor little thing, neglected because she looks like me . . ."

"And I've just been saying that she gets spoiled beyond all measure . . ."

Meanwhile the children had appeared, and their father pulled an elegant little lace-trimmed paper bag from his pocket and held it out to Lydia. She took it and passed it to her little sister: "There, Heth."

"Don't you want any?" asked van der Straaten. "Have a look first. They're chocolate creams. From Sarotti, what's more."

But Lydia threw a sidelong glance at Rubehn and said, "Candy's for children. I don't want any."

Everyone laughed, even Rubehn, although he felt that he was the cause of her refusal. But van der Straaten took little Heth on his lap and said, "You're your father's child. No nonsense or affectation. Lydia is acting the de Caparoux."

"Leave her alone," said Melanie.

"I shall *have* to leave her alone. And strangely enough, it's only for myself that I hate these aristocratic airs and graces. I don't mind them in my family, at least occasionally; quite apart from the fact that all sorts of changes are in the air for me too. For in my capacity as member of a commission of inquiry I have had to accept the obligation of adopting a more elevated social manner, and if things continue as they are, Melanie, in six weeks from now you will find yourself with someone on your hands who's almost a chief master of ceremonies. Six weeks is the lying-in period—so it's always been a significant length of time."

"A comparison, my dear van der Straaten, which only goes to prove that for the present you are still far removed from your new status."

"True, true," laughed van der Straaten. "Everything in its time; Rome was not built in a day. And now tell me, since I've only ten minutes left, how you intend to spend the afternoon and amuse our friend Rubehn. Forgive my asking. But I know that you can be dangerously careless about the joys of the table, and it occurs to me that your beans and lamb chops—even if the beans are stringy and the chops tough—will hardly see you through more than half an hour. Not even if you throw in strawberries and stilton for dessert. So I'm worried about you, especially as there is not the faintest chance of your seeing me back before nine o'clock."

"Don't worry," said Melanie. "There is no question but that we shall miss you sorely. You'll leave—you can't help leaving a gap. For who—just to name one thing—could make up for the imaginative richness of your flights of fancy? We can hardly follow them ourselves. And yet I guarantee to fill those poor lost hours that are causing you so much anxiety. I'll even tell you the program."

"Ah, now you arouse my curiosity."

"First we'll sing."

"Tristan?"

"No. And Anastasia will accompany us. And then we shall have dinner, or anyway, what passes for dinner. I expect it will be all right. Because when you're not there, we always try and console ourselves by having a better meal and a few extra sweets."

"I can believe it."

"And then it is my intention to acquaint our friend with all the treasures and beauties of the villa. Incidentally, following a recent agreement, I must now present him to you as Rubehn with an *e* instead of an *h:* so he's simply our friend Reuben now. He has been our dear guest hundreds of times (though not nearly often enough), but he still knows nothing of all this splendor except the dining room and the music room and the veranda with the screaming peacock, which of course he abhors. But I intend to humble his pride, based as it is on being the citizen of a free city and having lived overseas. I intend to start with our orchard, after the orchard to show him the palm house, and after the palm house, the aquarium."

"A good program, though the last item fills me with some apprehension, or at least inclines me to counsel caution. I must put you in the picture, Rubehn, and tell you what a horrendous experience we had last summer with that miserable collection of glass boxes that boasts the name of aquarium. No less and no more than an explosion, an inundation, and I shall hear Anastasia's screams till my dying day. Imagine, one of the large sheets of glass cracked—reason unknown, but probably something to do with Gryczinski giving his fuselier's sword the wrong directive; and there, before we could count three, not only was the whole aquarium floor under a foot of water, but all the monsters of the deep were wriggling all around us, and a large pike was investigating Melanie's instep to the deliberate neglect of Aunt Riekchen's. He must have been a connoisseur. And in a fit of mad jealously I had him killed and personally devoured his liver."

Anastasia confirmed the truth of this account, and even Melanie joined in the general merriment, although for some time past she had shown an obvious reluctance to listen to her husband's orations. During her conversation with Rubehn she had worked herself into such a state of excitement that she seemed intoxicated and almost indifferent to all the considerations and scruples that had tormented her only a short while ago. Once again she began to see the funny side of every remark and occurrence, even the most equivocal; without admitting it to herself, she had resolved to shake off once and for all the nervous sensitivity of the last few weeks and to live her life as confidently and freely as before.

Van der Straaten, however, was beside himself with pleasure at having discovered such a good exit line with his pike; he seized his hat and gloves and promised to urge the minister to get through the business quickly—insofar as it was possible to urge a minister in any way at all.

Those were his parting words. Immediately afterward they heard the crunch of the wheels and saw van der Straaten wave good-bye across the fence with the deliberately exaggerated solemnity of a man of consequence on his way to see a minister. And especially the minister of finance, who is twice as important as any other.

12

UNDER THE PALM TREES

The afternoon passed in the manner planned by Melanie and approved by van der Straaten. They made music for an hour and a half and then had their little dinner, which turned out to be more opulent than expected. As the sun was about to disappear behind the trees, they rose and went to pick a second dessert from the fruit trees.

The orchard occupied the sunniest part of the park and was laid out for various kinds of fruit; it consisted of a seemingly endless gravel path along the bank of the river Spree, separated from the rest of the grounds by a cordon of trained fruit trees. The espaliers were arranged with the most elaborate care, each single branch lovingly tended and bearing the choicest kinds of fruit, while the more common varieties—such as huge, pineapple-scented strawberries—grew on low wooden frames alongside.

Melanie had taken Rubehn's arm; Anastasia followed at an ever increasing distance. But Heth accompanied her mother on her velocipede, now far ahead, now close beside her, now turning again, quite unaware that with each turn the back of her dress billowed and fluttered in wild and comical abandon. At every turn Melanie would try to overcome her slight embarrassment by speaking more emphatically, until at last Rubehn took her hand and said: "Why don't you leave the child alone. Look how happy she is—it makes me quite envious to watch her. And you see, my friend, I'm not even laughing at her."

"You are right," Melanie replied. "It was silly of me—plain silly. Our shame is our blame. And when you think about it, she's both touching and charming." Just then the little tomboy came pedaling up again, and Melanie herself gave the command: "Right about turn! Don't get too near the river. Just look at her, how she flies! In the whole of history there's never been a cavalry charge with such flying colors."

During this conversation they had come to the place where a broad avenue joined the long narrow path along the cordoned trees. Here, in the center of the whole layout, a couple of palm houses with high glass domes had been erected, after the manner of Kew Gardens. One of them was joined to an old-fashioned greenhouse which had once belonged to the family but now, along with all the indoor and pot plants in it, had become the property of the old gardener; it formed the basis of a very profitable private business for him. His house was right next to the hothouse—a tiny cottage with only two windows, completely overgrown with ivy and sheltered by the branches of the ancient acacia that arched over it. Two or three steps led up to the threshold, and beside them stood a seat, its back also ivy-covered.

"Let's sit down," said Melanie. "Always supposing that we are allowed to. Because our old friend here is not always in a good mood. Isn't that so, Kagelmann?"

She had addressed these words to a small, rather ugly man, whose bald head was hidden under a summer cap but nevertheless sprouted a few lank strands of hair hanging from his temples right down to his shoulders. Everything about him was out of proportion; so that in spite of his short stature—or perhaps because of it—everything seemed too big: his nose, his ears, his hands. And his eyes too. But they were visible only when he removed his bleary horn-rimmed glasses, which he frequently did. He was a typical gardener: unfriendly, brusque, and grasping, especially toward his benefactor, the Commercial Councillor. Only when he saw Frau van der Straaten was he noticeably pleasant and good-humored.

He took the joking "if we are allowed to" in the best of spirits. Pushing back his wide-peaked cap with his right hand, in which he held a little pot of primulas, he said, "You don't have to ask, ma'am. A woman like you. A woman like you can do what she likes. You know why? Because everything you do suits you. And if everything suits a person, they can do what they like. It's whether it suits you or not that counts. Some folks say flowers make you silly and weak in the head. But flowers can teach you that what matters is whether a thing suits a person or not."

"What a gallant Kagelmann you are," laughed Melanie. "It's obvious you're not married, you old bachelor. But you were wrong, Kagelmann, not to. Not to marry, I mean. A man like you, hale and hearty, and in such a good business. And rich too. You know, people say you have an estate of your own. But I don't want to know, Kagelmann. I respect a man's secrets. But one thing is certain, your ivy cottage is too small, always supposing that one day you should change your mind."

"Yes, well, it's small, all right. But it's big enough for me. For me alone, that is. Otherwise . . . but I'm all of sixty now."

"Sixty. My goodness, sixty. Sixty is no age at all."

"True," said Kagelmann. "You can't really call it an age. And everything's still running right. Not bad at all. An' I still enjoy my food an' my old legs are still holding me up. But that's about it. And who is a man to marry? You see, ma'am, the ones that would do for me, I don't fancy them, and the ones I fancy, they wouldn't do.—I'd like one under thirty or thereabouts. Thirty's a good age; and thirty plus thirty, that's all right. But sixty into thirty won't go. The woman's gonna say: I'll borrow one."

Melanie laughed.

But Kagelmann continued, "Oh, you don't get to hear of things like that, ma'am, and you wouldn't credit what the world's like and what goes on. There was a fellow over there with Flatow, Cohn, and Satow—big leather people (and people say they get their stuff from America—well, it's all the same to me)—he was a gardener too, around fifty-six or thereabouts. Maybe only fifty-five. An' he got hold of this little madam, about thirty years old, a widow, an' always in black, an' a pretty little thing, an' she always used to sit in the middle tent, number 4, next to the emperor Wilhelm, where they have the music—piano and flute. Well then, an' what did he get out of it? Not a darn thing. An' there he is with his three brats, and the little madam, she up and off. An' guess who she went with. With a boy not twenty years old; and Teichgräber says he was only eighteen. Well, it's possible. But he was a sharp little fellow, Italian or something like that, though he only came from Rathenow. But a pair of eyes he had on him, I tell you, ma'am, just like fireworks, an' you could hear them crackle."

"Yes, it's sad for the husband," laughed Melanie. "But saddest of all for the woman. Because when a man has eyes like *that* . . ."

"An' nowadays it happens every day," the old man concluded without noticing her interjection. And he began shifting his flower pots and rummaging about.

But Melanie would not leave him in peace. "Every day?" she said. "Of course it does. Of course, anything is possible. But that shouldn't stop you. Otherwise no one could get married and there'd be no more life and no more people. After all, a sharp little gardener's boy might turn up anywhere."

"Yes, ma'am, you're right. But sometimes they turn up all the time, and sometimes they only turn up now and then. Getting married! Well, it must be nice, otherwise people wouldn't do it so much. But I think I know better. And it's my belief: better safe than sorry."

At this moment a one-horse cart made its appearance from the direction of the main avenue and turned to halt in front of

the seat where Rubehn and Melanie were sitting. It was a
low-slung vehicle, which carried the goods between the little
private greenhouse and the town.

Kagelmann put a few questions to the driver, who was
sitting on the shaft board in front. Then he called another
workman, and all three began unloading palm trees in tubs.
Although they were not very tall, their tops came well above
the edge of the cart, and from a distance their dark green
crowns looked like proud, waving plumes.

All three men worked busily for a few minutes; but when
everything had been unloaded, Kagelmann addressed himself to Melanie once more. Patting the two largest and finest
palm trees with his hands, he said: "Yes ma'am, these are my
two main supports, the two pillars of my business. An' always
on the go, like a country postman. Only more than a postman,
'cause a postman has Sunday off, or time for church, anyway.
But not my palms, not them. An' it always gladdens my heart
when there's nothing doing once in a while, an' I can get to
see 'em again. Like today. Sometimes I don't get to see my
palms all week."

"But why not?"

"Goodness you can't go wrong with palms, ma'am. Makes
no difference if it's a wedding or a funeral. And some folks
even christens with palms. An' when I say palms, well, it
could be laurel or box or what we call thuja. But palms, of
course, are the fanciest. An' there's only one other line of
business like it, identical like it, an' no dying or getting born
without it. An' it's always the same too."

"Oh, I understand," said Melanie. "You mean the carpenter."

"No, not the carpenter. He's always there too, that's true,
but it's not always the same job for him. A coffin ain't a
cradle, an' a cradle ain't a coffin. An' when it comes to a
regular four-poster, well, that's another thing altogether . . ."

"But Kagelmann, if it's not the carpenter, who is it?"

"The cathedral choir, ma'am. They're always there too,
an' always the same. Just like me. An' they've got their two
main supports, their two pillars of the business: 'God in His

wisdom hath ordained' and 'How peacefully they rest.' You can't go wrong with those hymns, an' it makes no difference whether a person's going on a journey or gettin' buried. Green is green, an' they're evergreen just like palm an' box.''

"All the same, Kagelmann, if you ever get married and take a bride yourself (but not here in the ivy cottage, it's too small) you shall have both—hymns *and* palms. And what palms! I promise you that. Without the palms and hymns it wouldn't be solemn enough. And solemnity is what counts. And then we'll go into the greenhouse, right under the dome, and we'll make a magnificient altar under the finest of all the palms. And that's where you'll be married. And we shall stand up under the dome and sing a beautiful hymn, a chorale: Fräulein Anastasia and I, and Herr Rubehn here, and Herr Elimar Schulze—you know him too. And you'll feel as though you were already in heaven and listening to the angels sing.''

"I believe you, ma'am, I believe you.''

"And if you want to thank us in advance for all these future glories, my dear Kagelmann, you can take us into the palm house now. Because I don't know my way around and I don't know the names, and this gentleman has been round the world several times and has studied palm trees at the source, so to speak, and he'd like to know what we have and what we don't have.''

As a matter of fact this was as inconvenient as could be to the old man because he wanted to get his tubs and flower pots back into the small greenhouse before dark. But the controlled himself, and pushed his cap to the back of his head as a sign of assent, and said, "Anything you say, ma'am.''

And they walked between low brick stoves along the central aisle, only wide enough for one person at a time, until they came to the opening to the large palm house. A few more steps brought them to what seemed like the entrance to a tropical forest, with the huge glass structure arching above them. This was where the finest specimens of the van der Straaten collection were to be found: palms, drakea, and giant ferns. A spiral staircase twisted upward, first into the dome, then around it, an on into one of the high galleries of the central nave.

No one had spoken as they walked.

When they paused under the high dome, Kagelmann re-membered that he had forgotten something important. The truth was simply that he wanted to get back, and he said, "Well, ma'am, now you know your way about, and you know the gallery. Where the little table is, an' the little chairs, that's the best place, just like an arbor an' all shut in. That's where the Commercial Councillor sits. An' nobody can see him. That's what he likes best." And the old man took his leave. But he turned round once more to ask whether he was to send the other lady in.

"Certainly, Kagelmann. We'll wait."

When they were alone, Rubehn took the lead and climbed up and when he reached the top he hastened to give his hand to Melanie, who was still on the winding stair. And then they went on across the little clanking iron slats that formed the gang plank until they came to the place Kagelmann had described—and described better than he himself might have thought. It was a magical arbor formed by the leafy treetops, and completely enclosed; orchids climbed all over the trees and up the ribbing of the dome, and filled it with their scent. Breathing was delightful but difficult among the dense foliage; at the same time it seemed as though a hundred secrets were being spoken, and Melanie felt her nerves giving way under the intoxicating scent. She was one of those people that depend on the conditions around them, on light and air, and that need freshness in order to feel fresh them-selves. Driving fast across the snow with a sharp east wind blowing—that would have restored her serenity and courage. But this soft, heavy air made her soft and limp, and the armor of her spirit loosened, gave way, and fell from her.

"Anastasia won't be able to find us."

"I don't miss her."

"But I shall call her all the same."

"I don't miss her," repeated Rubehn, and his voice trem-bled. "The only thing I miss is that song she was singing the day we crossed the river in the boat. Can you guess which one?"

"Long, long ago..."

He shook his head.

"Oh, could I but see on yonder heath..."

"Not that either, Melanie."

"Rotraud," she said softly.[26]

And at that she tried to rise. But he would not let her and knelt down and held her tight, and they whispered words as feverish and sweet as the air they breathed.

But at last, dusk began to fall and broad shadows slanted across the dome. And when there was still no sound, they climbed down the stairs and felt their way through a thicket of palms, first to the central aisle, then out into the open.

Outside they found Anastasia.

"Wherever were you?" said Melanie, embarrassed. "I was worried about you—and me. Yes, it's true. Just ask. And now I have a headache."

Anastasia laughed as she took her friend's arm and said, "Does that surprise you? One doesn't walk unpunished under palm trees."[27]

Melanie blushed to her temples. But the darkness helped her to hide it. And so they walked toward the villa, where the lights were already burning.

All the windows and doors stood open, and a balmy air wafted from the freshly mown meadows. Anastasia sat down at the piano and sang, and began a bantering conversation with Rubehn, who made an effort to fall in with her tone. But Melanie stared in front of her and was silent and far away. On the high seas. And in her heart the question rose again: where are we drifting?

An hour later van der Straaten appeared and called in good-humored mockery from the hallway, "Ah, the communion of saints. I should be afraid to disturb you. But I bring good tidings!"

And when they all rose—either genuinely curious or at least pretending to be—he continued his report: "His Excellency was *very* gracious. Everything's been gone into and agreed upon. All that remains is pure formality and minor detail. Or rather committees and paperwork. That's all I'm giving away for now. But I think I may say: today marks the beginning of a new era for the house of van der Straaten."

13

CHRISTMAS

The next few days brought many visitors, and the uncon-strained tone of earlier weeks seemed to have returned. If any constraint remained, no one noticed it except Anastasia—least of all van der Straaten, who was more than ever given over to his vanities, great and small.

And so autumn drew near, and the park grew ever more beautiful with the changing of the leaves, until in late September the day arrived when they usually left the villa.

Rubehn had not been seen for several days, because urgent business kept him in the city. A younger brother, accom-panied by an old confidential clerk in the family business, had arrived to hurry on the establishment of their new subsidiary; and by the beginning of October their combined efforts had succeeded in setting up a new branch of the great Frankfurt bank.

Van der Straaten took a lively interest in all these proceed-ings and regarded it as a good sign and a guarantee of businesslike conduct when Rubehn's visits grew rarer and, by November, almost ceased entirely. Indeed, "our new branch manager," as the Commercial Councillor was pleased to call him, now made his appearance only at small or very small receptions, and would probably have preferred to miss even those. He could not remain unaware that Reiff and Duquede, and especially Gryczinski, were treating him with cool formality. True, the lovely Jacobine tried, somewhat fur-tively, to reestablish friendly relations, and begged Rubehn not to neglect her brother-in-law's house entirely—both for her own sake and for Melanie's; but every time she men-tioned her sister's name she lowered her eyes in embarrass-ment and broke off hurriedly and nervously, for Gryczinski had given her strict instructions to either avoid talking to Rubehn altogether or at least to limit her conversation to a few words.

The little gatherings were much gayer without the Gryczinskis, when only the two painters and Anastasia were present. Then they laughed and joked as they had done in the
coffee house at Stralow. Van der Straaten had got to hear of
visits—frequent visits—by Rubehn to Anastasia's apartment,
and he used this information to indulge his old predilection
for making elaborate fun of everyone concerned. Speaking
for himself, he saw no reason why he should not be
genuinely delighted by this new relationship, based as it was
on a pure communion of musical tastes. Indeed, he would
consider it his duty to be delighted, if it were not for his belief
in the old maxim that each new right could come into existence only at the expense of some older right. In this case the
new right was represented by his friend Rubehn, and the old
by his friend Elimar; and although he was willing to grant
that the latter had remained very much his old self, indeed,
his old self to the nth power when it came to the pleasures of
the table, yet this in itself constituted an undeniable danger.
Because he was well aware that this increase of consumption
was commensurate with the consumption wrought by
Elimar's inward fires. But whether these inward fires should
go by the name of love, hate, or jealousy, only He could tell
who sees into the abyss.

Thus van der Straaten's volley of squibs hissed and
exploded all around, but those for whom they were intended
were the least affected by the flying sparks. The fact was,
matters stood very diferently from what the pyrotechnical
Commercial Councillor supposed. At the Stralow outing,
Elimar had committed himself far beyond his will and desire,
and now Rubehn's apparent rivalry had given him back his
freedom, which was infinitely more precious to him than
Anastasia's love; and she, on the other hand, was able to
forget the evident sinking of her star in the delight of finding
another highly interesting relationship developing before her
eyes and under her protection. Each day she reveled more
and more in her role of confidante; and, being exceptionally
well endowed with Mother Eve's propensity for things secret
and forbidden, she not only counted these winter weeks

among the most entertaining of her richly entertaining life, but also enjoyed the indescribable pleasure of being able to laugh at van der Straaten at the very moment when he, in his Pasha mood, thought he was making *her* the object of everyone's ridicule—including, of course, his own; for *au fond* she found him tiresome and uncongenial.

In fact, if our friend the Commercial Councillor had been more observant and less wrapped up in self-regard he should have suspected something, and Anastasia's smiling equanimity should have shaken his own. But on the contrary, he basked in his blind confidence to a degree which, given his distrustful and pessimistic character, would have been incomprehensible but for the fact that now as always he was blinded by preconceptions which were the very reverse of the true state of affairs. With his exaggerated perspicacity he often saw things which were not there, while missing what was obvious. He lived in superstitious dread of an annihilating blow to his happiness, but expected it neither today nor tomorrow; and the more certain and inevitable it seemed in the distant future, the safer and more carefree he felt in the present. And least of all did he expect the danger to come from the direction in which it lay and where any other man would have recognized it. But here again he lived under the spell of a preconceived notion—in this case an artificially constructed Rubehn, who shared a superficial relationship with the real Rubehn but nothing else. He saw Rubehn as the child of Frankfurt patricians, governed by ideas of correct behavior and family honor; capable of youthful indiscretions but never of betraying trust or breaking the domestic peace. He was, moreover, engaged to be married—the more firmly engaged the more he denied it. And over tea in the evenings when Anastasia was present and the subject of engagements came up, van der Straaten would be in the most complacent good humor: "You women hear the grass grow—especially this particular kind of grass. I should really like to know whom he's tied himself down to. One thing I certainly suspect: ten to one, she's a lady of the old aristocracy, something like Schrecken von Schreckenstein or Sattler von der Hölle." And then both ladies would protest, but they did it so cleverly and carefully that instead of proving anything, their protests only served to make van der Straaten more secure in his preconceived idea.

And so it went until Christmas Eve, when all our friends except Rubehn were assembled around the candle-lit tree in the first room of the picture gallery. Elimar and Gabler had insisted upon adding their contribution to the wealth of presents: a huge doll house, three stories high, with a laundry in the basement complete with boiler, wash tub, and mangle. It was an old-fashioned mangle with a wooden roller in stone casing; and it really worked. There was soon no doubt that the doll house was the triumph of the evening, and both children were in a state of bliss. Even Lydia had abandoned her superior, aristocratic manner and allowed Elimar to throw her into the air and catch her. For he was a gymnast and acrobat. And even Melanie joined in the laughter and seemed to delight in the happiness of the others—even to share it. But if you had looked more closely, you would have seen that she was making an effort, and sometimes she appeared to have been crying. There was something infinitely soft and melancholy about the expression in her eyes, and the Police Councillor said to Duquede, "Look, isn't she more beautiful than ever?"

"Pale and run down," said the latter. "There are people who always admire a pale and run-down appearance. I don't. Altogether, she's overrated, overrated in every respect, but especially for her beauty."

The presents were followed by the usual supper, and they finished the evening with a Swedish punch. Everyone was merry and having a good time. Melanie recovered her spirits, and her color returned. Riekchen and Anastasia stayed until the very end. Accompanying them to the stairs, Melanie called after Riekchen in her warm, captivating voice, "Be careful, Christel has just been telling me the ground is icy." And she bent over the banisters and waved.

"Oh, I shan't fall," said Riekchen. "Short people never fall. Especially when they're equally balanced in front and behind."

But Melanie did not hear Riekchen's last words. Looking over the banisters had made her dizzy, and she would have fallen if van der Straaten had not caught her and carried her back to her room. He wanted to send for the doctor. But she begged him not to. It was nothing, nothing serious, at any rate nothing the doctor could do anything about.

And then she told him what it was.

14

DECISION

It was three days before Melanie was sufficiently recovered to pay a visit to the Alsenstrasse. She had not been there for weeks. But first she intended to visit a Frenchwoman only recently settled in the city—Madame Guichard, whose hats and artificial flowers Anastasia had highly recommended. Van der Straaten advised Melanie to take the carriage because she was was still a little under the weather; but she insisted on walking. And so she put on her latest Christmas present, a mink coat and a little beaver hat with an ostrich plume, and she had just reached the bottom landing when she encountered Rubehn, who had heard that she was not well and was coming to enquire after her.

"Oh, what a good thing you've come," said Melanie. "Now I shall have company on my walk. Van der Straaten wanted to force his carriage on me, but I've been longing for fresh air and exercise. I've been longing for it so much . . . I feel so anxious and oppressed."

And then she interrupted herself and quickly added, "Give me your arm. I'm going to my sister's. But first I want to buy flowers for the ball, and you can come with me. Just half an hour. And then I shall set you free—quite free."

"You mustn't do that, Melanie. You won't do that."

"Yes, I shall."

"But I don't *want* to be set free."

Melanie laughed. "That's how you men are. Tyrannical and self-willed, even when you are being gracious, even when you mean to serve us. Come on now. I want you to help me choose the flowers. I have absolute faith in your taste. Garnet flowers, don't you think?"

And they went down the Grosse Petristrasse, through the square, and into a labyrinth of small streets. Close to the Jägerstrasse they discovered Madame Guichard's, a small shop with some of her French flowers displayed in the window.

And then they went inside. They looked through a few boxes and made their choice without wasting many words. Rubehn had indeed chosen garnet flowers, and a manageress who was present promised to have everything delivered. Melanie gave the Frenchwoman her card. The woman struggled with the long style and designation and with the name, but a smile spread over her face when she read "née de Caparoux." Her face—not pretty—suddenly lit up, and it was with an indescribable expression of happiness and melancholy that she said, *"Madame est française...ah, notre belle France!"*

Melanie had not remained insensible to this little incident, and when she took her friend's arm outside she said, "Did you hear? *Ah, notre belle France!"*

"It sounded so wistful. Yes, she's homesick. We're all homesick. But for where? For what?... For our happiness... For our happiness. Which no one recognizes and no one sees. How does it go in that Schubert song?"

"Where you are *not,* there happiness lies."

"Where you are *not,"* Melanie repeated.

Rubehn was touched, and involuntarily looked into her eyes. But then he turned away, because he did not want to see the tear that glistened there.

They parted just before they reached the big square at the end of the street. He, for his part, would have liked to accompany her further, but she would not have it and said softly, "No, Rubehn, you have been too much with me already. We mustn't provoke evil tongues before it's necessary. Not that I have any right to talk about evil tongues. Good-bye." And she turned round once more, bidding him farewell with a slight movement of her hand.

He looked after her, and a feeling of terror and of the enormous responsibility of disturbing another's happiness overcame him. What is to become of us? he asked himself. But then his expression grew gentler and more serene, and he said to himself, "I am not a fool who rushes in where angels fear to tread. She was no angel, and is no angel. Certainly not. But she is the most engaging human being, as engaging as any that ever trod this earth. And I love her far, far more than I thought, far, far more than I ever thought I could love. Courage, Melanie, courage. There are difficult days ahead, and I can see them gathering around you. But afterwards I think I can see them clearing. Courage, courage is all we need."

Three or four days later, on New Year's Eve, the Gryczin-skis gave a small dance, and Melanie was the belle of the ball. Jacobine stood aside and did not begrudge her older sister's triumph. "Superb creature. An Egyptian princess," rasped Major von Schnabel. He had been posted to the capi-tal from the provinces because he was such a fine figure of an Uhlan, and Gryczinski used to say of him: "A born dancing partner for a princess. What a pity there are no princesses left."

But Schnabel was not Melanie's only admirer. The far win-dow recess was occupied by a group of young officers: Wensky of the coffee-colored Ohlau Hussars, a passionate sportsman and steeplechaser (he had fractured his thigh three times in the same place); then Captain Stiffelius of the Engineers, a famous mathematician, as dry and bony as his equations; and between them Lieutenant Tigris, a little, yellow-faced Fuselier from the Zauche-Belzig regiment; for reasons no one had ever been able to discover he had been an attaché at the Paris embassy for several years, since which time he considered himself to be half French, a libertine, and a lady killer. He thought young girls "ridiculous." Although he had the eyes of a veritable lynx, he raised his pince-nez on its short silk ribbon and said, "Wensky, you are more or less at home here, cock of the walk, as it were. Who is that beauty with the garnet flowers in her hair? I could swear I've seen her before. But I can't place her. She's a mixture between the Duchesse de Mouchy and la Beauffremont. *Un teint de lys et de rose et tout à fait distinguée.*"

"You've hit the nail on the head, *mon cher Tigris,*" laughed Wensky. She's Gryczinska's sister, née de Caparoux."

"Ah, so that's why. Every inch a Frenchwoman. I knew I couldn't be mistaken. And look how she laughs!"

Yes, Melanie really was laughing. But anyone seeing her the next day would scarcely have recognized the beauty of the evening before, and certainly would not have heard her laugh. Unwell and haggard, at odds with herself and the world, she lay on her sofa reading; and when she had finished the book, she leafed back through the pages in order to remind herself more or less of what she had read. Her thoughts wandered. Rubehn came to ask after her, but she would not admit him and sulked as she did with everyone else. Only in weeping did she find relief.

Several weeks passed in this manner, and when she got up and began to speak again and to look after the house and the children, she did everything with a new sharpness and intensity; the energetic spirit of her former days had returned, but not the old mood. She was irritable, vehement, and bitter. And, what was worse, capricious. Van der Straaten mounted a campaign against this many-headed foe, and was effective on one or two occasions; but on the whole his efforts were a failure. He wisely countered her irritability with tolerance, but unwisely tried to conquer her caprice with displays of affection. It was this that forced the decision. Each day was more painful to her than the one before. For many years she had been proud and always confident of victory; she had played with the man whose plaything she appeared and pretended to be; now she winced and trembled nervously when she heard his distant step in the corridor. What did he want? What was the purpose of his visit? And then she had an urge

to flee and leap out of the window. When he finally appeared
and took her hand in order to kiss it, she said, "Go away.
Please. I'd rather be alone."

And when she was alone she would rush out, often without a destination, oftener still to Anastasia's quiet, secluded
apartment, and when the expected visitor appeared, all the
misery in her heart would break out in bitter tears, and she
would sob and moan that she could stand the lies and the
pretense no longer. "Stand by me, help me, Reuben, or you
won't see much more of me. I must get away, away; or I shall
die of shame and sorrow."

And he was just as shaken and said, "Don't talk like that,
Melanie. Don't talk as though I did not want exactly what you
want. I disturbed your happiness (if it was happiness) and I
want to restore it. Anywhere in the world, however and
wherever you want. Any time, any day."

And then they built castles in the air and dreamed and saw
a smiling future all about them. But they spoke of real plans
too, and parted with tears of happiness.

15

THE VERNEZOBRES

And what they planned was flight. On the last day of January
they were to meet at a railway station early in the morning,
and go far, far away, over the Alps to the south. "Yes, over
the Alps," Melanie had said with a sigh of relief, and she felt
as though a new life could begin only on the other side of that
great wall of mountains, which would separate and protect
her from her present life. And they had also discussed what
they would do if van der Straaten should want to interfere
with their plan. "He won't," Melanie had said. "And why
not? He's not always tenderly considerate of others, and
sometimes he enjoys flouting the world and its gossip." "All

the same, he'll spare himself—himself and us. And if you really want to know why—because he loves me. Oh, I have not thanked him well for it. Oh, Reuben, what a difference between what we mean to do and what we do! Ingratitude, unfaithfulness—how I hate them. And yet—I would do it again, all of it, all of it. And I don't want things not to be as they are."

And so the weeks of January passed. And now it was the night before the appointed day. Melanie had gone to bed early and told her old servant to wake her punctually at three. She could rely on her absolutely, although by virtue of her long years of service—and by virtue of those alone—Christel belonged to the van der Straaten legacies whom Duquede had organized into a silent opposition against Melanie.

It had barely struck three when she entered the room. But she found her mistress already up and could only help her to dress. Even in this she was not of much use, for her hands trembled and, as she put it, she had "a flicker in front of her eyes." But at last everything was ready, and Melanie, in her stout leather boots, said, "There we are, Christel. And now get me the bag so we can pack."

Christel fetched the bag from a dressing table by the window and unfastened it. "There, this is what's to go in. I've written it all down." And as she spoke, Melanie tore a page from her notebook and gave it to the old woman. Christel held the piece of paper to the light and read and shook her head.

"Oh, ma'am, dear sweet ma'am, that's nothing... Oh, dear sweet ma'am, you're so..."

"So spoiled, you were going to say. Yes, Christel, I am. But being spoiled doesn't make you happy. You people have a saying, 'Little but with love.' And people laugh at it. But they always laugh at what's most true. And you know, we're not going out of the world. We're only traveling, and when you travel, you should travel light. And you must admit, Christel, I can't leave the house with a huge trunk. If I did that, I might as well take my jewel case and the strong box as well."

As she spoke, Melanie held her hands over the fire, which had burned low. She felt cold and shivery. She sat down in

an armchair and looked at the glowing coals and back to
Christel who was packing the few things on the list, talking
and weeping softly to herself as she did so. And then everything was ready, and she fastened the bag and placed it at
Melanie's feet.

A few minutes passed and neither spoke. Eventually Christel came up behind her young mistress and said, "Good
Lord, ma'am, do you really have to . . . Don't go away. I know
I'm just a silly old woman. But sometimes silly people aren't
as silly as all that. An' I tell you, ma'am, you wouldn't believe
what people can get used to. Lord, people can get used to
anything. An' if a person's rich, an' has a lot of money, he can
put up with a lot too. I could, I can tell you. An' how do
people do it? An' how do they live? There's a ghost in every
house, so they say, nowadays. It's one of those modern
sayings. An' in some houses there are two, an' making such a
racket you can hear them in broad daylight. That's how it was
at the Vernezobres. Well, I'm fifty now, an' I've been here
twenty-three years. An' seven with the Vernezobres before
that. An' he was a Commercial Councillor too, an' everything
was just the same. Almost, that is."

"And what happened?" Melanie smiled.

"What happened? What always happens. She was thirty
and he was fifty. An' she was as pretty as they come. Plump
an' fair-haired, people used to say. Well, and him? I won't
say what people said about him. It wasn't very nice. And
then, of course, there was an architect, not a real architect,
just one of those men that build bridges for the trains to go
over, with railings an' little holes to see through. An' he'd be
there quick as a weasel when they went out to concerts or to
Pichelsberg or Saatwinkel, an' he'd always be carrying her
jacket, an' her fan, an' her parasol, an' then they were always
looking for strawberries an' getting lost an' never to be found
when the others wanted to go home. An' the master, he was
always worried, always thinking something had happened.
An' the others, well, they just used to whisper."

"And did they separate? Or did they stay together? I'mean
the Vernezobres," said Melanie, who had given only half her
attention to the story.

"Of course they stayed together. Once I heard 'em, 'cause I was in the room next door, an' he said, 'Hulda, it won't do" 'Cos her name really was Hulda. An' he was going to reproach her. But that was just what she wanted. An' she turned the tables on him and asked him what he wanted. All she wanted was out, she said. An' she loved him—the other one, I mean—and didn't love *him*. An' she wouldn't dream of loving him. It was enough to make a person laugh, she said it really was. An' she went on an' on, an' she really did laugh. An' then he climbed down, humble as a worm, an' only asked her to think it over. An' that's what she did, an' come the end of May, the Vernezobres got their doctor, one of those clever doctors who know everything, an' he said she had to go to the seaside—I can't remember the name of the place—but it's the one where they have the biggest waves. An' that was in the days when they were building the suspension bridge, an' people used to say he could do the figuring for it better than anyone else. An' our Commercial Councillor, he only came down Saturdays. They were free all week. An' by the end of August or thereabouts, she came back, all fresh an' cheerful, an' her cheeks were quite pink, an' she was all over him. An' he was right out of the picture."

While Christel was speaking, Melanie had thrown a few logs on the coals, and the fire began to crackle once more. She said, "You mean well. But it won't do. I'm different. And even if I'm not, at least I imagine I am."

"Well, things are always a bit different," said Christel. "An' she was only from down by the river at Neu-Kölln, right opposite the musical clock. But it wasn't the clock's fault; that was always playing 'Be ever true and honest.'"[28]

"Oh my dear Christel, true and honest! That's what everyone would like to be, unless they're really bad. But you know, one can be true by being untrue. Truer than by remaining faithful."

"Oh ma'am, you mustn't talk like that! I really don't understand it. But I must tell you one thing, when people talk like that an' I don't understand them, there's always something wrong. An' you say you're different. Well, that's true, an' even if it isn't quite true, at least it's half true. But the main thing is, the main thing, my dear little mistress has her heart in the right place, and is always wanting to be helpful and kind, and is always on the side of the poor. But that Vernezobre lady, well, she was always getting dressed up, always standing in front of the mirror that made everything look even prettier, an' she looked like a fashion magazine, an' all the same she was really stupid. Stupid as a hat stand, as the saying goes. An' she wasn't out of the top drawer, like you, ma'am; they were only dyers, her people, bright red. But there's one thing I grant you: yours is a different kind from the one the Vernezobre lady had, and doesn't give himself airs, and says whatever he thinks, and can't turn anyone down. At Christmas he gives twice as much."

Melanie nodded.

"There you are, ma'am, that's right; you're nodding, and if you go on nodding at what I say, then things 'll sort themselves out, and we'll be able to start unpacking. You go to bed and sleep until daylight. And on the stroke of twelve I'll bring you your coffee and your chocolate, all on one tray, and when I tell you how we sat here and all the things we said, it'll all seem like a dream. Because it's my opinion he really is a good man, a very good man, only a bit odd. An' there's nothing wrong with being odd. And a rich man can get away with it. If I were rich, I'd be even odder. And him talking like that and sounding like he was from the wrong side of the tracks, well, for heaven's sake, why shouldn't he? Why shouldn't he talk like that if it gives him pleasure? He likes Berlinese, that's all. After all, he is a Berliner . . ."

16

PARTING

Christel broke off with a start and retired to the next room, for van der Straaten had come in. He was still in the same evening clothes in which he had returned an hour after mid-

night, and his haggard features expressed anxiety and ex-
haustion. How he had heard of Melanie's plan remained a
mystery. But everything showed that he had made up his
mind to let things take their course. If he came, nonetheless it
was not to stop Melanie by force but to ask her to think it over
and to plead with her. He came not in indignation but in love.

He drew an armchair toward the fire and sat down facing
Melanie. "You want to leave me, Melanie?"

"Yes, Ezel."

"Why?"

"Because I love another."

"That's not a reason."

"It is."

"And I'm telling you, Lanni, it will pass. Believe me; I
know you women. You can't bear monotony—not even the
monotony of happiness. And the greatest happiness of all—
peace—is what women hate most. You are made for unrest.
You would rather have a conscience that's pricking you than
one that isn't. To a woman, the idea of 'sleeping the sleep of
the just' couldn't be more tedious and absurd. You simply
don't want to rest. Women always want something to tickle
or pinch them, and with your excessive sensuality—or your
heroism, if you prefer, you find delight in your sufferings."

"You may be right, Ezel. But the more right you are, the
more you justify me and what I intend to do. If it really is as
you say, then women are born gamblers, and staking all is
really part of our nature. Mine too, of course."

He liked to hear her talk like this; it sounded like the good
old days; and moving his armchair closer, in a confidential
manner, he said, "Don't let's be too narrow-minded, Lanni.
People say I'm bourgeois, and they may be right. But
narrow-minded I am not. And even if I don't take a noble,
idealistic view of the world, I don't take a petty, narrow one
either. Please, Lanni, don't rush into anything. My stock's
low at the moment, but it will recover. I don't flatter myself
that you—a beautiful and charming creature, singled out and
made much of by all the best and cleverest men—I don't
flatter myself that you married me from sheer affection, even

less from romantic love. You accepted me because you were still young and had never been in love; and your wits and commonsense told you that all those young attachés were no heroes or demigods either. And because the van der Straaten firm had a good name. So let's not talk about love. But you had no *objections* to me either, you found me a bit out of the ordinary, and you enjoyed talking to me and laughing and joking with me. And then the children arrived, and you must agree they are charming children—you take the credit for that, I admit; and for ten years you've lived with the idea—and the experience too—that there are worse things than to be a well-situated young woman, the apple of her husband's eye, a pampered young wife who can do whatever she pleases and doesn't have to make the slightest effort in return except to put on an agreeable face when she feels like it. And you see, Melanie, that's all I'm asking now—or perhaps I'd better say that's all I'm asking for the future. Because at this moment even the little I ask must seem too much to you. But things will change; they must change. And I repeat: I shall be satisfied with a minimum. I'm not asking for passion. I don't want you to look at me as though I were Leone Leoni,[29] or some other hero from fiction, with women downing poisoned chalices for him as though it were almond milk, and dying with a smile on their face, just to see *him* smile once more. I'm no Leone Leoni, I'm just a German of Dutch extraction, which doesn't make being German any better, and I've the broad cheekbones that go with my ancestry. I've no illusions, especially about my appearance, and I don't expect heroic acts of love from you. Not even renunciation. Renunciation comes of its own accord, and that's the best way. It's best because then it's an act of free will, and that makes it lasting and reliable. Don't rush into anything. Everything will fall into place."

He had risen and gripped the back of his chair, rocking himself back and forth. He continued, "And one more thing, Lanni. I'm not a man for niceties, and I hate all those boring considerations for nothing at all. But all the same, I'm telling you, have some consideration for *yourself*. It's no good always thinking what people will say, but it's even worse never to think of it at all. I've experienced that for myself. And now think it over. If you go *now* . . . you know what I mean. You can't go now. Not *now*."

"That's just the reason, Ezel," she answered softly. "I want things to be straight between us. I'm sick of this vile lie."

He had greedily sucked in every word; in moments of crisis one wants to hear even one's death sentence. And now it had been pronounced. He let go of the chair and threw himself into it, and for a moment he felt he was going to faint. But he quickly recovered. Wiping his forehead and temples he said, "Very well. That too. I shall get over it. Let's talk. Even about that. You can see how this is hurting me—more than anything in my life has hurt me. But all the same, I know it's the way of the world, and I've no right to preach morals at you. When I think of my own past! . . . It had to come, it was bound to, according to the family law of the van der Straatens. (And why shouldn't we have a family law too?) And I think I've always known it, since I was a child." After a while he continued, "There's a saying: the mills of God grind slow. And you know, when I was a little boy our old nurse used to say it, and it always made me uneasy. I expect it was a premonition. Now I'm between the two millstones, and I feel as though I were being ground down and crushed . . ."

Ground down? He slammed his fist into his palm and repeated the word once more, though suddenly in a different tone: "Ground down! There's really something quite amusing about it. And honestly, let the devil take all cowards. I refuse to go on tormenting myself. And I'm disgusted with myself for making such a song and dance. Pooh, the armchair moralists of the world exaggerate the whole business, and we are foolish enough to repeat their blather after them. And we always forget what splendid creatures we really are, and we forget how it always was, is now, and ever shall be. Was it any better in the days of my godfather Ezechiel? Or when Adam dug the ground and Eve span? Isn't the Old Testament one long shocker? Triple secrets of Paris! I tell you, Lanni, compared to those, we're newborn lambs, white as snow. Innocents! And now listen to me. No one need know, and I'll care for it as though it were my own. It's yours, after all, and that's all that matters. For if I may say so without offending you, I love you and I want to keep you. It won't matter. I won't let it. Only stay."

When he began to speak, Melanie had been profoundly moved, but as he went on, he himself destroyed that feeling by the words he used. It was always the same old song. Everything he said came from a generous heart, but the tolerance took a form that wounded her. In spite of his deep emotion he treated the incident as a trifle, with contempt and a definite streak of cynical amusement. He meant well: he loved Melanie and he wanted her to take advantage of his attitude. But her inner nature was more fastidious, and it revolted against such treatment. What had happened, she knew, would condemn her in the eyes of the world, would humiliate her; but at the same time she took pride in putting her whole life on the line, in the unreserved confession of her love. And now suddenly all this was to be a mere nothing, or little more than nothing—something quite ordinary, easy to overlook and disregard. She could not bear it. And she felt distinctly that what had happened was more pardonable than his attitude toward it. He had no god and no faith, and there was only one possible excuse for him; his desire to make it easy for her, his wish to make up at *any* price, had made him speak in a manner which did not reflect what was really in his heart. Yes, that must be it. But if it was, then she could not accept his gift of mercy. At any rate, she did not want to.

"You mean well, Ezel," she said, "but it cannot be. It's just that everything has its natural consequence, and this particular consequence means our separation. I know that worse things happen every day; less than half an hour ago Christel was chattering to me about it. But everyone has a law written in their heart, and mine tells me that I must go. You love me, and so you want to overlook it. But you mustn't and you *can't*. Because you're not the same every hour of the day, none of us is. And no one can forget. But memories are powerful, and a stain is a stain, and guilt is guilt."

She was silent for a moment and bent over to the right toward the fireplace to throw a few small pieces of coal on the flames, which were now burning brightly. Suddenly, as though a completely new thought had struck her, she said with all her former vivacity, "Oh Ezel, here I am going on and on about guilt, and it must sound as though I wanted to be a repentant Magdalene. I'm positively ashamed of having used such highfalutin words. But it's true—there's no situation in which we don't deceive ourselves and play-act. What is the real position? I want to go, not because I feel guilty, but because I am proud: I want to go in order to rebuild my self-respect. I can't bear the petty feelings that cling to all lies: I want my position to be clear, and to be able to look people in the eye. And I can only do that if I go, if I leave you and acknowledge my acts before the world. There will be a big scandal, and virtuous, self-righteous people will never forgive me. But there are more than virtuous and self-righteous people in the world; there are human beings as well, who look on human behavior with human understanding. They are the ones I put my hope in; they are the ones I need. And most of all I need myself. I want to live at peace with myself again, and if not at peace, then at least without discord and duplicity."

Van der Straaten looked as though he were going to reply, but she would not let him, and said: "Don't say no. That's how it is—it can't be otherwise. I want to hold up my head again and feel like myself. It's pure self-righteousness. And I know it would be better and more unselfish if I forced myself to stay, always supposing I could start by repenting. Repentance and remorse are what I should feel. But I can't. I have a purely superficial sense of guilt, and though my head may surrender, my heart goes on protesting. I admit it's a stubborn heart, and I'm not trying to justify it. But it's no use scolding it or railing at it. And so you see, there's only one help for me, only one way of escape from myself: I must start a new life and find in *him* what was missing from my old life, and that is truth. Let me go. I'm not trying to make excuses, but let me just say this: it's a good thing that the law that's separating us should coincide with my own selfish desire."

He had risen to take her hand and she let him. But when he tried to bend down and kiss her forehead she would not allow it and shook her head: "No Ezel, not like that. Let there be no more between us that could confuse or torment or frighten me; it can only make things harder without altering anything... I am expected. And I don't want to begin my new life by being unpunctual. Unpunctuality is a kind of disorder. And that's what I must avoid. I want order in my life, order and unity. And now good-bye, and forget."

He had acquiesced, and she took the little bag standing beside her and went. When she reached the tapestry door that led to the children's bedroom, she stopped and looked back. He took it as a good sign and said, "You want to see the children?"

Those were the words she had dreaded, the words she could hear within herself too. Her eyes widened, there was a tremor around her mouth, and she had not the strength to say no. But she controlled herself and only shook her head and went toward the door and out on to the landing.

Christel was already there, a candle in her hand, ready to take her mistress's little bag and accompany her down the two flights of stairs. But Melanie refused. "No, Christel, now I must find my way by myself." The second flight was in darkness, and she had to feel her way down.

"It's beginning straight away," she said.

The house was already unlocked. A cold wind blew from the direction of the Brüderstrasse, and feathery snowflakes fluttered in the air. She was reminded of the day—almost a year ago now—when the snowflakes were whirling as they were today, and she had been seized with a childish longing to rise and sink as they did.

Now she made her way toward the bridge to the Spittelmarkt. The only person in sight was the lamplighter; he ran ahead of her with his long narrow ladder, and when he reached the top he would look down at her, half sly and half inquisitive, not quite knowing what to make of her.

Beyond the bridge she met a cab coming slowly toward her. The coachman was asleep, and the horse was almost asleep too; but as there was nothing better in sight she gently tugged the man—he was still drowsy—by his coat, and eventually got in and gave him the name of the station. He seemed to understand and agree to take her. But as soon as she sat down, he turned on the box and grumbled through the little spy-hole that he was a night cabbie and frozen stiff, and had had nothing to eat since eleven o'clock, and was on his way home. So she had to plead with him until he relented. And then he started to whip up the poor beast and they went jolting down the long road.

She threw herself back and braced her feet against the front seat, but the upholstery was damp and cold and the little lamp was flickering out and filled the cab with dingy smoke. Something seemed to press harder and harder on her temples, and she felt sick at heart and nauseated by the wretched breath of poverty about her. At length she let down the window and began to enjoy the fresh breeze blowing in. And she enjoyed the awakening life of the city and would have liked to greet every baker's boy who went by singing and whistling with his wares high on his head. For at least it was a merry sound and helped her to struggle out of her depression.

Meanwhile they had come to the last crossroad. She looked out of the window, becoming more and more nervous, for it seemed to her that all the traffic going in their direction was overtaking her own miserable conveyance with ever increasing haste. First one or two vehicles, then many. She knocked and called out. But in vain. And in the end she felt as though it were her fault, as though her strength were ebbing away; she would be the last, she would be left behind, not just today, but tomorrow and for ever. And she was overcome by a feeling of infinite misery. "Courage, courage," she cried to herself. She took her feet off the front seat and sat up. And there, she felt much better. Resuming her outward poise had brought back her composure.

At last the cab stopped. Because no luggage was visible either on top or at the driver's side, no one came to assist her or to open the door. She had to open it herself from the inside. Looking about her she thought, "What if he's not here?" But she had no time to finish the thought. The next moment, Rubehn stepped forward from one of the entrance pillars and offered her his hand to help her down. Her foot on the straw-covered step, she put her head on his shoulder and whispered, "Thank God! Oh, *what* an hour that was. Please, please, my only beloved, help me to forget it."

And he lifted the beloved burden and set it down, and took her arm and her bag, and so they went up the stairs to the platform where the train stood waiting.

17

DELLA SALUTE

"To the south!" And they traveled by easy stages, often stopping for several days, because that was all that Melanie's shaken state of health would allow. They crossed the Brenner and reached Rome by the end of February. There they were to stay until Easter and await "news from home." They deliberately chose a neutral expression, for the news they expected was to decide their whole future, and they had to wait longer than they would have liked. But at last it came, the "news from home," and the very next morning saw them both at the door of a little English chapel. They had already made the acquaintance of the clergyman, and it was his gentleness that had caused them to confide in him. There were even a few friends present, and after the religious ceremony they all set out from the city where they had been shut up for many months; they wanted to leave its walls behind and enjoy the splendor of the crocuses and violets at the Villa d'Este. Everyone rejoiced, especially Melanie. She was happy, infinitely happy. Everything that had oppressed her heart had gone from her, and she laughed with childlike innocence as she had not laughed for a long time. People who can laugh like that never lose the capacity; even if they do, it always returns. And it outlasts guilt and builds bridges backwards and forwards into better times.

True, on this day she had begun to feel free, but she

wanted to be freer still. When it grew dark, they returned to their lodging. The excellent Roman landlady had already lit the fire in the chimney as well as the triple wick of the lamp, and Melanie decided to write to her sister Jacobine that very evening. She wanted to ask certain questions and at the same time to talk about her happiness and her journey.

And she did, and this is what she wrote:

My dear Jacobine,

Today was a real holiday; more than that—a happy day, and I feel like expressing my gratitude. And that is why I am writing. And to whom should I write but to you, my dear, darling sister! Or perhaps you do not want to hear that word any more? Or perhaps you are not allowed to?

I am writing these lines in the Via Catena, a little side street that runs down to the Tiber, and when I look down I can see a few lights shining on the other side. And these lights are in the Farnesina, the famous villa where Cupid and Psyche seem to lean down from every lintel. But I ought not to make jokes about such matters, nor would I, but for the fact that we went to the chapel today. At last, at last! And do you know who was among the witnesses? Our Captain von Brausewetter, your old dancing partner at the Dachrodens. And he was sweet and good and not superior at all. When you are an outcast, which is even worse than being unhappy, you get an eye for that kind of thing, and that painting, you know the one I mean, the one I made all those remarks and jokes about—well, I cannot get it out of my mind. It's always the same: casting stones, casting stones. But the divine voice that spoke to the Pharisees, that voice is silent.

But enough of that. I want to tell you what's been happening.

We traveled by easy stages, and at the beginning I was exhausted and took no pleasure in anything, or if I pretended to, it was only for Reuben's sake. Because I was so sorry for him. A tearful woman! Oh, it's absolutely the worst thing in the world. And especially when one is traveling. And so it went for a whole week, until we got into the

mountains. Then it got better, and when we drove along the
foaming Inn River and got to Innsbruck that same afternoon,
and found a wonderful place to stay—then it dropped away
from me and I was able to breathe again. And when Reuben
saw how everything was doing me good and making me feel
better, he stayed another day and took me to see all the
churches and palaces, and we finished up with the church
where the emperor Max is buried. He's the one on the Martinswand,[30] the one who lived in Luther's day. And he's
also the one Anastasius Grün celebrated as "the last
knight"—which was probably going a bit far. He was altogether too fat and portly for a knight, and, without flattering you, I think Gryczinski is much more like one.
Strangely enough I feel altogether much more Prussified
than I thought, so that I didn't like the picture of Andreas
Hofer much either. He wears a belt with a Tyrolean motto
round his middle, and, as you may have heard, he was shot
at Mantua. Some people criticize him because he's supposed
to have been afraid. I for my part have never been able to
understand how one can blame a person for not wanting to
be shot.

    And then we crossed the Brenner, which was all covered
with snow, and it was marvelous when we looked out of our
train window and saw two or three other trains below us on
the same mountainside, as tiny and insignificant as the food
boxes on a linnet's cage. And that same evening we got to
Verona. Last time I was there we just passed through, but
this time we stayed a day because Reuben wanted to show
me the ancient Roman theater in the town. It was a cold
day, and I was frozen in the icy wind, but still, I'm glad to
have seen it. How ever can I describe it to you? Imagine the
opera house, not on an ordinary night, but when they have
a charity ball—and the place where the orchestra sits is
curved like the rest of the place. It's completely egg-shaped,
and the whole thing is an amphitheater with the sky for
a ceiling, and I should have enjoyed it all even more if I
hadn't been persuaded to go to a restaurant close by and
have a salami lunch, which was much too Italian for me.

    The next week we got to Florence, and if I were Duquede,

I'd say it was overrated. It's full of English people and pictures, and the pictures are too much of a good thing. And then they have what they call the *cascine*, a bit like our Tiergartenallee or Hofjägerallee, and they are very proud of them, and you do see carriages with six and twelve and even twenty-four horses. But I didn't see any, and I don't want to confuse you with figures. Over the Arno there is a bridge full of stalls like the Rialto, and apart from the churches and monasteries the most important sight to see is the ducal palace. What they admire most is a little turret that sticks up in the middle, rather like a chimney with a wreath and a gallery around it. But it's supposed to be a very original idea. And in the end you come to agree that it is. And quite close by there is a long narrow lane running parallel with the main street, where they roast quail on spits. And everything smells of fat, and there's so much noise and so many flowers and piles of cheeses that one simply doesn't know what to do with oneself, whether to hate it or love it. But in the end one loves it, and I'd say it was really the prettiest sight I saw on our whole journey. Apart from Rome, of course. And we're in Rome now.

But, Jacobine of my heart, I can't tell you about it now because I'm already on my fourth sheet and Reuben is getting impatient and throwing confetti at me from the dark corner where he's sitting, although it's long past carnival time. And so I will stop and just ask a few questions.

Now that I want to ask them, though, the questions won't quite come off my pen, and you must guess what they are. It's not difficult. Be gentle when you answer, but don't conceal anything. I have got to learn to bear unpleasantness and pain. There's nothing else for me. I have no illusions about that. He that toucheth pith will be defiled. And the world will choose worse metaphors than that. All I want is that when they condemn me they should not quite forget the "extenuating circumstances." Because, you see, there was nothing else I could do. All I want is to be allowed to prove it. But I know my wish will not be fulfilled, and I shall have to seek consolation in my happiness, and happiness in retirement. And that's what I shall do. I have had enough of the noisy world, and I long for quiet and time to think. And I have those here. Oh, how beautiful this city is! Sometimes I feel as though it must be true that Rome is the source of all salvation and comfort—Rome alone. It is bliss to walk in this place, you see and hear things of a dreamlike beauty.

And now, my sweet Jacobine, farewell, and write as much as you can and in as much detail as possible. Everything interests me, and I long for news, particularly for news of . . . But you know what. No more of that.

> Ever yours,
> *Melanie R.*

She sent the letter to the post that same evening in the vague feeling that by doing it promptly she could compel her sister to reply promptly. But the reply did not come, and the implicit rebuff would have been deeply wounding to her but for the fact that a few days after she had sent off her letter, Melanie fell back into her former state of melancholy. She was sure she was going to die; she would try to smile, yet burst into torrents of tears. For she clung to life, and in the midst of her sorrow she enjoyed one immeasurable happiness: being with the man she loved.

She was right, indeed, to savor this happiness; for all Reuben's virtues shone more brightly as the days became gloomier. He was all consideration; he was never in a bad mood, never complained, and his innate courtesy concealed even his unselfishness.

And so the dismal weeks went by.

In the end, they consulted a German doctor, who advised Melanie to avoid staying still in one place and to seek as much variety as possible. He prescribed, in other words, a constant change of scene and air. Of course, such toing and froing was an evil in itself, but a lesser evil, and the only remedy for her inner restlessness.

And so new travel plans were made and apathetically received by the ailing Melanie.

Carefully avoiding train journeys and major roads, they journeyed through Umbria and higher up the east coast until they found themselves only ten miles from Venice. And lo and behold, Melanie was seized by an intense longing to await the birth of her child there. Suddenly she was a changed creature and laughing once more; and she said: "Della Salute! Do you remember?... It makes me feel at home. I feel refreshed. Salute—health, salvation. Oh come, let's go to Venice."

And they went, and it was there that the anxious hour arrived. And there was a day when the pointer hovered between life and death. But in the evening bells sounded across the water. "Where from?" asked Melanie, deathly weak. And when the answer came, "From della Salute," she sat up and said, "Now I know I am going to live."

18

HOME AGAIN

Nor did her hopes deceive her. She recovered, but it was not until the first days of autumn that the thriving condition of the child and—more important—her own health enabled them to leave the city to which they felt bound by so many hours of sadness and of joy. They journeyed to Switzerland, to seek a new temporary resting place in the loveliest of all valleys, the valley of Interlaken.

They spent quiet, happy weeks there. Only when a sharp northwest wind swept down from Lake Thun to Lake Brienz, followed next day by heavy snow that blanketed not only the Jungfrau but even the smallest mountain peaks, did Melanie say, "Now it's time. Not every face improves with age, and not every landscape with snow. Winter's not at home in this valley; at least, it doesn't suit it. I'm ready to go back to where people are accustomed to winter and understand how to live with it."

"I do believe," laughed Rubehn, "you're homesick for Rousseau Island."[31]

"Yes," she said, "and a lot of other things as well. Look,

from here it would take me three hours to get to Geneva and see the house where I was born. But it doesn't attract me. It's the north that attracts me, and more and more I feel that that is the country where my heart is at home. And so it must remain, whatever has happened in the meantime."

And one mild December day, Rubehn and Melanie arrived back in the capital accompanied by Vreni, a sturdy Swiss maid they had engaged at Interlaken to look after the child. They had made an excellent choice. Rubehn's younger brother met them at the station and conducted them to their new apartment, a charming mansard close to the west end of the Tiergarten, lavishly but tastefully furnished and almost next door to Duquede. "Are we going to be good neighbors?" they asked with simultaneous amusement the moment they walked in.

Melanie was very pleased with the apartment and its appointments, indeed, with everything; and the very next morning, when she was alone, she sat in one of the deep window bays and gazed out at the frosted trees in the park, where squirrels chased each other, leaping from branch to branch. How often she had watched them when driving through the Tiergarten with Liddy and Heth! Everything suddenly stood before her eyes, and she felt a shadow fall across the happy pictures in her mind.

But at last she felt drawn to go out. She wanted to see the city again, the city and familiar faces. But whose? The only person she could call on was her friend the music teacher. And this she did, but without deriving much pleasure from it. Anastasia received her with familiarity, almost with condescension, and Melanie went home understandably put out. Here too not everything was as it should be: Vreni was in a bad temper, the rooms overheated, and Melanie's good humor returned only when she heard Rubehn's voice from the hall.

He came in.

It was tea time; the water was already on the boil, and she took her beloved by the arm and chatted as they walked over the thick Turkish carpet. But he was oppressed by the heat.

She vainly tried to fan it away with her pocket handkerchief. "And here we are in the north," he laughed. "I ask you, did we ever have to put up with such equatorial conditions in the south?"

"Oh yes, Reuben. Do you remember the first time we went out to the Lido? I shall never forget it, anyway. I've never been so scared in my life as on that boat: first the heat and then the storm. And then the lightning! And if it had just been lightning! But it was like sheets of fire falling from the sky. And you were so calm."

"I always am, my sweet, or at least I try to be. Getting excited doesn't change anything, and certainly never improves matters."

"I'm not so sure you're right. In fear and anguish we pray, even people like us who normally take things as they come. And that reconciles the gods. Because they want us to feel how small and helpless we are. And don't you think they are right?"

"I only know that *you* are right. Always. And for your sake I'll concede the gods are right too. Does that satisfy you?"

"Yes and no. Part of it is love for me, and that's fine—at least, I like to hear it. But . . ."

"Never mind the but and let's have our tea. It's been waiting for us. And tea is always good for everything; it will even help us to stand this African heat. But to make absolutely sure I'll just open the window." And he did. The blind was half down and admitted the gentle evening air.

"How soft and mild," said Melanie.

"Too soft," he replied. "We shall have to be prepared for colder air streams."

19

INCOGNITO

Melanie was glad to be home again.

She did not underestimate what she would have to face,

and she shared the fear that Rubehn had expressed. But she was sufficiently sanguine of temperament to hope that she would overcome all the difficulties ahead. And why shouldn't she? It seemed to her that, as far as society was concerned, they had just about made amends for what had happened; the decencies had been respected, the formalities observed. She did not expect to encounter the kind of severity that society normally practices only when it feels absolutely compelled to—perhaps simply because it realizes that people in glass houses should not throw stones.

Melanie did not expect a rigorously puritanical reception. All the same, she agreed with the suggestion that they should remain incognito at least for the next few weeks, and not begin to pay even the most essential calls until after the New Year.

So it was natural that they should spend Christmas Eve within their narrowest circle. Only Anastasia, Rubehn's brother, and the confidential clerk came to see the Christmas tree with its lighted candles; the clerk was a silent, starchy bachelor, whose tongue normally loosened only at the third glass. When the candles were lit, little Aninette was brought in to join the party, and Melanie took the child in her arms and held her up to the lights. And the child reached for them and laughed and seemed happy.

They were all happy, especially Rubehn, and anyone who saw him that evening would not have found him lacking in warmth or geniality. He had shed all his American demeanour.

Meanwhile, a little supper had been served in the next room. The proceedings were opened by Anastasia, followed by the younger Rubehn, who proposed a few humorous toasts. In the end, even the old clerk got to his feet to bring a final toast: From the bottom of his glass and the bottom of his heart. The best things in life—he knew that from his own experience—were always incognito. What could be found in the streets and markets was worthless rubbish, or at any rate only common, everyday stuff; but things of true value were always hidden in quiet, secluded places. The loveliest flower—there could be no doubt about that—was the violet;

and the most poetical fruit—again without a doubt—was the wild strawberry. Both were hidden, both had to be searched out, both lived, so to speak, incognito. And therefore he drank to the incognito, or the incognitos, because singular and plural were all the same to him:

> They or he,
> A full glass for Melanie.
> They or her,
> A full glass for Ebenezer.

And then he began to sing.

They did not break up until late at night, and Anastasia promised to come back to dinner the next day. And on the day after that (Rubehn had just gone into town), Vreni appeared and reported—in evident excitement and her thickest Swiss accent—that Police Councillor Reiff wished to be announced. She did not calm down until her young mistress said, "Ah, how nice. Please ask him to come in."

Melanie went to greet her visiotr. He was quite unchanged: the same shining face, the same black frock coat, the same white vest.

"What a joy to see you again, dear Reiff," said Melanie; and with her right hand she pointed to the armchair beside her. "You were always a good friend of mine, and I think you always will be."

Reiff made some sort of declaration about his unalterable devotion and asked a string of questions. Eventually he dropped van der Straaten's name—either by chance or deliberately.

Melanie showed no embarrassment and merely said, "You must not mention that name, my dear Reiff, at least, not at present. It's not that it calls up hostile images. No, oh no. If it did, I shouldn't mind. But it's just because the name brings back no unkind memories; because the only thing I know is that I have hurt the man who bears it—that's why the sound of it torments and tortures me. It reminds me of a wrong which is not diminished just because, in my heart, I don't quite feel it to have been a wrong. So let's not talk about him. And let's not talk about . . ." And she fell silent. After a pause she continued, "I am happy now, really happy; mais il faut payer pour tout et deux fois pour notre bonheur."[32]

The Police Councillor stammered his agreement. He was confused because he had not quite understood.

"But you and I, Reiff," Melanie resumed, "we must find neutral ground. And so we shall. That's always been one of the advantages of a big city. There are always a hundred things to talk about. And not just in order to have something to say—no, we can talk from our hearts. Don't you agree? And I count on seeing you again."

Soon, the Police Councillor took his leave because he did not want to keep the cab that had brought him waiting too long. Melanie looked after him and was pleased to see him encounter Rubehn, a few doors on, on his way home from the city. The two men greeted one another.

"Reiff was here," said Rubehn, entering a moment later. "How did you find him?"

"The same as ever. Only more embarrassed than a Police Councillor ought to be."

"Bad conscience. He was trying to sound you out."

"Do you think so?"

"Without a shadow of doubt. They're all the same. Only their manners are different. And Reiff has this air of innocuousness. You have to be especially on your guard with that type. And though it may seem ridiculous, I can't help thinking that tomorrow he'll put us in his black book."

"You're doing him an injustice. He's fond of me. Or do you think that's just vanity and imagination on my part?"

"Perhaps. And perhaps not. But those fellows . . . their best friends, their own brothers are never safe. And if you seem surprised or complain, they turn sarcastic and shrug their shoulders: c'est mon métier, they say."

A week later the New Year had come and with it the time when the young couple intended to break out of their incognito. At least, Melanie did. She had still not been to see Jacobine. Remembering her unanswered letter, she did not expect much joy from this visit; but still, it had to be made, whatever the dangers. She needed to be sure what attitude the Gryczinskis would adopt.

And so she drove to the Alsenstrasse.

Her heart was heavier that usual as she climbed the carpeted stair and rang the bell. Soon she could distinguish figures flitting to and fro behind the glass door into the passage. At last the door was opened.

"Emmy! Is my sister home?"

"No, Frau van der Straaten . . . Oh, how sorry my mistress will be. But Frau von Heysing came to take her to look at the big picture. 'Nero and his torches,' I think it's called."

"And the Major?"

"I don't know," said the girl, embarrassed. "He was going out. But perhaps I'd better . . ."

"Oh no, Emmy. Don't bother. It's all right. Tell my sister—tell your mistress I called. Or perhaps you'd better take my card . . ."

With a brief gesture of farewell, Melanie left.

On the stairs she said to herself softly, "It's him. She's a good child and loves me." And then she put her hand over her heart and smiled, "Be silent, my heart."

When Rubehn heard about the visit he was not surprised, and still less when a letter arrived next morning. The elegant monogram. J.V.G. left no doubt about the sender, and the letter really did contain a few lines from Jacobine. She wrote:

My dear Melanie,

How sorry I am that we missed one another. And after such a long time! And when I hadn't answered your dear, long letter! It was such a charming letter, and even Gryczinski was really quite enchanted, even though he's so critical and always judges everything according to whether a person has the right views or not. There was only one bit he objected to, when you said that all comfort and salvation still comes from Rome. That annoyed him, and he said one shouldn't say such things even in jest. And when I stood up for you he wouldn't listen. Because most of the Gryczinskis are still Catholics, and I think he's so straitlaced and touchy because he wants to get rid of the whole idea and throw it off. Because you know they are still very difficult higher up,[33] and as you know, Gryczinski is too intelligent ever to want anything they disapprove of higher up. But of course things may change. Can it really be so important and such a burning question? And if it weren't for all the dead and wounded, what I'd like would be another war. (Incidentally, it's being said they're expecting one.) Because if we had a war, the whole question would disappear, and Gryczinski would be made a lieutenant-colonel. Because he's third in line. And a few of the old generals, or anyway the very old ones, will surely have to retire one day.

But there I go chattering on about war and peace and Gryczinski and me, and I haven't asked about you and how you are. I am convinced that you are well, and pleased with the change in all the essentials. He is rich and young, and with your views I imagine you won't mind his not having a title. And after all, with a young man there's always hope. And then, of course, Frankfurt is part of Prussia now. So I expect it will still come.

Ah, my dear Melanie, how much I should have liked to come myself see to everything—big and little, but especially little, and to see whom it looks like. But he has forbidden me and told the servent that 'we are not at home.' And you know I am not brave enough to contradict him. I mean really to contradict him. Because I did contradict him a bit. But then he shouted at me and said, 'I won't have it. I'm not going to be passed over for the sake of such nonsense. And you look out, Jacobine. You are a charming little woman (he really did say that), but you two are like twins, like twin cherries, and there is something of the same sort in *your* blood too. But I'm no van der Straaten, and I shan't play the forgiving hero. Least of all to my own cost.' And then he threw me a kiss de haut en bas and left the room.

And what did I do? Oh, my dear Melanie, I did nothing, I didn't even cry. I was only frightened. Because I feel that he is right, and that there is a strange kind of curiosity inside me. And that's where the people in the Bible are right— when they blame curiosity for so many things. Elimar—not that he's from the Bible—once said to me that nothing was more fun than drawing comparisons. I think he meant in art. But I've thought about it since, and I don't think it applies only to art. Incidentally, Gryczinski is going on a little General Staff trip this winter, or anyway in the spring. And then I'll see you. And when he comes back I'll confess. I'll be able to then, because he's always very affectionate when he comes back. And he's not at all a Bluebeard. And until then,

Yours ever,
Jacobine

Melanie dropped the sheet and Rubehn picked it up. When he too had read it, he said, "Yes, my darling, these are the days that they say bring no pleasure. Oh, and they are only just beginning. But never mind, never mind. Everything wears off in the end, and this kind of thing fastest of all."

And he went to the grand piano and played loudly and with a touch of humorous exaggeration, "My coat will guard you from the storm, guard you from the storm."

And then he got up and kissed her and said in English: "Cheer up, dear."

20

LIDDY

"Cheer up, dear," Rubehn had called to her, and she wanted to heed the call. But she did not, could not succeed, because each day brought new wounding rebuffs. No one was at home to her, her greetings were not returned, and before the winter was over she knew she had been outlawed by an unspoken common consent. Society had pronounced her dead; she was deeply cast down, and would have been in despair if it had not been for Rubehn's support in her distress. It was not merely the warmth of his love that upheld her, but also his serenity, of the kind that transmits itself to all around, or at least exerts a gentle influence. "I know these things, Melanie. When something quite out of the ordinary turns up in London, they call it 'a nine days' wonder'; and nine days expresses the maximum length of time the excitement can last. That's in London. But the rule is the same everywhere. Every storm blows itself out. One day we shall see the rainbow and celebrate the day of atonement."

"Society doesn't accept atonement."

"On the contrary. Society doesn't really like sitting in judgment. And it knows the reason why. And so it simply waits for a sign, and then it puts the executioner's sword back in its scabbard."

"But there has to be something to make that happen."

"There will be. There nearly always is, especially in cases that aren't all that serious. We have created one kind of impression, and we must strive to create another. A totally different one . . . but in the same field . . . Do you understand?"

She took his hand and said, "I swear to you, I will. And the expiation shall fit the sin. I don't really mean expiation—compensation would be better. And that's a rule of life too, at least I hope it is. In fact, that's the best of all rules. Not everything has to be a tragedy."

At that moment the servant brought a card: "Friederike Sawat von Sawatzki, known as Sattler von der Hölle, Candidate Canoness of the Convent of Himmelpfort in the Uckermark."

"Oh, now leave us alone, Reuben," Melanie pleaded as she rose and went to greet the old lady in the hall. "Oh, my dear Riekchen! How glad I am that you've come, that you're here! And how difficult it must have been for you . . . I don't mean just the three flights of stairs . . . You, almost a canoness and at Saint Matthew's every Sunday! But religious people, if they're really religious, are always the best. Not nearly as bad as they're made out to be. And now sit down, my one and only Riekchen, my dear old friend."

And as she spoke, she helped her take off her little silk coat and hung it on a hook that was too high for the little creature.

"My dear old friend," Melanie repeated. "That you always

were, always have been. A real friend who always gave me good advice and never said only what I wanted to hear. But it was no good, and I've never been able to understand how people can have rules or principles; principles are the same as rules, really, but they always strike me as even more difficult and unnecessary. I always simply did what I wanted, what I pleased, what I felt like at the moment. And that doesn't seem so terrible to me. Even now. But it is dangerous, I'll admit that, and I will try to change. I'll learn. I promise you. And now tell me all; I've a hundred questions burning inside me."

Riekchen had been embarrassed when she arrived, and she was still embarrassed. She lowered her eyes, then raised them again, and looked Melanie warmly and squarely in the face: "I just wanted to see . . . And I haven't come behind his back. He knows, and he encouraged me."

Melanie's lips quivered. "Has it embittered him? Tell me, I want to know. From your lips I can take anything. Reiff was here around Christmas. I didn't want *him* to tell me. There is a difference. It depends who is speaking. And whether they are speaking out of curiosity or from the heart. Tell me, has it embittered him?"

The little creature moved her head from side to side and said, "Whatever next! Embittered! If he were bitter, I shouldn't be here. He was unhappy and still is. And it pains him and gnaws at him. But he's calm again. In front of other people, that is. And that's how it will continue to be, because he was very fond of you, Melanie, as fond as he could be of anyone. And you were his pride, and every time he looked at you he was happy."

Melanie nodded.

"Look, my darling child, you couldn't help it because you hadn't been taught otherwise—you hadn't been taught what really matters. You didn't know how serious life can be. Anastasia was always singing: 'Who never ate his bread with tears,'[34] with Elimar turning the page for her. But singing and experience are not the same thing. And you've never eaten the bread of tears, and nor has Anastasia, or Elimar. And that's why you did only what you wanted to do or felt like doing. And then you left the children, such dear children, so pretty and so good, and you didn't even want to see them. You renounced your own flesh and blood. Oh, my poor dear, how can you ever answer for that before God and the world?"

Riekchen seemed about to continue. But Melanie jumped up and said, "No, Riekchen, that's enough. Now you are being unjust. Look, you've known me so well and so long, and I myself was hardly more than a child when I came to live in the house. But one thing you must grant me: I have never lied or pretended. On the contrary, I always had a horror of making myself out to be better than I was. And I still have. And so I tell you: what you said about the children—my sweet little Heth who looks like her father though she laughs exactly like her mother and is just as scatterbrained—what you said about the children isn't true."

"And yet you went without a parting look or word."

"Yes, I did, and I know quite well many other women would not have done it. But if you can be proud of something that's basically sad, then I'm proud I did it. I had made up my mind to leave, that was certain. And if I had seen the children, I couldn't have left. So I had to make a choice. Perhaps I chose wrong in the eyes of the world, but at least I played fair—I was open and honest. If you run away from your marriage for no other reason than because you love another man, then you give up your right to play the tender mother. And that's the truth. I went without a parting look or word because I've always found it repugnant to mix profane and sacred matters. I didn't want to create a kind of sentimental confusion. It's not my place to boast about my virtues. But there's one quality I do have: a fine sense of what is out of place and what isn't."

"And would you like to see them now?"

"The sooner the better. Every moment of the day. Will you bring them?"

"No, no, Melanie, you're going too fast. But I have thought up a little plan, and if it works, you shall hear from me. I shall either come or write, or Jacobine will write. Because Jacobine will have to help us. And now may God be with you, my dear, dear Melanie. Never mind what people say. I know you are a good child. Frivolous, but your heart's in the right place. And now God be with you, my darling."

And she left, refusing to put on her little coat because she wanted to break off quickly . . . But when she had gone down one flight, she stopped and struggled into the little sleeves by herself.

Melanie was deeply happy about this visit, which filled her with longing and expectation; sometimes it seemed to her as though the small being in the cradle next door meant less to her than her longing. She was one of those people who always have a favorite in their hearts.

So the weeks passed, and it was almost Easter when a note was delivered, of which the envelope seemed to promise good tidings. It was from her sister, and Jacobine wrote:

My dear Melanie:
   We are alone, and God bless all ordnance surveys. As you may know, they are those tall three-legged stands all over the country that one can see quite clearly from the train; all the other passengers in the compartment always say: My goodness, what is that? And you can hardly blame them, because they look like a painter's high stool, only it would have to be a very tall painter. Even taller and with longer legs than Gabler. He won't be back for a fortnight, which I am looking forward to very very much; in fact, I am already homesick for him. Because he most certainly has what it takes to please a woman. And in the old days you used to like him too, yes, my angel, you can't deny it, and sometimes I used to be jealous because you're more intelligent, and they like that. But to come to the point of my letter: Riekchen was here and begged me to arrange it, and so let's not wait a moment longer, and come tomorrow about noon. They will be here and Riekchen too. But we haven't said anything and we want to surprise them. I am happy to put

my hand to such a moving occasion. Because, what I think
is, there is nothing like mother love... Oh, my dear
Melanie... But I will not go on. Gryczinski never stops
saying that what matters in life is controlling one's feelings... I am not so sure he's right. And now good-bye.

Ever yours,
Jacobine

These lines threw Melanie into a state of agitation which she
could not and did not wish to hide. Rubehn found her in that
condition, and grew truly worried, knowing from experience
that such overexcitement is always followed by a reaction,
and that high expectation always leads to disappointment.
He tried to divert and distract her, and was truly glad when at
last the next morning came.

It was a clear day. The air was mild and only one or two
clouds floated in the blue sky. Melanie left the house even
before the appointed hour to go the Alsenstrasse. Oh, how
the air did her good! She kept stopping to breathe it in greedily and to enjoy the quiet signs of awakening life which
showed themselves here and there where a bud was beginning to swell. All the hedges were edged with green, and,
where the ground had been raked and the dead leaves
cleared away, the ground ivy put forth its small green leaves;
and once she thought a swallow shot past her with its shrill
and merry cry. And so she crossed the whole width of the
Tiergarten until she reached the little square called Kleiner
Königsplatz directly in front of the Alsenstrasse. Here she sat
down on a bench and fanned herself with her handkerchief
and distinctly heard the beating of her own heart.

"What a wilderness of confusion we enter as soon as we
leave the path of custom and diverge from rule and law. It
makes no difference whether we absolve ourselves. The
world is always stonger than we are, and in the end it defeats
us in our own hearts. I thought I was doing right when I left
my children without a look or a word, I wanted to avoid a
tearful melodrama: either–or, I thought. And I still believe

that what I thought was right. But what good is that to me? What is the result? A mother afraid of her own children."

These last words pulled her together. The streak of defiant pride in her gentle nature asserted itself, and she went quickly toward the building in which the Gryczinskis lived.

The two concierges, man and wife, and their two half-grown daughters must have heard of the impending event by way of the back stairs, for they had posted themselves at the half-open basement door and were peering over each other's heads. Melanie saw them and said to herself, "A nine days' wonder. I've become a sight to be seen. I've always hated that more than anything."

She mounted the stairs and rang the bell. Riekchen had arrived ahead of her, and the sisters kissed and said nice things about one another's appearance. And the air was full of excitement and happiness.

They now entered the living and reception room. It was large and airy, but narrow in relation to its depth. The two large windows were close together in a sort of bay, with no partition between them. There was a feeling of solemnity; the red curtains were half drawn, creating a soft mysterious light, which was reflected from the white walls. Across from the windows, a tall door led to the dining room.

Melanie sat down on the small sofa by the window, and the other two ladies sat beside her. Jacobine tried one of her little conversations. For she felt no deep emotion and regarded the whole thing as a matinee performance. But Riekchen noticed that Melanie's eyes were fixed on one spot, and at last she interrupted and said, "Don't go on, Binchen. I'll go and fetch them now."

A painful silence fell. Jacobine could not think of any more to say, and was sincerely glad when she heard the music of a passing regiment of guards. She got up, placed herself between the curtains, and looked to the right. "They're Uhlans," she said. "Don't you want to . . . " But before she could finish her sentence the large double doors opened, and Riekchen appeared holding the children by the hand.

The music outside faded away.

Melanie had risen quickly and gone toward the children, who stood bewildered and almost scared. But when she saw Lydia take a step backward, she stopped, and a feeling of terror overcame her. Only with difficulty could she bring out the words, "Heth, my sweet little darling... Come... Don't you know your mother any more?"

Summoning her whole strength she had moved close to the door and was bending down with outstretched hands to pick Heth up. But Lydia threw her a look of bitter hatred and tore the child back by her shoulder strap. "We have no mother any more," she said.

As she spoke, she dragged the half resisting younger child back through the door, which had remained ajar.

Melanie fainted.

Half an hour later she recovered sufficiently to drive home. She had refused all offers to accompany her. Riekchen's wise words and Jacobine's silly ones were equally intolerable to her in the mood she was in.

When she had gone, Jacobine said to Riekchen, "It made quite an impression on her. And Gryczinski mustn't get to hear of it. He doesn't approve of children as it is. And he would only say to me, 'There, you see what it leads to. Ingratitude and unnatural behavior.'"

21

IN SAINT NICHOLAS' CHURCH

The clock in the turret over the courtyard next door was striking two as Melanie entered her apartment. Her heart was bursting and she longed for the relief of talking to someone. Then, she knew, she would be able to weep, and that would help console her.

But Rubehn stayed out longer than usual, and anxiety and worry about her beloved husband added to the other fears in her heart. At last he came; it was late in the afternoon, and the sun sinking behind the bare branches threw a pattern of glaring light spots through the small mansard windows. But the room was cold and inhospitable. Moving toward her husband, Melanie said, "You bring so much cold with you, Reuben. And I so long for light and warmth!"

"How strange you are," Rubehn replied in evident distraction, although he tried to show his usual cheerfulness. "How strange you are. I see nothing but light, a real *embarras de richesse,* on all the sofa cusions, and on the arms of all the chairs, and the metal on the stove is glittering as though it were gold. And you say you long for light. Really, I find it quite blinding, and I'd be glad of less light or even none at all."

"You won't have to wait long."

He had been pacing up and down the room. Now he stopped and said sympathetically, "I'm forgetting to ask about the main thing. Forgive me. You were at Jacobine's. How did it go? Not well, I fear. I can read something of the sort in your eyes. And I had a sort of premonition early this morning when I went into town. It hasn't been a good day."

"Not for you either?"

"Nothing worth mentioning. A shadow of a shadow."

He sat down in the nearest armchair and mechanically reached for an album from the sofa table. He had frequently expressed the opinion that looking at albums was the lowest possible form of mental activity, and so it was not surprising that he looked into the distance as he turned the pages. He kept asking, "How was it? I'm anxious to know."

But she could see only too well that he was *not* anxious, and much as she had longed to pour out her heart, now she found it difficult to utter a word. More than once she lost the thread as she told him, in response to his wishes, of the deep humiliation she had had to endure from her own child.

Rubehn had risen and tried to calm her by throwing out a few random words, but he did it as though he were reciting a jingle.

"And is that all you have to say to me?" she asked.

"Reuben, my only love, am I to lose you too?" And she stood before him and gazed into his face.

"Oh, don't talk like that. Lose! We can't lose one another. It's true, Melanie, isn't it, we can't lose one another?" With that, his voice grew momentarily softer and more fervent. "And as for the children," he went on after a while, "well, children are just children. And by the time they are grown up, a lot of water will have flowed under the bridge. And you must remember, it was not exactly staged by the most brilliant director. Riekchen is kind and good, and you are fond of her, too fond perhaps; but even you are not going to maintain that the candidate for the Convent of Heaven's Gate has knocked on the gates of wisdom. At any rate, they didn't open for her. And Jacobine! If you will forgive me, there is something of the princess about her, but a princess who minds sheep."

"Oh Reuben," said Melanie, "you're talking about all sorts of things but you're not saying the right words. You're saying nothing to raise me up, to restore me in my own eyes. My own child turned her back on me. And the fact that she is still a child is precisely what makes it so shattering. That's what judges me."

He shook his head and said, "You're taking it too hard. And do you really think that mothers and fathers are beyond criticism?"

"At least for their children, yes."

"Not even for their children. On the contrary, children are always sitting in judgment, silently and inexorably. And Lydia was always something of a little Grand Inquisitor, at least of the Geneva variety, and she would make a good example for the study of heredity. She must be descended from one of the people who condemned Servet to the stake. She would have liked to see *me* at the stake, I'm sure of that. And now let's not talk about it any more. I have to go back to town."

"Oh, please, what has happened? What is it?"

"A meeting. And it will be impossible for me not to stay on afterward. Don't be frightened, and above all, don't expect me back. I hate young women who are always waiting at the window "to see if he's coming," and who keep on friendly terms with the night watchman to guarantee safe delivery. I simply detest that kind of thing. The best thing will be for you to go to bed early and sleep it off. And when we meet again tomorrow morning, perhaps you will agree with me that Lydia needs to learn her place, and that silly little chits of ten, including Miss Liddy, are in no position to judge the morals of their mothers."

"Oh Reuben, you're just saying that. It's not what you feel and you are far too intelligent and fair-minded not to know that the child is right."

"She may be right. But so am I. And anyway, there are more serious things to worry about. And now good-bye."

And he took his hat and went.

Melanie was still awake when he returned. But she did not ask about the meeting until the next morning, and then she made an effort to joke about it. He for his part replied in the same tone, and, as on the previous day, it was obvious that he was trying to hide his real feelings behind a screen of sprightly conversation.

And so the days went by. His vivacity increased, but also his absentmindedness, and sometimes he would ask the same question several times over. Melanie shook her head and said, "Please, Reuben, where are you? Tell me, what's the matter?" But he only declared that it was nothing, and that she was probing where there was nothing to discover, and that absentmindedness was a family trait, not a good one, but there it was, and one had to live with it and get used to it. And then he would go away, and she felt freer when he had gone. Because the right words were never spoken and he—who should have eased the burden of her loneliness—only increased its weight by his presence.

Now it was Easter. Anastasia called on Easter Sunday and stayed for half an hour, but Melanie was glad when the conversation came to an end and her friend left; she found her increasingly tiresome. And the second day of Easter came, as unfestive and unfriendly as the first; at luncheon Rebehn announced that he had yet another appointment; and then she could bear the anxiety in her heart no more and decided to go to church and listen to a sermon. But where? She knew no preachers except those she had met at christenings and weddings; many a time she had sat at table beside devout and not so devout clergymen, and when she got home afterward she would declare, "You and your anticlericalism! I've never had a more entertaining conversation in all my life than with Pastor Käpsel today. What a charming old gentleman! And he keeps filling up your glass, and toasting you, and drinking along with all the rest, and paying compliments. I don't understand you. At least he's more interesting that Reiff, not to speak of Duquede!"

But a sermon! She had not heard one since her confirmation.

In the end she remembered that Christel had spoken of evening services. But where? At Saint Nicolas'. That was it. It was a long way away, but all the better. She had so much time to waste, and exercise in the fresh air had for weeks been her only comfort. So she set out, and, walking along the Grosse Petristrasse, she looked up at the lights shining in the windows on the first floor. But *her* window was dark, and there were no flowers there. And she walked faster and looked behind as though she were being followed, and finally she turned into the churchyard of Saint Nicholas'.

And then she went into the church itself.

A few lights were burning in the nave, but Melanie kept on the dark side of the pillars until she found herself before the ancient, richly decorated pulpit. Pews had been placed in this part of the church, but only three or four. They were occupied by children from an orphanage, all girls in blue dresses with white kerchiefs tucked into their bodices; among them sat a few old women, their gray hair hidden under black head scarves: most of them had a stick in their hands or a crutch lying beside them.

Melanie sat down on the last bench and saw the little girls giggling and nudging each other; they kept looking round at her, unable to believe that such a fine lady should come to such a service. For it was a paupers' service, and that was why the lighting was so meager. And then the hymn ended, and the organ fell silent, and a little man appeared in the pulpit. She remembered him well from several lavish bourgeois funerals, and more than once, in her high spirits, she had declared that he spoke like an epitaph on a tomb—only not so briefly. But today he did speak briefly, eulogizing no one, and certainly not exuberantly; he was simply tired and exhausted because it was the evening of the second feast day. And so it was that nothing really touched her heart until at last he said, "And now, my children, we will sing the second-to-last verse of the Easter hymn." And as he said it, the organ began to hum and quiver as though it needed to take heart and work up its strength; but then at last the full, mighty sound reverberated from the lofty vault; the alms-house women joined in with their shaky voices, and two little girls shyly edged up to Melanie and gave her a hymn book and showed her the place. And she joined in:

> Lighten our darkness, God of Life,
> My staff in hour of need.
> Thou knowest I am sick with strife;
> Forsake me not, I plead.

At the last line she returned the book, thanked the children kindly, and turned aside to hide her emotion. And then she murmured words that were supposed to be a prayer, and no doubt were a prayer in the eyes of Him Who hears the voice of our hearts. Then she made her way out, down the side aisle, as quietly and unobtrusively as she had come.

Arriving home, she found Rubehn at his desk. He was reading a letter, which he laid aside as she came in. And then he came toward her and took her hand and led her to her place on the sofa.

"You've been out?" he said, sitting down again.

"Yes, my dear. In town...in church."

"In church? What were you doing there?"

"Seeking comfort."

He fell silent and sighed deeply. And she saw that the moment of decision had come. And she sprang to her feet, ran toward him, flung herself on the ground, and threw both her arms around his knees: "Tell me what it is! Have pity on me, on my poor heart! Look, everyone has given me up and my children have turned from me. Oh, hard as it is, I could have borne it. But that you should turn from me, that I cannot bear."

"I am not turning from you."

"Not with your eyes, though they no longer see me, but with your heart. Tell me, my dearest, what is it? It's not jealousy that's tormenting me. I couldn't live another hour if it were that. But there is something else that frightens me; something else, but just as bad: I've lost your love. I can see that, but what I can't see is why I've lost it. Is it the ostracism I'm living under, which you have to bear with me? Or is it that I've brought so little light and sunshine into your life and have merely turned your solitude into sadness? Or is it that you mistrust me? Is it the thought behind the old saying: it will be my turn next? Oh, tell me. I don't want to see you suffer. I shall be less unhappy if I know that you are happy. Even away from you. I'm ready to go, at any time. Ask me to, and I will do it. But save me from this uncertainty. Tell me what it is that weighs on you, what spoils your life and embitters it. Tell me. Please."

He passed his hand over his forehead and eyes; then he took the letter he had laid aside and said, "Read this."

Melanie unfolded the sheet. The writing was old Rubehn's, which she knew well. And then she read, "Frankfurt. Easter Sunday. The agreement has fallen through. Arrange whatever you can. I shall have to announce suspension of payment in a week at the longest. M. R."

As she read, Rubehn's face showed that he expected her to feel another profound shock. But how greatly he had misjudged her; she was far, far more than merely the spoiled darling of society. He had scarcely had time to realize his mistake before she leaped up in an ecstasy of joy and embraced and kissed him and then embraced him again.

"Oh, is that all ... Oh, now everything will be all right again. It may be a misfortune for your house, but to me, it's happiness, and now everything will right itself, far beyond my hopes and expectations ... The day I left him and talked to him for the last time, I spoke of people understanding. I feel as though it was only yesterday. And I relied on those understanding people for my future, I thought they would forgive me because I loved you. But that was a mistake, and even those who understood abandoned me. And I must say, they were right. Because love is not enough, and faithfulness is not enough either. It's not much to be faithful when you love and the sun shines and life goes comfortably on and demands no sacrifices. No, no, faithfulness alone is not enough. But *proven* faithfulness is different. And now I can prove myself, and I shall and I will; my time has come. Now I will show what I am capable of, and I will show that everything that has happened only happened because it had to happen, because I loved you; and not because I lived carelessly and thoughtlessly from day to day and simply wanted to keep on living my comfortable life even more comfortably."

He looked at her full of happiness, and the unselfishness in her words and countenance tore him out of his deep depression. He too began to hope once more, but anxiety and doubt accompanied his hope. Deeply moved, he said, "Dear Melanie, you were always a child, and still are at this very moment. A spoiled child and a good child, but still a child. You see, from the moment you first drew breath you have never known need—need is hardly even the word; as long as you have lived, no wish of yours has ever gone unfulfilled. And you lived as if you were in the land of Cockayne; your table was always laden with everything you wanted, with everything life can offer, even with flattery and affection. You were petted like a little Spaniel dog with a bell on a blue ribbon round its neck. And everything you did, you did in play. Yes, Melanie, in play. And now you want to play at self-denial, and you imagine that everything will work out somehow. Or perhaps you even think that poverty is charming and rather out of the ordinary, and you romance about the poetic cottage where there is room for a happily loving couple[35]—or at any rate where there is supposed to be room for them. Oh, it's edifying to read about the table scrubbed clean, and the bunch of may in every corner, and the linnet in its cage that has been trained to pull in its feed dish all by itself. And there is something to it; painted poverty looks just as nice as painted wealth. But when it stops being a picture or an idea and becomes reality and the rule, then the bread of poverty tastes bitter and need is a hard master."

It was useless. Again and again she shook her head and said in her cajoling manner that was so hard to resist: "No, no, you're wrong. It's quite different. I once read in a book—and it wasn't such a bad book either—that children, fools, and poets are always right. Perhaps they're right altogether, but they certainly are from their own point of view. And I'm really all three, and from that you may conclude just *how* right I am. Three times over. You say I want to play at learning self-denial. Yes, my dear, that's it, that's exactly the point. And you don't believe I can do it. But I shall, I'm sure I shall, as sure as that I'm raising this finger now, and what's more, I'll tell you why. You've already guessed one of the reasons: because I imagine it will be so romantic—so charming and out of the ordinary. All right, all right. But you might just as well say that it's because I have other ideas of what happiness is. Happiness isn't having a title or being dressed up like a doll. It's *here* or nowhere. That's what I've always thought and felt, and that's how I was and still am. But even if I were different, even if the trappings of life meant a lot to me, I should still have the strength to give them up. One feeling is always dominant, and for the sake of love there's nothing, nothing one cannot do. That's the way women are, anyway. And I certainly am. I've gladly given up so much, and now you think I can't give up a carpet! Or a vitrine. Oh dear, a vitrine!" And she laughed gaily. "Do you remember saying that nowadays everything has to be a commission of inquiry? That was ages ago. Meanwhile the world has moved on, and now everything is a vitrine."

He was not convinced. With his practical, patrician temperament, he could not believe that such feelings would last, but he said, "So be it. Let's try it. So it's a new life for us, Melanie."

"A new life! And the first thing to do is to give up this apartment and find something more modest. A mansard sounds quite unpretentious, but that only makes all these pier glasses and bronzes even more pretentious. I haven't had much education, and that's a good thing, because like most uneducated people I know quite a lot. And I shall start with Toussaint l'Ouverture, no, no, with Toussaint-Langenscheidt,[36] and in a week or a month at the most I shall give my first lesson. I wasn't born in Geneva for nothing. And now tell me, do you agree? Do you believe in me?"

"I do."

"Done."

And she shook hands with him, and laughing and joking she drew him into the next room, where Vreni had set the table for tea because it was the servant's day off.

And on this day of misfortune they enjoyed the first day of a new happiness.

22

RECONCILED

And Melanie meant every word she had spoken. She regained all her former vigor, and before a month had passed the modern, elegantly furnished apartment had been exchanged for a more modest one, and she had begun to give lessons. With her knowledge of French and, even more, with her outstanding musical talent and polished technique it was easy for her to find work; she was employed by a few great Silesian families who were just sufficiently distinguished to be able to ignore vulgar gossip.

And soon the need for her prompt, resolute action became apparent; the collapse of the great house of Rubehn came more suddenly than expected, and every form of restraint turned out to be necessary if the family was not to lose its social as well as its financial reputation. Every day the news from Frankfurt confirmed this; and Rubehn, at first only too prone to regard Melanie's eagerness as a capricious show of sacrifice, soon found himself compelled to follow her example. He took a post as American correspondent in a bank, which offered him only a small starting salary; and he was surprised and delighted to find that the poetic wisdom about love in a hut[37] turned out to be true in his own case.

The following weeks were idyllic. Every morning, as they made their way from the edge of the Wilmersdorf fields along the Tiergarten, they would pass their old apartment and look up at the elegant mansard and breathe more freely as they thought of the somber, anxious days that lay behind them. Chatting as they went, they would take the narrow shady paths through the park until they came to a slanting willow, which almost blocked the way between the Royal Monument and Louis Island; here they joined the wide Tiergartenstrasse. They nicknamed the tree "the toll gate," because an organ grinder had set up his pitch just beyond it and every day he exacted his toll. He was beginning to know them, and would regularly doff his military cap, though he glared at most passersby with angry contempt as if they were tax evaders. But he could not quite change his spots; one day when the young couple had forgotten—or perhaps deliberately withheld—the charge that he considered his due, they heard him give his handle three vehement and furious turns and then abruptly break off, so that a few unfinished notes grumbled and scolded after them. Melanie said, "We must keep in everybody's good books, Reuben; friendship is scarce nowadays." And she turned back and went to the old man and gave him his money. But he did not thank her, because he was nursing his indignation.

And so the summer passed and autumn came, and when the trees began to change color and the sycamores and planes

to shed their leaves, the two who walked under them day
after day found that their lives had altered, and altered for the
better. When they passed the old veteran, greeting him respectfully, they would say that their new friendships were still too
uncertain to give up proven old friends, but the beginnings of
new friendships were being made. People were taking notice
of them, and their social life was reviving. There were those
who had taken malicious pleasure in seeing the glorious financial empire of the Rubehns collapse, and who—according
to whether their education and inclination tended more toward the classics or the Bible—had spoken of Nemesis or "the
finger of God"; but even these now deigned to take up the
good-looking young couple "who were so happy and so
bright and never complained and were so fond of one
another." Yes, so fond of one another. That was what finally
turned the scales, and whereas formerly their love had only
awakened envy and doubt, now the general mood was re-
versed. And no wonder! The state of mind that first condemned and then pardoned was basically the same: at first
people had reveled in the thrills of indignation; now they
spoke with scarcely less satisfaction of "the inseparables" and
sentimentalized their "true love." A small number of esoteric
characters, however, attributed the whole affair to elective
affinities; proceeding from a scientific basis they declared that
the weaker element must always yield to the stronger, which
is thereby justified in its course of action. It was simply a case
of the law of nature triumphing once again. This development spelled the end of van der Straaten's triumph, which
had lasted through the winter; he shared the fate of all favorites for a season: to be forgotten even more quickly than they
have been acclaimed. Mockery and malice now pointed their
arrows at him, and, on the rare occasions when the case was
still recalled, people would say, "He asked for it. How could
he do such a thing? She was seventeen! True, he's supposed
to have been a lion once. Fair enough. But when a lion begins
to feel too comfortable . . ." And they laughed and rejoiced
that things had turned out as they had.

Did van der Straaten get to hear of these and similar remarks? Perhaps. But they meant nothing to him. He had explored his own character too skeptically and ruthlessly to be surprised even for a moment at society's changes of taste, at its making and breaking of idols. You could say of him, "He heard what was said, even though he did not hear it." There was only one thing he valued less than people's judgment, and that was their pity. He had always been an independent character, free and stalwart, and so he had remained. Nor had he changed in his tolerance and charity.

And the day came when this was revealed, even to Melanie.

October was almost out, and only a few red and yellow leaves hung from the trees, now almost bare. Most of the leaves lay in drifts on the paths, and ready for raking wherever they were dry enough; for the weather had changed again during the night, and after a long series of rainy, stormy days a splendid autumn sun was shining. It could be the last sunshine of the year.

So little Aninette had been sent out, and today she stayed out longer than expected. At last, about four o'clock, the maid appeared in great excitement and reported her most recent adventure in her heavy Swiss dialect. "She'd been sitting on the seat where the four lions guard the bridge and had just said, 'Look, Aninette, that's the autumn gossamer, it wants to spin a cocoon round you, but it'll never get you. And Aninette was just shouting for joy and laughing and reaching for Vreni's earring when two gentlemen came over the bridge, well into their fifties, and over the hill, you might say, and one of them—a tall, skinny fellow—said, 'Look at that silver necklace; that's a Swiss girl, and I bet that child belongs to the Swiss ambassador.' But then the other said, 'No, it can't be; I know the Swiss ambassador and he hasn't any children or family . . .' And then the other says to me, 'Well then, whose child is it?' And I says, 'It's Herr Rubehn's and it's a girl and her name's Aninette.' And then I see him change color and look away. But in a minute he turns back and says, 'She's just like her mother, and laughs like her, and has the same black hair. Beautiful child. Don't you think so?'

But he wouldn't agree and only says, 'Don't overrate her. There are plenty more like that. Dozens.' Yes, that's what he said, nasty old fellow—there are more like that. Dozens. But the nice gentleman, he took her little paw and stroked it. And he praised me for being so good and smart. Yes, that's what he said. And then they went away."

All this did not fail to make an impression, and in the following days Melanie continued to hark back to the encounter. Over and over again Vreni had to describe every detail, and this went on for weeks until the various preparations for Christmas made them forget the whole affair.

And now the holiday had arrived; it was Christmas Eve, and, as before, Rubehn's brother and the old clerk were invited; they had not been able to make up their minds to return to Frankfurt. Anastasia had been invited too.

Melanie had a number of domestic arrangements to make before the guests arrived, and she was quite startled when, the daylight barely gone and long before the appointed time, she heard the bell ring. If it should be the guests already! Or even one of them! But her worries did not last long, for she heard questions and parleying outside, and then Vreni appeared carrying a fair-sized box. It bore no address: only the word *Juhlklapp*[38] was written on it.

"Are you sure it's for us, Vreni?" asked Melanie.

"I think so. I says to him, 'Herr Rubehn lives here. And Frau Rubehn.' And he says, 'That's right. That's the name.' And so I took it."

Melanie shook her head and went into Rubehn's room; together they set about opening the box. None of the usual Juhlklapp ingredients were missing; and it was not until they saw a large apple at the bottom that Melanie said, "Careful. This is where it must be." But there was nothing to be seen, and she was just about to lay aside the apple with the other contents when a chance movement of her hand dislodged the two halves, which had been carefully fitted together. "Ah, voilà." And so it was; the core had been removed and in its place lay a little packet wrapped in tissue paper. She picked it up and slowly, expectantly, removed one wrapping after another until she held a little locket in her hands, quite plain, with no ornament or decoration. She pressed the spring, and the locket opened, revealing a picture she recognized; it fell from her hand. It was a miniature of the Tintoretto that she had once looked at in amusement and high spirits, saying of its subject, "Look, Ezel, she's been crying. And she looks as though she doesn't really understand what she did wrong."

Ah, now she felt that all this had been said on her account as well. She picked up the picture from where it had fallen and gave it to Rubehn and blushed.

He balanced it in his hand; then he closed the spring and said in English, "King Ezel in all his glory." Then he continued, "Always the same. Well meaning but clumsy. I shall wear it. As a pendant on my watch chain."

"No, I shall. Ah, you don't know how much it means to me. And it is to remind and warn me . . . all the time . . ."

"If you like. But don't take it more tragically than necessary and don't go brooding over that tedious business of crime and punishment."

"You are being supercilious, Reuben."

"No, I'm not."

"All right. You're proud, then."

"Yes, I am, my sweet Melanie. I am. Proud of what, though? Of whom?"

And they embraced, and an hour later the Christmas candles were burning for them in undisturbed brightness.

The Poggenpuhl Family

1

The Poggenpuhl family consisted of Major von Poggenpuhl's widow and her three daughters—Therese, Sophie, and Manon. Since they had moved to Berlin from Pommersch-Stargard seven years ago they had lived in a corner house in the Grossgörschenstrasse, a new building only just completed and still damp in the walls when they arrived. It belonged to August Nottebohm, a decent, portly fellow who was a retired builder's foreman. The Poggenpuhls had chosen the Grossgörschenstrasse not least because its name commemorated an event in military history, but also because of its so-called "magnificent view." The front windows looked out on the monuments and family tombs of Saint Matthew's churchyard, and the rear windows gave on to the backs of several houses belonging to the Kulmstrasse, one of which bore the legend "Schulze's Sweets" in huge letters of alternate red and blue. It is possible, even probable, that not everyone would have appreciated these two views. But Frau von Poggenpuhl, née Pütter (she came from a poor but highly respected family of clergymen) was equally well pleased with both. The view from the front appealed to her because she was rather sentimental and fond of talking about death; and the view from the back, because she suffered from a perpetual cough and lived almost entirely on barley sugar and cough pastilles, despite her efforts to economize. So whenever visitors came it was the custom to speak of the tremendous advantages of this apartment, whose only real advantage was that it was very cheap and that Herr Nottebohm had promised never to put up the rent for the major's widow. "No, no, Frau von Poggenpuhl," was more or less what he had said on that occasion, "as far as that's concerned, you have no need to worry, nor the young ladies either. My, my, when I think back on it all! You will pardon me, Frau von Poggenpuhl, but little Manon was only a little bit of a thing when you moved in that Michaelmas . . . and when you came down on New Year's Day with our first rent payment and all the other apartments were still empty because of the walls being damp—which was nonsense, of course—I said to my wife, because that was before we had any money at all, 'Line,' I said, 'that's our first takings and it'll bring us luck.' And so it did; because from that quarter on we've never had an empty apartment and always respectable people, that I must say . . . And then, Frau von Poggenpuhl, you'd be the last person I'd start on—putting up the rent, I mean. After all, I was out there too; my word, that really was a hellish business. I've still got a bullet in here. But the doctor says it'll drop out one day, and then I'll have a souvenir."

And that was the end of Nottebohm's speech, the longest he had ever made. He could not have had a more sympathetic listener. The "hellish business" referred to the battle of Gravelotte, where Major von Poggenpuhl had died an honorable death late in the evening when the Pommeranian Division had been sent in. He had led the battalion in which Nottebohm had served. He—the major, that is—left nothing but his fine old name and three bright coronation talers. They were found in his purse and later given to his widow. These three coronation talers were the family's inheritance and therefore, naturally, their pride as well. Sixteen years later when the youngest daughter Manon (born a few months after her father's death) was to be confirmed, the three talers, whose preservation during all those years had been no mean feat, were made into three brooches, one for each of the daughters, in memory of this confirmation day. All this was done with the participation and help of the clergy; for Superintendant-General Schwarz loved the family, and in the evening after the confirmation he had joined a few old comrades and friends in the Poggenpuhl apartment and raised the presentation of the brooches to the level, if not of a religious ceremony, then at least of a solemn celebration. It had impressed even Nebelung the porter, a rather crude fellow full of prejudice against "that aristocratic gang." If he was not exactly converted to the more benign views held by his landlord and employer Nottebohm, he was at least brought a little closer to them.

It goes without saying that the arrangement of the Poggenpuhl apartment also reflected the circumstances in which, for better or for worse, the family now found itself. There was no plush-covered upholstery, and the only carpet was a small Schmiedeberg rug with a somewhat fuzzy black woolen fringe. It lay in front of the sofa in the parlor, which was the room nearest the passage and therefore served as the reception room. The narrow curtains with darns here and there were in keeping with the rug. But everything was very clean and well kept. A long mirror with a strip of gilt beading on its white frame had recently been bought at an auction; it probably came from some old patrician family home in the Mark. Although the otherwise meager furnishings appeared to have been scraped together (or perhaps because of that appearance) the mirror invested them with an aura of expiring grandeur—expiring, but nevertheless bearing witness to past glories.

Above the parlor sofa there hung a large, knee-length portrait in oils of a Major von Poggenpuhl in the Sohr Hussars. In 1813 at the battle of Grossgörschen he had broken through the enemy formation and had been awarded the order Pour le Mérite. He was the only Poggenpuhl ever to have served in the cavalry. The major's face, half martial and half benign, looked down upon a shallow glass bowl filled with primulas and a circle of forget-me-nots in summer and with visiting cards in winter. Directly facing the major, against the opposite wall, stood a bureau with a shelf. To enable the family to show some sort of hospitality to visitors, half a bottle of Cape sherry was enthroned here, surrounded by a number of small liqueur glasses; all these stood on a gold-rimmed plate which never stopped rattling.

Next to this parlor was the living room with a single window, and, behind that, the so-called "Berlin room," which was really just a passage, though spacious. Three beds stood along one of the longer walls—three only, although they were a family of four. The fourth couch was of a somewhat more peripatetic character and consisted of a sofa frame strung with cane; the two younger sisters took turns to ensconce themselves on this piece of furniture.

Behind the "Berlin room" (Nottebohm had drawn up the ground plans himself) there was a kitchen and an attic for hanging out the washing. This was where the old servant Friederike had her being. She was a faithful soul who had known the "master" and had been Frau von Poggenpuhl's confidante through all the family's ups and downs, including the move from Stargard to Berlin.

That was how the Poggenpuhls lived and how they proved to the world at large that, with the right outlook and, of course, the necessary skills, it was possible to exist contentedly and very nearly according to one's station in life even in the humblest circumstances. This was admitted even by the porter Nebelung, albeit with reluctance and much head shaking. All the Poggenpuhls—the mother possibly to a lesser degree than the rest—possessed the happy gift of never complaining, of making the best of life as well as being good reckoners, though there was never anything unpleasantly calculating about their calculations.

In this the three sisters were all alike, but in other ways they were very different from one another in character.

Therese, already thirty, might seem somewhat unpractical at first sight, and that is what she was often taken to be. The only art she appeared to have learned was that of reclining gracefully in a rocking chair. But she was really just as capable as her two younger sisters; it was only that she labored in a different vineyard. Because of her particular character, she was convinced that the task of holding high the Poggenpuhl banner had fallen to her, and it was her duty to take her place more deliberately than her sisters cared to in the world to which they rightfully belonged. So she was at home in the families of generals and ministers of state in the Behren- and

Wilhelmstrasse; their tea tables never failed to resound with approval and applause when she gave one of her maliciously humorous accounts of her younger sisters and their adventures in the "would-be aristocracy." Even the old commander who had ceased to be particularly impressed by any earthly matter would cheer up and be quite merry and agreeable; and the Undersecretary of State who lived diagonally across from the general's family and was on friendly terms with them would always be quite carried away by the delicate satire of the young lady who was so poor but so properly conscious of her class, although—or perhaps because—he himself belonged to the very newest aristocracy. A further consequence of Therese's triumphs in society was that if anything needed to be asked for, she could afford to ask for it; but it must be noted that she never asked for anything for herself; or if she did, then she took care to choose something that could be granted effortlessly—and which therefore gave particular satisfaction to her benefactor.

Such was Therese von Poggenpuhl.

The two younger sisters were quite different; they had adapted themselves to their condition and to the modern world, and they worked more or less as a team.

Sophie, the second, was the family's prop and stay because she possessed something that hitherto had not distinguished the Poggenpuhl family, namely, talents. It is possible that under more favorable economic conditions these talents would have been regarded somewhat dubiously and would have been considered unbecoming to someone of her station in life; but in the Poggenpuhls' straitened circumstances her natural gifts were a daily blessing for the family. In her calmer moments even Therese would admit that. Sophie—who was physically unlike her sisters as well, having an amiable poodle face framed in little curls—was good at almost everything: she was musical, she drew, she painted, she wrote verse for birthdays and nuptial eves, and she knew how to lard a hare; but all this, much as it was, would not have been half as significant for them all if it had not been for Manon, the baby of the family.

In contrast to Sophie, Manon—now seventeen—had no gifts at all except the gift of making herself universally popular, especially in bankers' families. She preferred the non-Christian ones, and her favorite was the highly esteemed house of Bartenstein. Most of these families were prolific, so that there was never any lack of girls in their early teens who needed to be instructed in the rudiments of some branch of art or learning. Any conversation, whether short or long, about the various disciplines would regularly end with Manon's nonchalantly proffered remark: "I think my sister might possibly be able to help out there." This remark was perfectly justified, because in fact there was nothing Sophie was afraid to take on, from physics to spectrum analysis.

So that was the distribution of roles in the Poggenpuhl family. As has already been indicated, it brought with it certain financial advantages, and sometimes these advantages considerably exceeded the tiny pension that formed their basic income. None of the three young ladies lost any part of her dignity thereby. On the contrary, they were all (but especially the two younger ones) as carefree as they were grateful; they tactfully avoided any kind of exaggerated compliments, let alone flattery, and everyone respected and thought well of them because everything they did—and that was the important point—was done absolutely unselfishly. Their wants were few, especially with respect to dress (though this did not preclude a pleasing appearance; they knew how to manage on a minimum). All their thoughts and hopes centered on the "two boys," their brothers Wendelin and Leo. The elder was already a first lieutenant of over thirty, the younger still a mere cub, barely twenty-two. It goes without saying that both had joined the East Pomeranian regiment (now, incidentally, stationed in East Prussia) in which their father's career had begun—and ended, with honor and renown, on that memorable eighteenth of August.

To increase the family renown as much as lay in their power was the object for which the trio of sisters strove with all their might.

As far as Wendelin was concerned, he cooperated with his

sisters' efforts in every way, especially as he knew how to economize; there was hardly a doubt that he would achieve the highest goals. He was clever, ambitious, and level-headed. By keeping her ear to the ground in the houses of their military excellencies, Therese had gleaned that it was really just a matter of whether Wendelin's next posting would be to the War Office or to the General Staff. Things were not as happy in the case of Leo, who was less talented than his older brother and whose only aim in life was to cut a proper dash. Two duels, in one of which a junior legal counsel had suffered a shot through both cheeks and the loss of several front teeth, bore witness to the fact that Leo was rapidly approaching his ideal of what a proper dash should be; and there was no reason why his career should not have justified hopes as great as those placed on Wendelin's talents, had it not been for the specter of dismissal that stalked beside it: Leo was in perpetual danger of being cashiered because of his steadily mounting debts. He was everyone's favorite, but at the same time he was everyone's problem child; and everything the family thought and did was directed toward helping him avert yet another catastrophe. No sacrifice seemed too great, and although their mother sometimes shook her head, the daughters never doubted that, "if only it were possible to keep him going for the necessary length of time," the next great battle against the Russians, the Zorndorf of the future, would be won through Leo's intervention.

"But he's not even in the Guards," said their Mama.

"No. But that's neither here nor there. The next battle of Zorndorf will be won by the infantry."

2

It was a winter day, the third of January.

Friederike was just returning from her regular morning shopping expedition, a basket of rolls for breakfast in one hand and a jug of milk in the other. Both rolls and milk came from the basement shop across the street. In spite of Friederike's woolen gloves, the cold had numbed her fingers, and as soon as she came into the kitchen she took the tea-kettle from its hole in the stove and warmed herself at the glow. But not for long; she had fallen back to sleep before dawn, and so she was half an hour behind with her work—and of course she intended to make up the time.

So she took the coffee mill down from its shelf and went briskly to work. When she had ground the coffee beans, she tipped them into the filter bag so that they would be ready later for her to pour on the water; finally she put the kettle back on the fire, picked up the basket of firewood (the bottom of which, incidentally, threatened to drop out at any moment), and went off to the front part of the apartment to light the fire in the living room with the single window. She knelt before the stove and piled up wood and briquettes so skillfully that she managed to light the whole structure with a single match, which she applied to a wad of neatly twisted newspaper.

Scarcely half a minute had gone by before she heard the fire popping and crackling inside the stove, and as soon as she was sure it would burn, she rose from her place before it to apply herself to the second task of the morning, which was dusting. Whatever effort she made, the three young ladies were never quite satisfied with the result; and so, conscientious though she normally was, she went about it rather superficially and contented herself with putting a moderate amount of shine on the row of pictures hanging over the sofa. Although they were all contemporary portraits, Leo always called them "the house of Poggenpuhl's gallery of ancestors." Three or four were cabinet-sized photographs; but the older ones belonged to the days of the daguerrotype and had faded so much that their artistic merit could be assessed only under exceptionally favorable lighting conditions.

But the "ancestors" did not have the whole wall to themselves. Immediately above them hung a fairly large oil painting, artistically of the third or even fourth degree of merit. It depicted the most important historical moment in the life of the family. Most of the canvas was covered with gunsmoke, but in the middle it was possible to discern fairly clearly a church with a desperate nocturnal battle raging in the churchyard.

It was the assault on Hochkirch; the Austrians were admirably "kitted out," but the poor Prussians' clothing was in a lamentable condition. The immediate foreground was occupied by an elderly officer in his underclothes and waistcoat; there was no question of boots, but he held a gun in his hand. This old gentleman was Major Balthasar von Poggenpuhl, who had held the churchyard for half an hour until he too joined the corpses on the ground. This picture—probably on account of its sentimental value to the family—was set in a broad, handsome baroque frame, while the glazed photographs and daguerrotypes had to be content with simple gilt borders.

All the members of the family—even Leo, who was something of a skeptic in artistic matters—extended their reverence for "the Hochkirch major" (as this officer was called to distinguish him from the many other majors in the family) to include the pictorial representation of his glorious act; only Friederike, in spite of her complete adherence to the family cult, was on a kind of war footing with the half-clad old hero. The reason was simply that it was her duty, at least every third day, to run her ancient, cobweb-thin dust cloth over the highly irregular baroque frame—with the very frequent, if not absolutely regular, result that the picture slid down from the wall and fell across the backrest onto the sofa. It was always put aside until after breakfast, when it was hammered back into place; but that did not do much good and could not be expected to, for the whole expanse of wall had been damaged too often, and quite soon the newly inserted nail would come out again and the picture would slide onto the sofa.

"Lord," said Friederike, "he probably stood there like that all right, it was a good thing he did. But to put him in a picture like that . . . it just won't stay in place, it just won't."

After this monologue she screwed the stove door tightly shut. That was always the last thing she did. Then she put her dustpan and dust cloth back into the firewood basket and softly began her retreat through the long bedroom into the kitchen. But there was no need to be so careful, because all four ladies were already awake, and Manon had even half opened a window into the courtyard, proceeding on the assumption that a temperature of several degrees below freezing was still preferable to air in which four people had slept through the night.

A bare quarter of an hour, and coffee was served. The ladies were already in the warm living room, the major's widow on the sofa, Therese in her rocking chair, and Manon with a tool box, hunting for a longer nail for the old Hochkirch major who had fallen down again.

"Friederike," said the major's widow, "you really ought to be more careful with that picture."

"Oh, ma'am, I am, I barely touch him; but he's always so wobbly . . . Lord, Manon dear, if you could find a really long one; or better still, if you could knock in a proper hook. Lord, it isn't as though I didn't remember all the time, but when he suddenly starts sliding, it always gives me a turn. And sometimes I wonder whether perhaps he's not properly at rest."

"Oh, Friederike, don't talk such nonsense," said Therese, a little sharply. "*Him,* of all people. As though he could fail to be at rest! Whatever do you mean? I tell you, *he*'s at rest all right. I only wish everyone could be at rest as he is. A clear conscience is the best pillow. You ought to know that. And as for a clear conscience, well, he's certainly got that . . . But wherever did you get these rolls again? They look as though someone had given them a fright, worse than the one you had. I don't like shop rolls. Why don't you go to young Karchow? He's a proper baker."

This difference of opinion occurred every third day between the maid and the young lady. Friederike enjoyed complete freedom of speech, and she would not have remained silent now and would have stoutly defended her dictum that "one must keep in with the basement shop people" if it had not been for a sudden knock on the front door. "The postman!" the three sisters cried altogether; and a moment later Friederike reappeared with the mail: a newspaper in a wrapper, an advertisement for firewood and peat, and a real letter. The advertisement went straight onto the stove; the paper probably contained a review of a recent exhibition of Sophie's watercolors and was pushed aside; only the letter caused a general rejoicing. "From Leo," cried the sisters, and handed the letter to their mother. But she gave it back to Therese. "You read it. He's such a good boy. But he always gives me a fright. He always wants something. And now we've just had Christmas and the New Year and the rent..."

"Oh Mother, you always start to worry right away. It's obvious you're not a soldier's daughter."

"No. Certainly not. And a good thing too. Who else would hold together what little we've got?"

"We would."

"Oh, you...! But now read the letter, Therese. My heart's positively thumping."

Dear Mama,

Christmas was hopeless. I might have got leave from the regiment, but the fare! There's all this talk about cheap fares nowadays, but I think they're much too high, quite unnaturally high! And Wendelin also said, "Leo, it can't be done," and so it couldn't; and so, as you know, I went down to my landlord Funke the butcher, and watched their family celebrations. Everyone was deeply emotional, even Funke. It seems quite incredible, because especially over Christmas they never stopped slaughtering, and sometimes I simply couldn't stand the sound of the poor brutes squealing any more, and Funke always supervised it himself. Incidentally, the freshly made sausages and the pig's head brawn were quite excellent. As far as food is concerned, one couldn't do better than here in Thorn. But the mind starves and so does the heart. All in all, starvation seems to be my lot. Oh Mother, why weren't you born a Bleichröder?[1]

"Monstrous," said Therese, interrupting her reading. "There's Manon with her everlasting Bartensteins, and now Leo's starting too."

"Having the Bartensteins is not at all a bad thing for us. Why don't you go on?"

. . . Well, so Christmas was no good. However, there are
other important days in the year. And the most important is
the fourth of January, the birthday of our dear old mother,
née Pütter. And that's the day after tomorrow, and I
shall report booted & spurred to deliver my good wishes
personally.

"It's not possible! No money for Christmas, and after the
New Year, just when all the bills come in, he intends to make
such an expensive journey!"

"I expect there'll be an explanation, Mama," said Manon.
"Probably in the letter. Just go on listening."

. . . because signs and wonders still happen, and sometimes
I feel as though atheism and all the other disagreeable
phenomena of our times were on the way out. Even the aristocracy will rise again, and the *poor* aristocracy will go to the
very top, and that means the Poggenpuhls, of course. Because there is absolutely no doubt that in that sphere we
represent a kind of perfection, the pure breed, as you might
say. But back to our subject, as they say in parliament. So
now lend me your ears and hear: on New Year's Eve I was a
beggar (albeit a happy one, because we got through seven
bowls of punch at the mess, outsize ones!); and on the
morning of January first, I was a god, a Croesus. Because
Croesus is always tops, or what is called the climax. It was
only ten o'clock when there was a knock on the door. I
dragged myself from my morning dreams and felt a certain
leaden condition, but not for long. For who stood before
me? Oktavio? No, not Oktavio. For today we shall call him
Wendelin. And what he said was as follows: "Leo," he said,
"you're in luck. Our ship has come home. With money."

"For me?" I asked.

"No, not for you. At least not directly. But for me. The
Military Weekly sent me my cheque this morning."

"Is it a lot?" I interrupted in the highest excitement.

"The Military Weekly always sends a lot," he replied
quietly and laid three twenty-mark notes before me. Daz-

zled, as though they were not notes but the purest gold, I was about to rush at him blinded with gratitude; but he restrained me with noble reticence and said, "All yours, Leo. But not for swigging. Tomorrow morning you're off to Berlin."

"Kind Wendelin! He's sending him because he knows he's your favorite," Manon interrupted at this point, and she stroked her mother's hands. But Therese continued:

You are to arrive at four in the afternoon, behave nicely, and next morning you're to help celebrate her birthday. Next to the emperor's birthday, Mother's birthday is the most important date in the calendar. That's in the Poggenpuhl catechism. And now get dressed and take an hour's walk. You look like Saint Sylvester when his last hour had come." And with these words he left me like a prince. And I shall do as he commanded and arrive on Tuesday afternoon. Four o'clock. *Tout à vous, ma Reine Mère.*

> Your happy, crazy,
> well beloved
> *Leo I*

The two younger sisters clapped their hands; even Therese, much as she deplored their boisterousness, was pleased about the visit. Only their mother said, "Oh dear, and I'm supposed to feel happy. But how can I? I suppose he'll just about get here with the money, but while he's here we'll have to give him a treat for a few days, and even if he doesn't ask much, he'll have to go back on the third day, and we'll have to pay."

"Don't always keep on about that," said Therese.

"Yes, Therese, you always imagine a liveried servant will come and bring you a money box with the inscription: To the valiant House of Poggenpuhl; but those are all fairy tales, and the man at the ticket office who sells the tickets is an inexorable reality."

"Oh Mama," said Sophie, "you mustn't spoil the pleasure of looking forward to it. There are still signs and wonders—he said so. And if they don't happen, then I'll get an advance on my last lot of pictures, and if that doesn't work . . ."

"Well, then we've still got the sugar caster," Manon interposed.

"Yes, that's always going to get us through. But one day it will be gone."

"Which wouldn't matter either," Manon continued consolingly. "The Bartensteins will give us another. Only the other day Frau Bartenstein said to me, 'Dear Manon, is there really nothing that you want?' Yes, Mama, that's how it is, and I'm only sorry that just when Leo arrives this evening I shall have to go to the wedding eve rehearsal. But perhaps I could take him along. I've thought about it for some time, and I'm sure Flora would be really pleased."

"You keep forgetting that he wears the emperor's uniform."

"Oh Therese, that's petty and old-fashioned and totally out of date. Our crown prince is the crown prince and he wears the emperor's uniform too, and if he hasn't been to the Bartensteins, then he's been to other people just like them."

"Well, we shall see," said Therese; her attitude to the Bartensteins was critical, but she was nevertheless glad of their existence.

3

The next day came, and late in the afternoon, when it was beginning to grow dark, a cab stopped at the house, and mother and daughters saw Friederike and Leo merrily exchanging greetings; then Friederike took the officer's little case from the driver's box and walked toward the door, past Agnes Nebelung, who had stationed herself by the sidewalk because she wanted to see the lieutenant. Leo followed.

Kisses were exchanged on the stairs, where the sisters were standing one step above the other. Their mother stood at the top. "Hello, old thing," and another kiss. Confused and disjointed sentences flew about, and then Leo went through the parlor into the living room with its single window. Here he threw off his greatcoat and sword; his tunic had ridden up, and he tugged it into place in front of the looking glass. Then he performed a smart about-turn and said, "Well, my dears, here I am again. How do I look?"

"Oh, superb."

"Thank you. That sort of remark always does one good, even if it's not true. One might almost say it refreshes. But à propos of refreshment: in spite of the fresh air, I'm colossally thirsty. For seven hours I've had nothing but an anchovy roll. You wouldn't have a glass of beer?"

"Of course, of course. Friederike can go and fetch a tankard of real beer..."

"No, no. Nobody's to fetch anything. Why should they? Water will do just as well." Manon handed him a glass of water and he swallowed it all in one gulp. "Brrr. But it's good."

"You're in such a hurry," said Manon. "It's not good for you. I think you should have a cup of coffee now. It's half past four and at seven we'll have something to eat."

"Excellent, Manon, excellent. Only perhaps we could change the order of events. I've just put down that water. If I have coffee right on top of it, that'll be too much fluid—an unnecessary dilation of the stomach, tantamount to a weakening effect. And I need my strength. Or, let us say, my country needs it."

"So you think..."

"Permit me to think along the following lines: a reversal of the accepted order. First a bite, then coffee. For if my thirst was great, my hunger is almost equally great. Seven hours..."

"You've already said that."

"I know. Truth will out. Come on—what have you got?"

"A duck."

"Splendid."

"But it's still hanging up by the attic window and hasn't been plucked or drawn. So it'll be about two hours . . ."

"Rather a long time."

" . . . But I think I've got the solution. We'll take out the liver, and in a quarter of an hour it can be fried and on your plate. Would you like it with apple or with onion?"

"Both. Never refuse anything, unless decency absolutely demands it."

"Oh, so you think such cases exist?" said Therese.

"Of course I do, of course. But now, dear old Mama, tell me how you are. Have you still got a pain round here?"

"Yes, Leo. Every night."

"Heaven knows, those doctor fellows are absolutely useless. Look at my forefinger. I twisted it the other day—actually about three months ago—and I've still got the same weakness in it. I may have to ask for my discharge."

"Oh, don't talk like that," said Therese. "Poggenpuhls don't ask for their discharge."

"But they get it."

"No, they don't. He (and she pointed to the Hochkirch major) will never be forgotten, nor will the Sohr major, nor Papa either. The emperor knows our worth."

"Yes, Therese. And what *is* our worth?"

"Our principles and the certainty that we'll be loyal to the last drop in our veins."

"Oh well, I suppose so . . . But listen, Mother, have you tried healing?"

"Healing?"

"Yes. Faith healing. They puff and blow on you and mutter things, it's sort of sympathetic medicine. It always works. We've got an old Polish woman up there, and as soon as she starts puffing and blowing everything gets better . . . A propos, is the Christmas market still on?"

"I think so; some of it, anyway."

"There's bound to be a few stalls left, and we absolutely must go, girls. 'Count, just *one* three pfennig piece.' It's time I heard a classic remark like that again. And then we'll go to

Helms and have a grog or hot chocolate with whipped cream
and then off to the Reichshallen."[2]

"Oh, what a splendid idea," said Manon. "Don't you think
so, Sophie? You're so quiet . . . Why don't you say something
too . . .? I don't expect it would do for Therese, the Reichshallen are too common for her. But two sisters should be
enough, and I'm really looking forward to it. Only you must
arrange it so that we get to the Bartensteins at nine o'clock or
not much later. Yes, Leo, you'll have to take us as far as the
Vossstrasse."

"Certainly. But why? What goes on there?"

"Wedding eve rehearsal. Seraphine Schweriner, a cousin
of Flora's, is getting married in a fortnight, and we've been
rehearsing ever since Christmas. I've got a part—two, actually: first a girl with a baton, and then a Slovak mousetrap
seller. They say I look charming."

"Of course."

"And Sophie's painted a transparency and written the
prologue. But she won't recite it."

"Perhaps you'll have to do that too."

"Possibly. But I don't want to. Prologues are such a bore.
People are always glad when they're over. But whether I do it
or not is something we can discuss on the way—that is, if any
kind of conversation is possible on the way. You really have
to watch out now; it's always so foggy in the evenings.
Altogether, the Berlin air . . ."

"Oh don't talk nonsense, Manon. Berlin has the best air in
the world. I can tell you, I'm glad to have a chance of sniffing
about a bit in it once more. Fog! Fog's no problem. Fog's just
an external, and externals don't mean a thing. It's the inner
life that counts, that's where the creative force is—fresh,
happy, and free; I'll leave out the "devout" bit, if you'll
excuse me, Therese . . . Good God, our little hole up there, it
has the purest air, there's always an East wind or whatever,
and if you've got a weak chest" (and he thumped his own)
"you catch pneumonia before you know where you are. All
right, so it has the purest air, no question about it. All the
same, I tell you, everything there is stuffy, narrow, small. If

the colonel sneezes, the sentry hears him and presents arms. Horrible. If it weren't for the odd spot of gambling and the Jew girls..."

"But Leo..."

"Or one of the two or three Christian girls. But the Jewish ones are prettier."

"But you must have some intellectual activity?"

"Heavens, I should hope not. There's no time. But every now and then I work out my debts, and I sit there adding and subtracting, adding and subtracting, to see how I can get by. That's my only intellectual activity. It's quite serious—you might almost say scientific."

"Oh dear, Leo," said his mother with an anxious look at him. "I'm sure that's the only reason you came. Is it a lot this time?"

"A lot, Mother? It's never a lot. How can it be? No one's as silly as that. A lot—that would be the last straw. But it is a little. And although it's very lucky that it is so little, in a way that's just what makes it so annoying—the most annoying thing about it, really. Because you say to yourself, 'Good God, it's so little, how could you have had any fun on so little?' And you haven't really had any. And then the other trouble begins; even though it is so little, you just can't pay it. And no one to help, not a soul! And when I look at the others! Every one of them has an uncle..."

"Oh, we have an uncle too!" Sophie interrupted. "And Uncle Eberhard is a man of honor..."

"Granted. But kind as he is, Uncle Eberhard does nothing to prove he's an uncle; or anyway, not enough. And then, my dears, the ones that haven't got uncles, well, at least they've got a grandfather, or a godparent, or a canoness.[3] Canonesses are best of all: they believe any story you tell them, and even if they haven't got much themselves, they'll give you everything, down to their last penny."

"Oh Leo, don't talk such nonsense. How can they give everything away?"

"Everything, I say. A proper canoness can give everything away because she doesn't need anything at all. She has a roof over her head, and fish, and game, and turkeys run about the courtyard, and pigeons sit on the roof, and there's a huge vegetable garden which they look after themselves of course, because they have nothing else to do, and there's always a turnip to be found or a carrot; and there's always a fire in the kitchen because they get their firewood free. And that's why—yes, I must say it again—that's why they can give everything away; because they need nothing and what they need they've got."

"But they have to have clothes."

"Clothes? Good heavens, no. They don't have clothes. They have one dress and it lasts them thirty years. Of course they wear something; they're not the type to go about like Eve in the Garden of Eden . . . Ah, there's the liver—it smells delicious, exquisite. And now, my dears, we'll divide it up; Mother has the middle bit because it's the tenderest, Therese the right end and me the left end, and Sophie and Manon . . ."

"Oh Leo, don't put on an act. You know quite well you're having it all. That's how you've always been: you want to make nice—as long as no one takes you at your word."

"Don't make revelations about my character, Sophie. You had better give me a roll instead, to eat with my liver, or else it'll be too rich. And I'm right all the same about our relatives; not a kinswoman, not an aunt, hardly a female cousin, at least, not a proper one—it's enough to drive a man crazy, as Mephisto said somewhere. Mother, do you know Mephisto?"

"Of course I know him. You Poggenpuhls always think you're the only ones with any wisdom or knowledge, and all acquired through inspiration. Because it's not as though you got it at school. And you of all people, Leo! When I think of your teachers' reports! Wendelin was another matter. You know why? Because he takes after the Pütters."

"Oh Mother, you really are the tops. What would we do without you? And I'm almost ready to believe that the Pütters really are superior. But in one respect they're just like us; they haven't a penny and that's my misfortune. Oh Mama, no money anywhere, no cover—and that for a young fellow and a lieutenant! It's a devilish situation. And there I was inviting you to go to Helms and the Reichshallen!"

"He's incorrigible," laughed Sophie. "Whatever next! First of all, you're our guest, and your only duty is to do the honors. And surely you'll feel able to act as our escort?"

"Goodness, you're good girls, all of you. And so broad-minded; and you understand that this is how it has to be; and still you go on giving me your love and respect. At least I hope you do, otherwise I shouldn't accept. And now I think we should go. You're coming, Mama, aren't you?"

"No, Leo. Every extra person makes a difference. And then my coat—if we're going to a café, it's too shabby."

"Oh, that doesn't matter."

"And then I get rheumatism so easily—just here—and you never know where you're going to find a table, and it might be in a draft. And if I sit in a draft I always get my rheumatism, and then I have to go to bed. Or if I don't get my rheumatism, I get my colic, and that's even more miserable."

4

Leo really did go to the Christmas market and to Helms and the Reichshallen with his two younger sisters. Then he accompanied them to the Bartensteins, took his leave of them, and arrived home a little after nine. It was his plan to have a long chat with his mother and Therese, and to tell them all about his impressions of Berlin, for he was one of those fortunate people who only have to set foot in the street to have an adventure—or to imagine they have. But things turned out differently from what he had expected; for Therese had gone into town to buy a few extra trifles for their mother's birthday, and Mama herself, so Friederike told him as soon as he entered the passage, had already gone to bed. "Hm," he grumbled; and, having no other choice, he was just about to settle down to a little quiet meditation in a corner of the sofa when his mother sent for him to come and talk to her at her bedside. That was a great deal preferable to "contemplating his inner life," as he put it, while waiting for Therese.

"Are you feeling unwell, Mama?"

"No, Leo, not really. I just lay down because I wanted to build up my strength a bit for tomorrow. Get a chair and bring it close and then fetch the lamp so that I can look at you. Because you've got a nice Poggenpuhl face, and if there's something that isn't as it should be, I can always tell by looking at you, and get an idea of what's going on."

"Oh, Mama, you always think I'm fibbing. I'm not as bad as all that. I'm not even very talented in that line—all I do is exaggerate a bit."

"Never mind. And you were always my favorite, and the others have never begrudged it. But you are irresponsible, and you always think 'something will turn up.' And you see, that's what worries me. Turn up! How can anything turn up, where is it to come from? It's really a miracle that we've managed to scrape along so far."

"But, Mother, that's just it; that's where our hope lies, I might almost say, our certainty. If a miracle could happen yesterday, why shouldn't it happen today or tomorrow or the day after tomorrow?"

"That sounds quite good, but it's not right. If we take miracles and grace for granted, then we vex Him from Whom all grace comes, and in the end He won't send us any more. God doesn't want us just to accept everything and thank Him (and sometimes we do that very perfunctorily); He wants us to deserve His grace, or at least to show that we are worthy of it, and He wants us to keep our eyes fixed not on what *might* happen through a miracle, but on what *must* happen according to reason and calculation and probability. That kind of calculation has His blessing upon it."

"Oh, Mama, I never stop calculating."

"Yes, you never stop calculating, quite true; but you calculate afterward, not before. You start calculating when it's too late, when you're in trouble right up to your neck, and then

you try to calculate your way out, and all you do is to calculate yourself further in. You don't and won't see what you don't
like; and when something seems flattering or pleasing to you,
then you turn it into a probability. People have done so much
for us—for you too—and now, I think, the time has come for
us to say, 'We must help ourselves!' If we keep on saying,
'But we're the Poggenpuhls' we shall make a nuisance of
ourselves and in the end we'll turn into whiners, which is
something I should not like to see."

"We're far from that, Mama."

"Not as far as you think. Uncle Eberhard is a very fine and
generous man. I really must say it: he's a true nobleman; but
even he is gradually beginning to cool off a bit and grow
impatient. He doesn't say so right out, just because he *is*
generous, but you can read it between the lines."

"Oh, Uncle! The old bone of contention! Look, Mama, I ask
you: he really does do too little, and what he does is all just
for the sake of God. What he ought to think is: 'I've had my
time, and now it's someone else's turn! It's true he gives us
something every now and again, but his sacrifices on the altar
of the family are not in proportion either to his income or to
his sermons. He ought to write less and give more. After all,
he had a colossal stroke of luck and now he's been living in
clover for twelve years and more, or sitting pretty, as some
people call it."

"How is it that nothing can make you change your mind
and that you simply will not see how things really are with
Uncle. He married a rich widow and lives in a *Schloss*,[4] and
when his wife wants to invite Prince Albrecht or one of the
Carolaths, there's a great to-do and half the nobility of Lower
Silesia comes to dinner too, and it looks as though Uncle
Eberhard were giving the party. But he's not the one giving it,
she is; he only lends his name to it, and hardly even that,
because lots of people call her by her first husband's name
when they talk about her behind her back. He was a Silesian,
and of a very distinguished family, much more distinguished
than the Poggenpuhls—you've all got to face the fact that

there *are* more distinguished families . . . I tell you, kind as she is, she still keeps him short, and he hasn't got much more than his general's pension, and out of that he still has his old debts to pay off . . ."

"Old debts? You see, Mama, now you're the one saying it! So he has old debts too. And he was made a general just the same and now he's got a rich wife . . ."

"He still has his old debts to pay off," his mother repeated, taking no notice of the interruption. "And so what he has left is just pocket money."

"But a tidy sum . . ."

"Possibly, or let's say, certainly. And if he's careful with it nevertheless, it may well be because he doesn't trust you, or, if he does, then his wife doesn't, and she influences him."

"That's just it, that's what's so galling—the indignity of petticoat influence! And then, Mama, I won't even talk about myself—perhaps I'm an *enfant perdu*; that may be so. But Wendelin, that model of a boy, if I may call my respected brother by such a name—surely he must be pleased with *him*, and even Madam Aunt should be. It just shows how stingy they are. It's obvious."

"Is that what Wendelin says too?"

"No. Not him. He doesn't need to. Wendelin has the gift of feeling king of infinite space on a pitcher of water. Wendelin will get on anyhow. But even for him there's a difference. There's a difference between getting on effortlessly and getting on through perpetual abstinence. People who go in for abstinence usually have a screw loose—they become famous, or at least they *may* become famous, but even when they *are* famous, they usually behave like little schoolmasters. Possibly Wendelin may be an exception."

"But do you really believe—with any kind of certainty—that he'll get to the top?"

"Certainly, Mother. In less than six months he'll be on the General Staff. The stuff he wrote about Skobeleff made everyone sit up. And a year or two after that they'll send him to Saint Petersburg, and there he'll marry—at least that's what I'm assuming for the moment—a Yousoupov or a Dol-goruzka; they all have at least ten thousand serfs and diamond mines as well. What do you think? Not a bad forecast? Come on, admit it! But if Uncle were different—or Aunt, if you prefer; though we can't expect much from her—she's only a relative by marriage and she was from the petty bourgeoisie, which is always bad; at least *you're* middleclass—well, then he'd be there already. He'd be in Saint Petersburg, and I'd be posted there, and I'd go with him to the Caucasus or to Merv or Samarkand—and none of that will happen, or at any rate it's being cruelly delayed, only because we haven't the wherewithal, the filthy lucre."

"Goodness, Leo, one would think, to listen to you, that everything would fall into your lap if only the wind changed. Dreams! Plans! You were like that even as a little boy!"

"Yes, Mother, and that's the way to be—for people like us, that is. If you've got something, well, then you can take life as it really is, you can be what they call a realist nowadays. But if you've got nothing, if you live in the Sahara, then you simply can't exist without a mirage of palm trees and odalisques and suchlike. A mirage, I say. And even if there's nothing there when you get up close, at least you've lived for an hour, and hoped, and got your courage back, and then you can go on wading through the sand quite happily. And so the visions that lead us on, however deceptive and unreal they may be, are really a mercy after all."

"Yes, the young can live like that, and perhaps they have a right to. And I'll grant you another thing: hope is sometimes better than fulfillment, and people who can go on hoping, at least they've had their share of happiness. But all the same: you hope too much and work too little."

"I don't work much, that's true, and I won't boast about it. But I'm cheerful by nature, and in the end that's better than any amount of work. Cheerfulness attracts people, it's like a magnet; so I think in the end there'll be something for me too."

"Well, I hope there may. And now go into the kitchen and tell Friederike to give you some supper."

5

Leo made no objection; he really was hungry. The duck liver at lunch had not been much, and the cup of chocolate at Helms even less.

So he went out and found Friederike. She was sitting by the kitchen lamp with an inkwell close beside her, doing her bookkeeping. She sat pondering, pen poised between thumb and forefinger. It was a new, wooden pen (probably a Christmas present) with an eagle—or it might have been a dove—carved on the end. As far as could be ascertained in the semidarkness that reigned in the kitchen, everything there was tidy and clean, if not exactly gleaming. The only gleaming object was the tea kettle standing in it's hole in the stove; its lid rattled perpetually. Never to be without boiling water was a luxury peculiar to the Poggenpuhl family. It was a carefully calculated luxury, because it enabled them to dispense modest hospitality at any time. This hospitality could take various forms, but at the top of the list—almost a specialty of the house—was a clear soup with a French name that could be quickly concocted with the help of a few slices of toast and a pinch of nutmeg. Every single member of the family excelled in its preparation to such a degree that even Flora would ask for it when she dropped in for an hour's chat in the evening, having first charmingly declined offers of "cold meats" and suchlike; and she was wise to do so.

"Well, Friederike," Leo now said as he pulled up a kitchen chair and leaned over the back, "Mama sent me along, and she even spoke of supper. What's the supper situation? I'm hungry and I'd be grateful to God for anything. And to you too."

"Well, Master Leo, there isn't much."

"But what is there?"

"Well, a meatball left over from lunch yesterday, and a few pickled herrings with dill and sliced gherkins. And then there's an Edam cheese. But there's not much of thát left. And then perhaps I could make you a cup of tea. The water's still bubbling."

"No, Friederike, not tea. What's the good of that? But the rest sounds good, and I might as well stay here and have it in the kitchen. Mama is tired and worn out. And then you can tell me a bit about the girls. They're always writing to me. Manon always writes four pages, but there's never much in the letters. How are things?"

"Well, Master Leo, how should they be? Miss Therese, well, you know what she's like . . . but, mind you, I haven't said a thing. And then little Sophie. Little Sophie, she's a marvel. And little Manon's always bright and cheerful, there's no denying that."

"And she's in with the rich bankers, and that's very wise and sensible of her. Bankers are really the only people one should know; only it's a pity they nearly all belong to the Old Dispensation."

"Yes, Master Leo, that's how it is, and I've spoken to her about it; but she says: 'Friederike, if you want something, you mustn't be choosy, you've got to take what comes.'"

"Very sensible; a wise girl; I like that, and I've no objections. Because I'm in with them a bit too, I've started a little flirtation in the same direction. Fine, black-haired figure of a gal, with a waist like *that*, and eyes—well, Friederike, I tell you, her eyes . . . real almond eyes, and actually everything about her reminds you a bit of a harem. Ever heard of harems?"

"Course I've heard of harems. They're what the Turks keep their wives in, no windows, just tiny little holes, so they can only peek out now and then."

"Right. And mine looks just like one of those Turkish women, or anyway, very nearly."

"But will it be possible, Master Leo? Will the family give their consent?"

"Which? Mine or hers?"

"Oh, I mean the Poggenpuhls."

"I don't care, Friederike. And then . . . look, the Poggenpuhls aren't all that dumb either, and if it's really a lot, they'll be quite happy to consent to anything."

"Is it a lot then?"

"Ah, I'm not sure myself yet. Those Orientals are so horribly careful, always making marriage contracts that don't give you a thing unless you manage to produce half a dozen straight off. And it can't always be done as quickly as that."

"Oh, Leo, dear, you'll surely . . ."

"Yes, Friederike, so you may say. But nature plays strange games with us; and then when they *are* born (charming little angels, because when they're quite small they're always little angels) then they go and die; and look: there you are, back where you started, and all that trouble has been for nothing."

"Yes, yes, such things do happen. But have you come to an understanding, then, the two of you?"

"God forbid, and I haven't said a word to her, and I'm only talking like this because one's always got a knife at one's throat, and then one starts building castles in the air and then one feels a bit better and thinks, 'Well, one day I suppose I'll find a way out of this misery . . .' But Friederike, I think you might make me some tea after all, that is, if you've got a drop of rum left."

"No, Leo, dear. Rum there isn't. Only a Gilka."

"Hm, that's not really a very good mixture. Still, after all, why not? I can't pour it in, of course, but it would be quite acceptable to drink on the side. And that herring has made me a bit thirsty. And à propos of what I told you about the beautiful Jewess with the black hair: you must keep your mouth shut about that, and you mustn't mention it—not to Mother and not to my sisters either—anyway, not to Therese. It wouldn't matter so much telling Manon, since she's practically in it too with her everlasting Bartensteins, and she's always trying to get me to go to their place with her. The old man there is supposed to be very rich too, incidentally, and I haven't made up my mind yet what I'm going to do. Then one's troubles would all be over at one go, and that's the main thing. But if nothing comes of it, well, then, Friederike, then it'll have to be blacks, real, genuine blacks, because then I'll have to go to Africa."

"Oh Lord, Leo, dear! And I've just been reading about that. Oh, my goodness me, but they kill everybody there and cut poor Christian folk's throats."

"They do that here too. It's the same everywhere."

"And all those wild animals. Snakes and crocodiles, so even though it's so hot, you can never go for a swim."

"Yes, that's true. Still, you get everything free, and if you shoot an elephant you've got as much ivory as you want, and then you can get them to make you a billiard cue. And believe me, to be free like that has its advantages too. Have you ever heard of people being arrested for debt? Of course you have. Well, you see, there's nothing like that there, because they don't have debts or IOUs or interest or usury, and when I'm in Bukoba—that's a middling kind of place, sort of like Potsdam—well, when I'm there, the equator—which you've probably heard of and which is a good thousand miles long—well, this equator might run right through my body."

"For Heaven's sakes..."

"And that sort of thing is quite impossible here, and that's why I want to go there, unless something turns up here really soon."

"Oh Lord, Master Leo, then it would be better to..."

"Exactly, Friederike, much better. And all that Poggenpuhl stuff that Therese's always making such a fuss about... Heavens, that reminds me: wherever has Therese got to? You said she was just going into town to buy something for Mama's birthday... Oh God, birthday! I say, Friederike, I suppose I'll have to get something or other for the old lady too, otherwise she'll think I never think of anybody but myself. What do you think I could give her, what does she need?"

"Lord, Master Leo, come to that, Frau von Poggenpuhl needs everything!"

"Everything? That's too much, that's impossible, that's above my means. After all, I've got to get back again, and I haven't enough money for that as it is... But you mentioned some Edam cheese just now. Is there any left?"

"Of course there is."

"Oh, good. But first we must get this birthday present business settled. Though I've got to get back—that's the first consideration."

"Well, Master Leo, how much do you want to invest?"

"Want to? A million! But how much can I, Friederike, how much can I? That's the trouble, there's the rub. More than . . . more than . . . well, I'd prefer not to mention any figures. But it's got to be something nice, something imaginative."

"Well, I'd say a primula."

"Good. A primula. A primula fits the bill exactly. Primula —or *primula veris*, because that's the Latin name—more or less means the beginning of spring. And mother will be fifty-seven. And you see, that's exactly what I'd call imaginative."

"And then, Master Leo, perhaps a bag of ginger nuts as well: she really loves those. But they must be crisp, and not sticky and tough as old boots."

"Very well. A primula and ginger nuts, good and crisp and all white with sugar on the outside. But it's so late now, I doubt if they'll have any left."

"No, not today. But I'll get them tomorrow morning early. She won't have her presents before nine, because first the place must be warmed up, and tidied up a bit too."

As she spoke Friederike began to clear the plates and glasses from the table, and in their place she put half an Edam cheese, which was not really much more than a red rind. But that did not matter. Leo had already taken out his little pocket knife because that was the handiest, and was scraping out the good bits with dexterity; as he did so, he kept declaring that finding something where nothing was really to be found was perferable to anything else, and that there was something imaginative about it too. "Yes, Friederike, that's the way to live. Pick up the small joys until the great stroke of luck comes along."

"Ah, as long as it does come along . . ."

"And if it doesn't, then at least one's had the small strokes."

And with that he placed the hollow cheese on his left forefinger and spun it around, first slowly and then faster and faster, like a little half-globe.

"Look, up here, that's the Northern Hemisphere. And down here, where there's nothing, that's where Africa is."

6

Leo had had his bed made in the parlor, where he slept uncomfortably but soundly on the small cane sofa that normally had its place in the bedroom. He only woke for a moment when Friederike came through to light the stove, but quickly fell back into a quiet morning slumber when he heard the wood crackling and, a moment later, the stove door rattling in the single-windowed living room next door.

It was already half past eight when Manon came to wake him. "Up, Leo; it's high time. We can't keep Mama in bed any longer." Then he leaped up, and accomplished his morning ablutions with soldierly speed. The long mirror over the console table was quite impressive enough for the purpose; everything else was all the more primitive: a kitchen chair held a wash basin, towel, glass, and water jug; all the other requisites came out of his suitcase.

"Good morning, ladies"; and with these words he went in to his sisters and gave each of them a kiss. It was already agreeably warm in the little room. The presents for Mama still lay higgledy-piggledy on an old piano, because naturally they were not going to be set out here but in the parlor, which still needed to be put in order. When this had been duly accomplished, a proper survey became possible: there was a morning cap, two pairs of cotton gloves, and a pair of felt slippers. Friederike had contributed a pot of heather, and Leo's primula stood between the two felt slippers, together with the paper bag. Leo himself quickly tore a page from his notebook, wrote a few lines, and inserted it between the two pale mauve flowers of the primula. "A picture of my fate," he said to Sophie who was standing beside him. "Two blossoms, and pale mauve." Their mother had been growing impatient in the bedroom, from which she was now released and led to the table with the birthday presents. Leo and the two younger sisters kissed her hand, while Therese contented herself with a kiss on the cheek. "Goodness, children, such a lot of things!" said the dear old lady. "And everything so well chosen. Yes, the felt slippers are just what I needed; I'm always so cold. And the primula—and with a message too!" She took the piece of paper and read, "'A primula from your . . .' Yes, yes, Leo, it's you. You didn't finish the last word, but it wasn't necessary. Well, God loves us all, and perhaps he'll come to your aid too one day."

"Of course, Mother," said Therese. "You mustn't depress him like that. He must keep his self-esteem and tell himself that a Pomeranian nobleman will always find his place in the world. I am full of confidence."

"And will you go surety on it?"

"No, that you must do yourself. And if you do it properly, as befits a Poggenpuhl—and there you can follow Wendelin's example—things will go well for you. We have a star in our crest."

"I wish I had one on my epaulettes."

"All in good time. And now take Mama's arm and take her in to breakfast."

They must have sat an hour over their coffee. Leo had to tell them about his life at Thorn, especially about his visits in the country around, to the German as well as the Polish aristocracy.

"And do you win any moral victories over them?" asked Therese, referring to the latter. "Are you gaining ground?"

"Ground? Honestly, Therese, we're quite satisfied if we beat them at skat. But there are ways of doing that. Those Poles, I can tell you, they're damned crafty fellows, artful dodgers, the whole boiling . . ."

"You use such a lot of Berlinisms, Leo."

"I do; and because one can never get enough of them, I suggest we set off as soon as possible and go into town to see if we can find a few more. If you have eyes and ears, you can always pick up something. I feel like looking at a Littfass column[5] again. 'Save three hundred marks!' or 'Golden Number 100'; or 'Tapeworm cure.' I simply adore reading that kind of stuff. Who's coming with me? Who has time and feels like coming along?"

Therese silently turned aside.

"Hm. Therese is abandoning me, and Sophie has her household chores. But I think I can rely on Manon. And then we shall go and see the Rezonville panorama (the French are really good at that kind of thing) and at twelve we'll be on Unter den Linden and watch them change the guard with the full band playing, and if we're lucky the old emperor will be at his window and wave to us. Or at least we can imagine he's waved."

With these words Leo and Manon got to their feet.

"Don't be late; two o'clock!" warned Sophie; and they promised.

Leo and Manon returned on time, and punctually at two they went in to lunch. The table had been set in the parlor. There was a cake in the middle flanked by the heather on the right and the primula on the left. The Sohr major looked down from his frame and smiled.

Immediately after the soup the glass plate with the little bottle of wine for visitors was taken down from the desk and placed before Leo; with great dignity he said, "If this is for *me*, I must decline; but if it's because of Mama's birthday so that we can drink her health, then it can stay."

And while they were still arguing about it and overcoming Leo's resistance, Friederike appeared with the duck.

"Which bit would you like?" asked Sophie.

"Drumstick, please. I think asking for the drumstick is always the best policy. First of all it makes a good impression because it sounds modest, and secondly the top joint tends to come along with it. And then the question of the actual quantity is not to be taken lightly either."

So he did himself proud; everyone was ready to humor him. Then he proposed a toast to their mother's health. She had to take a sip, but the girls only touched the knuckles of their forefingers to one another's glasses.

"It's absolutely true, everything tastes better at home. There's no maternal duck like this in the whole of Thorn. And the stuffing—two kinds, even, chestnuts this end and currant

stuffing the other. My dears, I almost believe it's all pretense:
I think you've got something hidden away somewhere,
you're not as poor as all that."

"Oh Leo, don't say things like that, don't talk like that. It
always frightens me. You're quite capable of imagining that
it's really true..."

"No, no. I know perfectly well how things really are. I just
happened to think of something I once read in a newspaper, a
story about an old woman who had sewn a whole fortune
into—well, I won't say what she'd sewn it into. And then I
also thought of Uncle Eberhard, our uncle the general, and
that he could really..."

At that moment the door bell rang and Friederike came to
announce the general.

"Lupus in fabula." But before Leo could utter the words,
their uncle stood in the doorway bringing his fingers to his
temple in a semimilitary salute. "My respects, sister-in-law."

The girls hurried toward him, Leo naturally following; but
when the old lady tried to rise, her strength failed her, she
was so touched by the kindness of her brother-in-law for
whom she had always had a special love and admiration.

"Stay put, my dear Albertine. That's what comes of too
much youthful exercise. And I bring you greetings from my
wife too... And fancy finding Leo here. Gracious, boy, you
look terrific, and exceedingly well nourished. Ah, I see, I
see..." and he pointed to the duck.

"You must join us," said Manon.

And their uncle fell in between them. Tucking his napkin
round his neck (which he himself described as an old-
fashioned habit), he began to gnaw at a wing with much
relish. "Exquisite. And by the way, it's a well-known fact that
really delicious food is only to be found in small households.
I'll tell you why. Because in a small household people still
cook with love. Yes, my dear Albertine, with love. And that is
what counts, after all."

"You're always so kind, Eberhard, always just the same.
And if you like it... But tell me first of all, what brings you
here? To Berlin in winter?"

166 THE POGGENPUHL FAMILY

"Ah, Albertine, what brings me here? I might say your birthday. But perhaps you wouldn't believe me, so I'd better come out with the truth at once. Business brings me here, mortgages, things to write off, and this and that at the bank. Boring, really. And on the other hand quite interesting."

"Oh, very, very, " sighed Leo, and he was about to elaborate. But Therese raised her finger to stop him.

"...and," their uncle the general continued, "since the journey had to be made, of course I chose the fourth of January so as to be able to wish many happy returns to my dear sister-in-law."

"And you must stay with us," said the major's widow. "We haven't much to offer, but we do have a view of Saint Matthew's."

"I know, Albertine," said the general. "It's very nice here. But to be quite honest, I prefer the Potsdamer Platz, because there's lots of life there. And lots of life is the best thing a big city has to offer. That's what we miss in Adamsdorf. So I've put up at the Fürstenhof as usual; they know me there and, honestly, it looked as though they were all really pleased to see me arrive."

"I expect they were."

"And when I lean out of my window in the morning with a sofa cushion under each elbow and the fresh winter air blows from the Hall'sches Tor (and I can afford to do that because I'm used to fresh air: there's quite another wind blowing from our old Koppe at home), and I can see the Café Bellevue and Josty, where they all sit reading their papers in that glass projection from early morning on, and the horse trams and omnibuses all coming from different sides as though they were all going to collide at any moment, and the flower girls (only they're not really flower girls—they're men with wooden legs), and then in all that noise and confusion they suddenly start calling out late extras, the way they used to call out fire alarms in the old days, and in such croaky voices that it sounds as though the end of the world were nigh, to say the very least—yes, my dears, when I have that scene before me, then I know I'm among human beings once more, and I don't want to miss that."

Leo gave a silent nod.

"So forgive me, Albertine, if I refuse. The Fürstenhof is more conveniently located too. But let's all do something together all the same. It's three o'clock now. What shall we do today? Kroll![6] Good, that's an idea. There's bound to be a Christmas show on there, Snow White or Cinderella. Cinderella would be better. With Snow White you get the glass coffin. And on the whole I'm not keen on coffins. I'm more in favor of cheerfulness."

"Well, Uncle," said Leo, "then perhaps a theater would be best. They're doing The Quitzows[7] in two places today, the real ones at the Royal Theater, and a parody at the Moritzplatz. What do you think of going to the Moritzplatz Quitzows?"

"No, Leo, that won't do, fond as I am of that kind of thing. But we owe something to our name. Look, the Poggenpuhls were more or less the same kind of thing in Pomerania as the Quitzows were in the Mark, and so I think that from esprit de corps we shouldn't sit there cheerfully watching a parody of the whole affair."

Therese rose in order to give her uncle a kiss. "It always gives me great satisfaction, Uncle, to meet with such sentiments. Leo gets more shallow every day. You know why? Because he's chasing after the Golden Calf."

"Yes," said Leo. "I am. I only wish it would get me somewhere."

"It will," Manon consoled him; her thoughts immediately turned to Flora.

"But what are we talking about?" Leo continued. "It's all beside the point. We're still on the Quitzows, the real and the false. The false ones have been turned down, so . . ."

" . . . the real ones, then," the general concluded. "The real ones at the Royal Theater. That's where we'll go. And afterward we'll go somewhere where we can have a chat and try and establish what the play was really all about. It's supposed to be a good play, if only because it does justice to both sides, which is always a difficult thing to do. But I've heard this much: Dietrich von Quitzow is supposed to be more interesting than the Elector Frederic. Of course. Bound to be. A man who thumps the table with an iron mail fist is always more interesting than a chap who just preaches an afternoon sermon. You never get anywhere like that. I imagine Dietrich like Götz von Berlichingen, who wasn't afraid of the emperor and made fun of the Heilbronn Council. That's always been my favorite scene. I suppose we'll get tickets all right—I don't mind if we have to pay a bit extra. If your name is Poggenpuhl, you have to show some feeling for an old comrade."

"It's a good thing, Eberhard," said the major's widow, "that the walls have no ears. You aristocrats are all alike. And you Poggenpuhls...yes, of course, I know, you're among the best of them. But even you! The Hohenzollerns gave you everything, and as soon as the question of the estates comes up, you stand up against them."

"Quite right, Albertine. That's how we are. But it's not as serious as all that. When it comes to the crunch, you'll always find us ready. There's the Hochkirch major next door, still without his coat on, and that's to his credit and I should almost be prepared to say it suits him; and here (and he pointed to the picture over the sofa) we have the Sohr major, and your dear father, my brother Alfred, buried at Gravelotte. Those are our deeds, and they speak. But when times are quiet, like now, then we get a bit restive, and we like to think back to the old days when there was no War Ministry and no blue letters[8] and a man went to war off his own bat. I suppose I shouldn't say so, and I'm only talking off the top of my head, but I think it must have been more fun in those days. The commoners brewed Bernau and Cottbus beer, and we drank it. And that's how everything was. There was more go and gaiety to life—for commoners too, when you come to think of it. No competition yet, in those days. True, Leo?"

"And how. Much more dash in those days. Perhaps one day it'll come back."

"That's what I think. But not for us. It'll never be our turn again. It may seem like it now—but that's just the last flicker... But now our plan of campaign for tonight. First of all I'm going to the Fürstenhof to write a few lines to my wife, and at half past six you come and meet me there. You too, sister-in-law."

"No, Eberhard. That sort of thing's not for me any more. I've got rheumatism and I'd rather stay home. When you've all gone, I shall first of all read the newspaper and then the evening blessing. Or else Friederike can read it. She's beginning to wonder why we've been living like the heathen since New Year's Eve."

7

They managed to get seats, good ones in the fourth row of the stalls. Mitterwurzer, who happened to be giving a guest performance in Berlin, played Dietrich von Quitzow. The scene with Wend von Ilenburg in the second act made a tremendous impact. The interval came soon after, and the general, who had been growing increasingly agitated, turned to Therese on his right and said, "Strange—just like Bismarck. And both of them—there's coincidence for you—born practically next door to one another. I believe you can shoot from Schönhausen to Quitzöwel with an air gun, or a country postman can walk it in a morning. Marvelous part of the world, that. Lombard country. Ah well, you've either got what it takes or you haven't. What do you think, Leo?"

Leo would have liked to reply, but, uninhibited though he normally was, he now felt somewhat embarrassed, because he could see, in the rows in front and behind his party, people putting their heads together and whispering. His uncle saw it too. But he did not take it amiss and merely thought, "I know their sort. Berlin fusspots."

The performance finished shortly before ten, and after a brief consultation on a rather draughty corner they agreed to remain as close by as possible and to have supper in a theater restaurant in the Charlottenstrasse. The place was almost full, but they managed to find a table. Glancing briefly at the menu, they came to a rapid decision. Everyone chose sole, except for Therese, who declared herself in favor of macaroni with tomatoes. An instant later five pint mugs of beer were planted before them as though this were a matter of course, and it was only when the mugs were half empty that their order made its appearance; whereupon the general, who had grown somewhat edgy, regained his equilibrium. He drew his plate a little closer and squeezed lemon juice over the crisp coating of breadcrumbs. Savoring the first bite as a connoisseur, he said, "Yes, Berlin is becoming a world city. And what's more, it's becoming a port. They're beginning to talk of building a big one somewhere near Tegel—and I must really say this sole tastes as though we'd already got one, or at least as though we were sitting in Wilkens' Cellar in Hamburg. That's one of my memories of forty-eight, when I was a very young lieutenant like Leo now, only with less pay."

"I can hardly imagine that, Uncle."

"Well, we'll drop the subject. It can easily become personal, and when things get personal there's always a risk of squabbling. But art—art you can discuss; art is always peaceful. And my dears, what about the Berlin dialect in that play? It started off as soon as the Straussberg people came on when the watcher was on the lookout for them. And that was supposed to be around 1411!"

"I imagine," said Therese, "that the author—a man of good family—must have studied the subject. Perhaps he found the turns of speech and the expressions that surprised you in old legal documents."

"Oh, my dear child, the Berlin slang they spoke just now isn't a hundred years old, some of it isn't even twenty. But I suppose it's difficult. The one I liked best was the Polish countess, Barbara, I think she was called, a beauty—no doubt about that. On the program it said, 'Natural daughter to King Jagellos of Poland.' I can well believe it. She'd really got something. Eyes like coals. And that Dietrich, damn it all, what a spoiled fellow he must have been to jilt a Polish king's daughter like her just like that! I don't know of many similar cases, perhaps Charles XII and Aurora von Königsmarck. But that wasn't really a similar case. Because the Charles XII business was different, there was a snag there . . ."

"A snag? What snag, Uncle?"

"Oh, Manon, dear, that's not for young ladies to hear. And in such a public place..."

"Then whisper it in my ear."

"Can't be done. You see, these kind of things are tricky; you have to wait till you pick something up by chance—let's say on an old piece of wrapping paper, or in an ·old newspaper—the column with the court cases or miscellaneous historical items. For in my experience what we call waste paper contains quite an important body of history, more than many history books. I might call on Leo to support me, but he's busy staring at that elegant young man over there through his monocle—there, at the second table from ours. And now he's even nodding to him."

Indeed, Leo had been somewhat inattentive for the last few minutes, and now he rose from his seat and went toward the young man of whom his uncle had just spoken. It was not difficult to see that each was equally surprised to find the other there, and after exchanging—so it seemed—a few questions to orient themselves, Leo led his unexpectedly rediscovered friend to the Poggenpuhl table and said, "My dear Uncle, allow me to present Herr von Klessentin. An old comrade of mine from the cadet school... My three sisters..."

Herr von Klessentin had graceful, easy manners and the bearing of a typical lieutenant; he bowed to the general and to the young ladies, and then remarked that he well remembered the general's coming out to Lichterfelde on a visit.

"Quite right, von Klessentin. I used to go out there quite often—after all, I had to keep an eye on things from time to time." And with that he pointed at Leo. "Not that it did much good. But won't you join us? This is the best table, a bit away from the rest and no drafts."

Klessentin bowed, fetched his beer mug, and took a seat between the general and Therese.

"We've struck root here," the general continued, "because it's so near the theater... Were you there too?"

"Yes, sir."

"...and I could almost swear I saw you in the orchestra stalls on the left—in row six or seven."

"Sorry, sir. I was considerably closer to the field of action."

"Further forward?"

"Yes, sir. On the stage itself."

Everyone, including Leo, gave a start of curiosity but also of shock, and they were glad when their uncle continued in a cheerful tone, "Ah, then we must congratulate you, von Klessentin. Behind the scenes: *à la bonne heure*, not everyone is so fortunate. But on the other hand—excuse me—I can't help being surprised that such a thing is even possible under the present regime, which—so far as I know—is very strict in matters of morality. Or have you personal relations with Count Hochberg's family?"

"Unfortunately not, sir. And it's not a matter of special personal relations. I'm simply a member of the company. Dietrich Schwalbe—you may remember him in the last act: it says standard bearer in the program, but foster brother to the Quitzows would have been more correct; only delicacy probably prevented them from using that term—anyway, that Dietrich Schwalbe is me."

Therese recoiled slightly toward the right, while the two younger girls listened even more attentively than before and looked at their brother's newly rediscovered friend with rapidly growing interest. Leo himself still seemed a little uncertain, and he was glad when his uncle continued with great joviality, "Glad to hear it, von Klessentin. One can serve one's king anywhere. It's the loyalty of the service that counts . . ."

Klessentin bowed.

"But you surprise me, because I studied the program at least three times, and I didn't notice your name . . ."

"It's not there, sir. On the program I'm simply Herr Manfred—my Christian name. It's the custom. Manfred is my *nom de guerre.*"

"*Nom de guerre,*" the old man laughed. "Excellent. A Klessentin leaves the army and goes on the stage, and at the very moment he relinquishes the profession of arms, he acquires a *nom de guerre.* What a bit of luck you had such a pretty Christian name. But pretty as it is, I should like to enquire whether a poetical—a historical Christian name like that couldn't lead to complications. Manfred in particular, couldn't that get you into an awkward situation?"

"I wouldn't go so far as to deny the possibility, sir. But when I think of all the vast number of plays and parts that there are, I can think of a possible complication in my case only if I had to play Lord Byron's Manfred. Then, it's true, the program would have to read, 'Manfred...Herr Manfred'; and that, I admit, might startle the public a little and cause momentary confusion."

"I see, I see. Confusion which you would nevertheless be able to overcome."

"I think I can say yes to that, always supposing that I ever find myself in such a position. But that's almost out of the question, because it's right outside my sphere."

"Are you sure of that?"

"Absolutely, sir. Byron's Manfred..."

"And then, excuse me, von Klessentin, the elder brother in *The Bride of Messina*...the one, if I remember rightly, who isn't quite so guilty..."

"...Yes, sir. But—forgive me—actually, he's Don Manuel."

"Oh, quite right, quite right. Don Manuel. Don Manfred or even just Manfred, I got it mixed up... And so you think this Manfred, and probably this Manuel as well, are both parts quite outside your sphere?"

"Absolutely, sir. Byron's Manfred is a colossus of a part, lofty, great—like Lord Byron himself; I myself, on the other hand, I'm still a beginner."

"That will change. That's the same everywhere. A cadet today and a general forty years later. All in good time."

"I wish to God that that's how it was. But it isn't. I've started on a stage career now and I must stick to it; if you keep chopping and changing it makes a bad impression. But since I've been at it, I've come to realize that Herr Manfred is never going to be a great stage name... It is possible—or at least very desirable—that sooner or later I shall make a good match; after which event I wouldn't hesitate for one moment to retire from the boards. I really like acting, I could almost say I love it; but all the same—a house in the Tiergarten with a dolphin fountain playing continuously and watering the lawn . . ."

"A house like that is what you would prefer, my dear Klessentin. I should call that a healthy reaction. May God grant you His blessing on it. Yes, a park with deer and a waterfall and old plane trees, golden yellow in autumn— that's what I fell for too. But while you're still at it, can't you ever get promotion?"

"Unlikely, sir."

"And if not—please forgive my curiosity, but I'm interested in all such things—well, if not, what kind of roles should we look for you in? When I'm back on my estate and I pick up the morning paper and I read: 'Tomorrow, Wednesday, *Wilhelm Tell*, then, having had the pleasure of your acquaintance— because I'm enormously taken with you, Herr von Klessentin: forgive me for saying so right out—then I'd like to know which slot in *Tell* I'm to find you in; you're too young for Attinghaus, and not demonic enough for Gessler; Rudenz, perhaps?"

"You are still several degrees too high. There are, of course, a few exceptional cases, like this evening, when I was Quitzow's standard bearer and therefore slightly distinguished from the crowd; but on the whole, sir, you will have to look for me in groups or categories: first citizen, second murderer, third Pappenheimer: that's my fate. Especially in *Tell*, of course, I'm up on the Rütli with the others, close up against the moon rainbow and afterward against the sunrise. All the same—so far I've always only played Meier von Sarnen, and just once I was Auf der Mauer, and my ambition doesn't stretch beyond Rösselmann. It's a slow climb. But—and I'll hide nothing from you—even a very modest advancement such as that upsets other interests. And I don't care that much about it."

"Bravo, bravo. That's exactly how I've always felt. Never push, never go forward over dead bodies."

"And then, sir, it's said that even little men have their great moments, and that's especially true on the stage. There's hardly one among my humbler colleagues who doesn't say to himself: 'Yes, Matkowsky! Matkowsky plays Mortimer and the Prince in Calderon's *Life is a Dream,* and he plays both of them well, very well; but Friesshardt (excuse me, but he's the soldier who stands watch over Gessler), or Devereux, who knocks Wallenstein down with his pike, or the witch in *Faust*—please excuse me, ladies, I seem to be drawing all my examples from this sphere—or the Third Witch in *Macbeth*—those are parts that *I* play, and I play them better than Matkowsky' . . . well, I've had moments of happiness like that myself."

"Very, very interesting, Herr von Klessentin. And now you must go one further and tell me: apart from Meier von Sarnen, of whom, to be quite honest, I have only the dimmest conception—apart from this Meier von Sarnen, then, you must tell me the names of your other parade horses, large or small, because one can go on parade perfectly well on a pony."

"I'm flattered that you take such a friendly interest in me, and I'll gladly tell you all, only I hope that my disclosures won't make me forfeit that friendly interest. Strangely enough, my talent—if one can even speak of talent—leans toward the grotesque. And so I might say that so far my little triumphs have been in the *Midsummer Night's Dream,* and especially in Shakespeare's *Henry IV, Part II.* By a fluke—lucky or unlucky—I have had to play the whole lot of Falstaff's recruits in turn—the so-called cannon fodder. With the exception of Feeble, that is. Once His Majesty even distinguished me by applauding—which naturally made me very happy. But so far, the public has appreciated me most in the role of Bullcalf."

Therese reacted to this word with a haughty movement of her head which was not lost upon Klessentin. So he quickly added, "Once you start to confess—and here I must apologize all over again to the ladies—things are inclined to come out which may seem more or less offensive. And especially when it comes to Shakespeare. This very *Henry IV* contains persons and names—Mistress Quickly, for instance—

well, Mistress Quickly herself might pass, but there's a blonde called Doll who practices her profession there, a girl with a surname ..."

"Oh, I know, I know!" laughed Manon.

"You do *not* know," said Therese with all the severity of an elder sister watching over the education and upbringing of a younger sister for whom she has assumed responsibility.

"Yes, I do, I do, and Leo will bear me out. In fact, he'll have to, otherwise the poor fellow will never have another chance to open his mouth again. He's been entirely wrapped in admiration, a silent listener, and I bet that all this time he's been wondering which parts would suit *him* best."

Sophie put her finger to her lips. But Manon either did not see her or did not want to, and she continued, "And we shall see the day when, after the example of Manfred ... Herr Manfred, we shall read Leo ... Herr Leo on a program. But of course the part must be a pope—I'll not be satisfied with less. Yes, Leo, I mean it. And maybe I'd really like to see you on the stage ... Why not? I think the important thing is to be famous, never mind in what field."

Therese interrupted, "That was the principle adopted by the man who became famous for setting fire to the temple at Corinth ..."

"Ephesus," Leo corrected her. "Corinth is where the cranes were ..."

"It's all the same. A temple is a temple. And by the way, Uncle, I hope you'll forgive me for encroaching on your prerogative, but it's time we left. Herr von Klessentin will forgive me too; but our dear Mama ..."

"Of course, of course. And especially today, on her birthday ... Leo" (and with these words Uncle Eberhard drew a banknote from his wallet), "please capture the waiter and clarify things with him. Von Klessentin, perhaps you'll walk along with us a little way?"

"It would be an honor, sir. But at the same time I hope you'll forgive me if I take my leave when we get to the corner of the Friedrichsstrasse. An appointment—two fellow officers from my old regiment. I would try," and he turned to the

young ladies, "to suborn your brother, because once a man's
in Berlin he wants to enjoy the Berlin air; but I doubt whether
his chivalrous principles will permit him to desert the
flag..."

"I am afraid it will be impossible, Herr von Klessentin,"
Therese said with a meaningful smile. "And as far as the
Berlin air is concerned, I think it is purer in our Gross-
görschenstrasse than in the Friedrichstrasse..."

"Purer, but not more authentic, my dear young lady."

Meanwhile Leo had paid the bill and joined them, and they
left in a body—the general with Therese, Leo with Manon,
and Klessentin with Sophie, who had spoken least but whose
expression had shown particular interest all evening.

During the ensuing conversation with her escort, she asked
him about Fräulein Conrad, of whose engagement she had
heard recently. "Her fiancé," she said, "is supposed to be a
very stern critic. I think it must be hard always having a critic
at your side. It takes the wind out of your sails."

"Not always. If you're a sailor, nothing will stop you from
sailing."

"I'm so glad to hear you say that."

With these words they reached the corner of the Leipziger
and Friedrichsstrasse, and Klessentin took his leave; the
Poggenpuhls walked on toward the Potsdam Gate and the
Fürstenhof. Leo had not only presented an exact account of
his financial transaction, but also—much to his uncle's
amusement—tried to return the change. "Until tomorrow,
then," and with those words they parted.

8

It was nearly midnight when the brother and sisters arrived
outside their house. Sophie had the key and unlocked the
door. They were all somewhat excited, so that their voices
were raised as they came up the stairs, with the fortunate
result that Friederike—already a little anxious at their long

absence—came to meet them on the second floor and brought a light.

"Is Mama still up?" asked Leo.

"No, Master Leo. The mistress went to bed just after nine. She said she was so cold. But she's just lying there. She's not asleep."

During this short exchange Leo had taken off his greatcoat and the young ladies their wraps. Together they went into the large bedroom to wish their mother good-night. Friederike retired to her kitchen.

The major's widow was more sitting than lying in bed, and she seemed more cheerful than usual. "But children, how late you are . . . time for decent folk to be in bed. I was beginning to think something had happened to you . . ."

"And it did, Mother."

"Well, that's bound to be bad news. Perhaps you've lost your fortune. But I'll hear about that soon enough. Come, Manon, give me your hand and look at me. And now pull up your chairs and tell me all about it. And you, Leo, you can sit on the foot of my bed. I'ts not as hard as being sentenced to the slats.[9] That still used to happen when I was young. You've been gone nearly six hours. It's lucky I've got Friederike to have a good chat with."

"I expect you've had a thoroughly good one. You're always so familiar with her, far more than one should be with a servant."

"Is that what you think?" said the major's widow, sitting up even straighter in her bed. "My blue-blooded Therese, what a lot you think and know. But now I will tell you what *I* think. I think that simple loyalty like that is the most beautiful thing in the world, for the giver as much as for the receiver. Children's love for their parents—even if they are good children—that doesn't last. They think of themselves, and it's not for me to blame them, and I wouldn't want it otherwise; but an old piece of household furniture like Friederike, all she wants is to help and be a support to you, and all she asks is an occasional 'thank you.' And I tell you, Therese, there's a good deal of Christianity in that."

"Yes, that's what you always think, Mother."

"No, I don't think it, I know it. Let's leave it at that. I'd rather Leo told me all about your evening."

"Well, Mama, if I'm to tell you about it, I can only do it by dividing it into three parts, like a sermon."

"Please, Leo..."

"All right then, simply in three parts, without any attributes or comparisons. Part 1: Uncle and the Quitzows. Part 2: Uncle and Herr Manfred (Manfred is my friend Klessentin from the cadet school). And part 3: Uncle and...but that comes later. I'm not going to play my best trump right away by putting it in the heading."

"Oh Leo, that's just another bit of nonsense. In the end there'll be nothing to it."

"On the contrary. As you will soon see. But now, attention please! First of all: Uncle and the Quitzows."

"Dear Uncle. Of course he'll have been enchanted by all those high-flown speeches."

"Not at all, Mother. On the contrary, I should say that although he admired Dietrich von Quitzow, it wasn't really his kind of thing. But it's a moot point. All I can say is that when the Straussberg people came on with bag and baggage, he began to talk—rather loud, or anyway loud enough to be embarrassing—about Mühlendamm and flea markets. What he seems to have liked best was a pretty countess, a certain Barbara, who was on very good terms—to put it mildly—with the Dukes of Pomerania, and was then prepared to take on our Dietrich von Quitzow as well. But there she had her come-uppance. Even in those days the Mark represented the higher morality, the very same to which she owes her subsequent greatness."

"Don't be sarcastic."

"And here too Uncle showed his Pomeranian descent: he was fired with ardor at once. And when we met Manfred Klessentin in the theater restaurant after the performance, he immediately wanted to know who the countess really was. I mean the actress who played the countess."

"A fine story..."

"And here we have the perfect bridge passage to part 3 under the imposing heading: Uncle Eberhard and the hundred mark note. And, what's more, a brand new one. Yes, Mama, that was a big moment. True, it no longer exists as a whole—I mean the bank note, of course—but still, there are very respectable remnants. Here they are. As you can imagine, I resisted for quite a while, but when I saw it would upset him..."

"Leo, you've never lied like this..."

"Self-mockery isn't lying, Mama. But it just shows how wrong you are to be so everlastingly worried. 'Even at the graveside he raises the banner of hope'[10]—the poet's great words were not spoken in vain and should never be forgotten. I gladly admit that I felt a certain anxiety all evening about the return ticket, because I think I may say that I prefer to give than to receive..."

The girls laughed.

"... However, God never forsakes a German, least of all a Poggenpuhl, and it's always darkest before dawn. I have always found it so. And so I'm back on top of the world, happy as a sand boy, and that, God willing, is how it'll be for some time to come. Because the return journey won't eat up much, even if I travel first class."

"But Leo..."

"Calm down, my dears. I am *not* going first class; it just makes me happy to think—just for once—that I could. It's all just make-believe and chimeras. But now this *is* serious: I want to know how much of my fortune I'm to leave behind: any sum you name, and I don't want it paid back and no interest. I just want to enjoy this state of affairs unalloyed and to the hilt, just once I want to trump Wendelin. But why don't you say something? You too, Mama?"

"Well, I'll take the thought for the deed, Leo. And now go into the front room and take Manon with you; she can help you pack. But don't be too long about it. I know you always start chattering, and then you don't know how to stop. And now good-night, and we'll say good-bye at the same time. Don't come in to me tomorrow morning, and give my love to

Wendelin, and tell him it was nice of him to let you have the trip. Tell him he's the best of the whole family, not a bit like . . ."

"Leo . . ."

"Yes, not a bit. But you can stay as you are. All old mothers are alike: they always love the good-for-nothings best, as long as their hearts are in the right place. And yours is. You're no good, but you're a dear. And now good-night, my boy."

He stroked her and gave her a kiss; and then he and the youngest sister, his special confidante, went into the next room to prepare everything for his departure next morning.

When they had finished packing, Manon took Leo's hand and said: "Sit in the corner of the sofa. I've got something to say to you."

"Brrr. It sounds terribly serious. Is it?"

"Yes, it is a bit. Though hardly as you see things. And now listen very carefully. The thing is, I'm a bit worried that because of your everlasting debts you are taking the wrong step. And in Thorn too. Please, don't rush into anything! You've dropped a few hints recently, first in your letters, and now while you've been here too—last night, for instance, on the way home. You know I don't think like Therese on these delicate matters. She thinks the Poggenpuhls are the pillars of society, the bulwark of the state, and of course that's ridiculous. But you lean in the opposite direction: you set too little store by our ancient name, or—which is the same thing—by the *reputation* of our ancient name. But names and reputations mean a lot."

"I'm prepared to agree with you there, Manon; but who doesn't have a name, nowadays? And look what *makes* names! Pears' Soap, Blooker's Cocoa, Johann Hoff's Extract of Malt! Chivalry and heroism are nowhere by comparison! Take Maréchal Niel, for instance. I believe he took Sebastopol, and if I'm not mistaken he was a genius at military engineering; a military celebrity, anyway. And yet if there weren't a rose named after him, no one would remember he'd ever existed. Let's take something much nearer home; let's take the great name of Hildebrand. I believe there were three famous painters of that name—or perhaps the third was a sculptor, it makes no difference. But when people speak of Hildebrand, especially around Christmas, nobody thinks of paintings or busts, but only of little dark blue packages with a picture of a ginger snap, tied up with a bit of string. I tell you, Manon, I have my Poggenpuhl pride just as much as you and nearly as much as Therese; but if I'm to enjoy it, then, in addition to my Poggenpuhl name, which for all its fame unfortunately only runs into single figures, I need at least four zeros. Or maybe five, really."

"I don't mind your calculating like that, Leo. I'm not too fussy myself on that point. Yes, I admit it, you've *got* to think along those lines. But I'm afraid you're not on the right ones. There are the Bartensteins, there's Flora . . . Yes, that really would be something. Flora Bartenstein is an intelligent and beautiful girl, and on top of that she's my friend. And she's certainly rich. Now there's something that *would* be worth considering. But in Thorn—that business you're always writing and talking about—though only mysteriously and in hints. I ask you, Leo, what's it all about? In Thorn . . . ! What's her name, for a start?"

"Esther."

"Well, that would do. Lots of English girls are called Esther. And her surname?"

"Blumenthal."

"Ah, that's not so good. But maybe even that would pass, because it's a dual-purpose name, you can use it *à deux mains*, so to speak, and when you are a staff officer (which is still in the distant future, I'm afraid), at Court or in whatever other circles you move in they'll say, "Major or Colonel von Poggenpuhl's wife is a Blumenthal," and they'll think she's the Field Marshal's granddaughter. When a Poggenpuhl marries a Blumenthal, the least of the advantages he can expect from his ancient name is surely to move straight to the right wing of all the available possibilities."

"Bravo, Manon. I see your objections are melting away."

"Not entirely; I can't concede that much. I'm simply trying
to make the best of Esther and Blumenthal. Besides, I understand your position, I can feel the pressure you're under, and
I'm glad you want to escape. But if it's at all possible, stick to
your own stamping ground: don't let it be on the Vistula, and
not Esther. Whatever she's like, she can't be a patch on Flora.
Besides, the whole Bartenstein family—there are three
brothers, two in the Voss-strasse—are especially well thought
of. The one whose family I know is a man of honor, and
incidentally a humorist too, and I'm quite sure he'll get a title
when the government floats its next loan. Not that it means
anything to me; on the contrary, it's almost a disadvantage
from my point of view, because I hate all half-way measures,
which is what it comes to in the end. But in the eyes of the
world . . ."

"I'll think about it, Manon. For the moment I find it en-
trancing to have the choice, as you might say: or at least I can
pretend I have. What I'd really prefer is to remain as I am for a
while; there's nothing better than being a bachelor. Only a
widower with his perspective into the past and the future
could conceivably stand higher in my eyes. But that takes
time. And now good-night. Mama will be wondering what
we've been up to together."

And with these words they parted.

But Manon went to her mother's bed to see if she was
asleep.

"You've been crying, Mama."

"Yes, my dear. But they were happy tears. They did me
good."

9

Manon was up early to lend her brother a hand with his
departure, but the other two sisters contented themselves
with stretching an arm out to Leo through the crack of the
door as he passed down the corridor.

"I can recognize you just the same," said Leo. "The fat arm belongs to Sophie." This diagnosis was correct but painful to Therese, and so the moment of departure was clouded by a touch of ill humor. Friederike, of course, had also risen, and she carried the suitcase to the nearest cab rank. Leo chose a cab, settled into it, and called out, "Friedrichsstrasse!" to the driver; then he pressed something into Friederike's hand. Little opportunity as she had had with the Poggenpuhls of developing a fine feeling for the value of tips received in the half-light, she recognized it immediately as a Prussian taler. Her shock was almost as great as her joy.

"Goodness, Master Leo..."

"Yes, Friederike, not all days are alike, and if I had any say in the matter..."

"No, no..."

"...and if I had any say in the matter, I'd take that hollow Edam cheese, which you've probably still got, and fill it right up with gold pieces. Well now, with God's grace, let's be off." And he gave her his hand once more before the cab set off at a reckless but soon diminishing pace.

As Friederike walked home from the corner of the Potsdamer-strasse, a number of thoughts passed through her mind. "It really does go to your heart," she said. "And when I think of the rich folks I used to work for, they never treated me like a human being. And when you compare them with the Poggenpuhls! They really don't have a penny, and sometimes I feel really bad when I have to say: 'Well, ma'am, we really do need a new floorcloth.' But there's something about them all, even Therese: she's a bit high and mighty at times, but in the end she's really not so bad. And as for little Leo! He's a good-for-nothing and a fibber, the poor old lady's quite right there, and he has his faults, they all have, except for Frau von Poggenpuhl... ah, she's had to struggle too hard, that knocks it out of you... But they treat you like a human being, and that's true of the whole lot. I'm glad I've got this situation. It isn't as though I was starved, and when things are a bit short sometimes, they just take a mouthful and leave it all for me.

But then I don't want it either; when I see how they go on, it sticks in my throat and won't go down. Oh dear, oh dear, money ... And a taler! Where can he have got that? Uncle must have really forked out ...''

When Friederike got back to the apartment, she found both the elder girls already at the breakfast table and Manon kneeling before the stove to light the fire. As soon as she had got it going, their mother entered and took her usual place on the sofa.

"Well, did he get off all right?"

"Yes, Mama," said Manon. "And he asked me to give you a kiss for him and to tell you you were the best person in the world, even though you're not a real Poggenpuhl."

"No, that I'm not. Heavens, children, if I were, we'd never make ends meet at all ..."

"Oh, never mind that. We're all right anyway. Courage, that's all. I'd just made up my mind to speak to Flora, and then all of a sudden Uncle turned up ..."

"Yes, he's come to our aid again. But we mustn't imagine it will always be like that ..."

"Not always, Mama. But nearly always."

"Yes, you're a harebrained creature, just like your brother. And I expect young Klessentin was just the same. There you see what comes of it. So now he's called Herr Manfred. And if a miracle doesn't happen soon—and you've said something of the sort yourselves—we shall read 'Herr Leo' on a theater program too one day. How did you like young Klessentin? How did Uncle get on with him or he with Uncle? It must have been quite awkward."

"No, Mama," said Sophie. "Why should it? You have to look at it the right way. I'm a noblewoman too, and a Poggenpuhl, and I paint plates and cups and give singing and piano lessons too. He acts on the stage. It's really the same thing."

"Not quite, Sophie. It's doing it in public. That's the difference."

"Oh, what does 'public' mean? When they have dancing at the Bartensteins and I play my three dances because it would be disobliging to refuse, that's in public too. As soon as we leave our rooms we are in public and playing our parts."

"All right, all right, Sophie. You win; I believe you. But young Klessentin—what sort of things does he act? I've never read about him."

"He gets only very small parts, and he told us what some of them were. But—and this is what's comforting—he added straight away that there isn't really any difference, and that small parts are sometimes just as important as big ones. And everything he said sounded so charming and so contented and good-humored that Uncle Eberhard was quite taken with him and congratulated him."

"Yes, I can quite believe that. Dear Uncle is a darling, and he can't bear stuck-up people who give themselves airs; and anyone who says, 'I'm for the small things in life' wins his heart at once. He doesn't like it when people puff themselves up and behave as though they couldn't live without brocade on the walls. He has practically no personal wants and is content with whatever he's offered, and that's why I am going to ask him to take pot luck with us for lunch. Because I expect he will drop in again. What could we give him? It's your week, Sophie; what do you think?"

"Well, pale ale soup with sago, I think; he loved that last time. And then we've still got a small dish of baby parsnips left, and we could have some slices of smoked goose with that."

"No, I don't think that would do," said Therese. "The smoked goose is from Adamsdorf; it was a present from Aunt."

"Never mind. One smoked goose is just like another. And if he does notice, it will be a little compliment. And then as a third course we could have cream meringues from the Eschke patisserie across the street. And then bread and butter and cheese."

Their mother regarded the whole thing in the nature of a symbolic act, as she knew very well that Uncle Eberhard would have a snack before coming; so she was content with the menu and only asked her daughters to return punctually by two o'clock: for they still had New Year's calls to pay in town. Otherwise it would get too late; but she would hold onto their uncle until then.

And when everything had been settled in this manner, the breakfast table was cleared, and they withdrew to the back room in order to dress for their calls.

All three sisters left the apartment simultaneously to catch the horse tram at the stop by the Botanical Gardens. They were very familiar with the tariff. When they had all gone, the major's widow set about "doing herself up," and she had scarcely finished when she heard a genial and somewhat noisy conversation out in the hall: there was no doubt that her brother-in-law the general had arrived.

"Good morning, Albertine. Forgive me for coming a bit early; though, as I see, I am not *too* early. Everything spick and span already, everyone in 'full dress'" (he used the English expression), "if you can say that about a lady. Because 'full dress' is probably masculine and I think it means white tie or tails. Tails is what we used to say in the old days."

"Oh, Eberhard, you mean well and you always have a kind word to say, and you've even noticed that I've got on my very best party cap with a new ribbon. But my dancing days are over."

"Oh no, they're not, Albertine. You're still a good-looking woman. And you're not even sixty yet. And even if you were, what is age? Nothing at all. Look at me. Just now I met a battalion of your railway regiment—I call it yours because you've got it on your street—and I can tell you: as soon as I heard the first bang on the kettle drum, it went right through me and my old bones felt young and spry again. The cards are in our own hands, and we're as young as we want to be. But you shut yourself up too much; you'll be an antique fit for the Egyptian Museum before you know where you are. Look at yesterday, for instance. Why didn't you come along?"

"My dear Eberhard—the theater—I'm past that kind of thing."

"Absolutely wrong. That's what everyone thinks. But once you're back in the firing line, you find you enjoy it as much as ever. I tell you, Albertine, if you'd seen this Quitzow, this Dietrich von Quitzow, a study after Bismarck, but compared to him Bismarck's a new-born babe. Eyebrows like a bootbrush, he had. What fellows they must have been! And his brother is supposed to have looked even wilder, because he only had one eye. Polyphemus. Wasn't he called Polyphemus?"

"I think so, Eberhard. At least, there was someone called that."

"And then after the theater. In the pub. Well, the children will have told you about it, and about this Herr Manfred, this Klessentin. Charming young fellow, dashing, fresh, with a touch of humor. Oh Albertine, sometimes I feel as though everything were just prejudice. Well, we don't have to get rid of it; but if other people have a bash, quite honestly, I can't see much objection. There are two sides to everything. Noble birth is all right, Klessentin is all right, but Herr Manfred is all right too. In fact, everything's all right, and when you think of it, everyone's an actor."

"Oh, not me, Eberhard dear."

"No, not you, Albertine. You've had it knocked out of you. But me—I'm an actor. Look, I play the easy-going, good-natured old buffer, and I wouldn't even say that the part was unsuitable for a general. There have been quite other types who all play-acted too, emperors and kings among them. Nero played and sang and made them set fire to Rome. And now you can see it in the panopticon for fifty pennies. Just think, how cheap everything is now! And I've just remembered that ten years ago they were even showing *Nero's Torches*—a huge painting. I was still in the service in those days, and I can still see that great canvas in my mind's eye. Perhaps you saw it too."

"No, Eberhard. I've never seen anything like that. I have to deny myself such things. You know why."

"Don't talk about denying yourself. I can't stand that expression. No one should deny themselves, and if they don't want to, they don't need to. Well, see here: it was a picture as

big as the sail on a Spree barge, or even bigger, actually; and
at the side, on the right, there was what the pundits call
'Nero's torches,' and some of them were already burning,
and the others were being lit. And what do you suppose,
Albertine, what do you suppose those torches really were?
Christian folk, they were, Christian folk bandaged up in
rags soaked in pitch, and they looked like mummies or like
big babies in swaddling clothes, and this Nero, who had
organized all these horrors, he was lying quite peacefully on a
golden chariot drawn by two golden lions, and a third lion lay
beside him, and he was scratching its mane as though it were
a poodle. And now look: this very same Nero, who could
afford to do a thing like that, and who ruled the whole
world—right up to our area here around Berlin, I believe—
this Nero sang and played too, just like that Herr von Klessentin; and so I ask myself, 'Well, why shouldn't he, that
young fellow? If an emperor can play, why not Klessentin? A
blameless young man who's probably never lit a torch at all,
let alone a torch like that.''

The major's widow stretched out her hand to her brother-
in-law and said, "Eberhard, you're just as you always were.
And Leo's going to be the same. Your brother Alfred was
always serious, a bit too serious—which may have been due
to our circumstances."

"Don't talk about circumstances, Albertine. Circumstances
—I can't stand that word."

"And it's funny the way children often have the same
character as their collateral relations. And I can only hope that
his life—I mean Leo's—will turn out like yours; the same
luck . . ."

"Don't talk about luck, Albertine. That's another word I
can't stand. A man should stand on his own feet. But no,
forget I said that . . . Just call it luck . . . You're quite right . . . I've
been lucky. First in the service. Of course I always did what
was expected of me, but after all, I wasn't exactly a Moltke . . .
Thank God, by the way, there aren't many of those, they'd
eat each other up, and when things came to the crunch
there'd be none left . . . Just one is best, then there can be no

competition and no envy. But now let's leave Klessentin and Nero and Moltke and talk about something else. Where are the girls?"

"They've run out. But I promised to make their excuses to their kind uncle. They had to make some calls they'd put off—it was high time. But you'll see them. I'm counting on your staying and being our guest—whatever we have ourselves . . ."

"Ah, ah, ah. I can't stand that. Whatever we have ourselves. What does that mean? A plate of soup . . ."

"Sophie was talking about pale ale soup with sago . . ."

"Excellent. Almost enough to upset my program. But I've still got various things to do and get. All nonsense, actually. Nothing that couldn't be done better by sending a postcard. But my wife wishes it. And a woman's wish is an order, otherwise it's war. And we military are always beaten: the more dashing we are, the greater the defeat. So I must be off. And much as I should have liked to see all three girls again, it rather suits me not to have them here. Because I want to take one of them back to Adamsdorf with me—my wife expressed the wish—and the only question is (assuming you agree), which one?"

"And you think that question can be settled more easily between you and me?"

"Yes, Albertine."

"Well, then I think Therese. She went to Pyrmont last summer with your wife, and she knows all about everything and has more or less got used to her."

"All quite true. All the same, a change might be indicated. Let me speak openly to you. Therese is an excellent girl and a lady. But she's more of a lady than my wife likes. My wife comes from the middle class, like you, and she has simple habits and opinions, all of which I can only approve of. And Therese—you must forgive my saying so—has a rather marked tendency to emphasize her Poggenpuhlishness. I don't want to criticize, and I personally have no objection. But my wife thinks it's a bit exaggerated, and there have been a few arguments about it between them."

"I understand, Eberhard. And your wife is right. I have the same trouble with her here. She has a sense of responsibility and she takes her ideas about nobility and its obligations rather seriously. But it's very difficult in circumstances..."

"No, no, no..."

"...when one lives as modestly as we do. It always leads to differences of opinion and quarrels. But if not Therese, who then? I shouldn't like to lose Manon."

"No need to, Albertine. Manon is your baby, and you must keep her. My wife—with your agreement, I repeat—has decided on Sophie. She liked her very much when she saw her here, and she liked her letters, including the ones she wrote to Therese. All very sensible. And my wife has a predilection for sensibleness—no fiddle-faddle or polite phrases and pomposity. And as for false pretenses, she really hates those."

"Thank goodness Sophie has none of that. Her life has always been work, and she holds things together when they're falling apart..."

"They mustn't. They mustn't. Nothing must fall apart. All right then: Sophie. Because my wife wants all sorts of new things, and what she particularly wants is a new set of plates with our crest on them. At first, I admit, that surprised me considerably. But she explained it to me. 'I am a Poggenpuhl now,' she said to me the other day, 'and so it's not proper that all our things should have the Leysewitz crest. I think people are talking about it, and we must avoid that.' Sophie paints so well: she can paint the Poggenpuhl crest for us, and that will keep her happy and she will be glad to use her gifts in the service of the family. And then she's so musical. I'm looking forward to hearing a Schubert song played as dusk falls; it will cheer up the house, which is too quiet now, and we can invite people to come and listen."

"And when do you think she should start?"

"Now, today. With me. She's to be at the hotel at three with her trunk. By herself would be best. Farewells are disturbing, and kissing is ridiculous. The train leaves at four, and we'll be in Adamsdorf by eleven."

And with that he rose, sent his best wishes to Therese and Manon, and took his leave.

10

Dear Mama,

We arrived here safely just after eleven last night. Right at the end, on the way from Hirschberg to here, I was enchanted by the drive in the open carriage although it was cloudy, and the mountains I had so looked forward to seeing were invisible. But there was still life in the villages, and through the mist you could see the lights of the factory at Erdmannsdorf where they work all night. It all looked medieval and romantic as though an ancient Piast family[11] lived there. Here in Adamsdorf everything was quite still, except for a dog barking in the distance and another dog answering him. The courtyard was absolutely quiet too, and for a moment I felt afraid; but that feeling dropped away as soon as I got into the drawing room, where Aunt greeted me in the friendliest manner. A marvelous woman, I can't understand why Therese never really got on with her. Perhaps I'll discover some snags too, but I hardly think so. If only, my dear old Mama, life had been as kind to you as it has to her! I mentioned the drawing room. Well, it *was* the drawing room, but it is really more of a hall. Adamsdorf was originally a Benedictine abbey, and the previous owner incorporated a lot of the old buildings when he rebuilt it. This hall was once the refectory. It has three Gothic pillars down the middle, and there was a fire burning in the hearth and every time the flames flickered up the light was reflected on the vaulted ceiling. Apart from Aunt there was only a cat, a big, beautiful creature which walked round me purring all the time and then jumped up on my lap. It gave me a fright; but Aunt reassured me and said that it was a demonstration of affection, and that Bob (I suppose it is a tom) was normally rather sparing of those; he has a suspicious and jealous nature. We were frozen, so Uncle askéd for an eggnog: they make it with Hungarian wine and egg yolks here. It was quite delicious. And what was more important, I slept marvelously after it, and when I got up quite early and raised the blinds, the whole long line of mountains lay before me all covered in snow. During the next few days we are to make an excursion to the Heinrich Cabin, and then to come down the mountains on sledges. They say it is absolutely beautiful, but I'm a little frightened. Keep well. Love and kisses to you all, and to the boys in Thorn when you write to them.

> With my fondest love,
> *your Sophie*

Schloss Adamsdorf, January 16

Dear Mama,

I am completely settled here. Aunt goes on being kindness itself; I don't need to reassure you about Uncle; and even Bob remains faithful to his attachment. He goes a bit far, because his shows of affection are always a bit like an assault. Suddenly he jumps at me—you can see the tiger in him. The trip to the Heinrich Cabin has been put off because we are to wait for another fresh fall of snow, because they say that the thicker the snow the better the run down into the valley, and it's less dangerous too; in the thick snow the sledge flies over the rocks as though they were molehills.

Our life is rather quiet, there are few visitors. Except for the Adamsdorf parson, who calls occasionally, we see only other clergymen from the neighborhood, and an old colonel from the town; and then a district court judge and his wife. I always enjoy these visits very much, but even without them I have plenty of entertainment, because Aunt likes to talk about her life, especially her childhood, which was spent in poverty. In addition to all that we have a curious picture gallery here; the basic stock consists of various paintings from when the house was an abbey: some saints (not many), and then portraits of abbots and priors, and even a Prince Bishop of Breslau. Mixed up with them there are all sorts of specifically Prussian things: Frederick the Great (three times), Prince Henry, General Tauentzien, and at the end a dozen portraits from the family of Aunt's first husband. All Leysewitzes. No Poggenpuhls at all, not even a portrait of Uncle. A few days ago I seized an opportunity to remark on this, and he laughed and said, "Yes, Fiechen[12] (that's what he always calls me), no Poggenpuhls at all, but that's a good thing: it's a terrific jumble already, and if we had to cope with the Hochkirch major and the Sohr major as well, there'd be total confusion." Uncle has so much good sense: he has absolutely no desire to see members of his own family competing with the old Silesian nobility. And it's probably because of that that no more has been heard on the subject of crested plates. I think Uncle Eberhard must have been against it from the start, and finally gave in—I won't say gladly but at least without a long struggle. But a new task awaits me which makes me very proud and happy. But I'll tell you about that in my next letter.

If you get any letters from Leo or Wendelin, please send them on—first of all for my sake, of course, but for Uncle's too; he is genuinely interested in them both, and expects both of them to do well—Wendelin of course, but Leo too. Only today he said that Leo was born lucky, and that that was the best thing that could happen to a person. Aunt got quite solemn and disagreed, but she calmed down when he said—very charmingly and with a courtly gesture, "Did I deserve you or was it luck?" She gave him a kiss, which I found touching, because it wasn't an amorous kiss (I don't like to see older people doing that), but just genuine affection and gratitude. And quite right too. Because as sure as this marriage has made him happy, it's made her happy too.

From all this you can see how happy I am here, though occasionally I feel homesick for you and wish I could stroke your hands. Don't worry too much. Everything will turn out all right. Uncle specially asked me to tell you that from him too. Today he told me there was a motto which went, "Take care, but not too much: everything will be as God wills." And he said you broke this injunction more often than was right and proper. And by the way, if you imagine I agreed, you are mistaken; on the contrary, I said, "Only the person who feels the pain can know how much it hurts." And then he gave me a kiss too. He is a wonderful man, and I can't make up my mind which is better, he or she. But now farewell.

Your Sophie

Schloss Adamsdorf, January 19

Only a card today, dear Mama. Yesterday it snowed: it's all piled up round the house like a wall. But since this morning there is a clear blue sky, a light frost, and divine weather. One day soon we are going to drive or walk to the top of the ridge and then toboggan down. The parson and an assistant judge from the town are coming along. I am looking forward to it immeasurably. Keep well, all of you.

Your Sophie

Heinrich Cabin, January 22

Only a card again, but with a picture (the Heinrich Cabin) this time. Because this is where we are, and we shall probably stay another day, we shall *have* to. And its my fault. What happened was this: almost as soon as I had got my sledge and was whizzing down, I lost the way and would certainly have plunged into a crater—they call it the 'little pond' because there's water at the bottom—when another sledge which was going the right way saw me and deliberately ran into me from the side. The crash (a lucky one for me because it saved my life) flung me off my toboggan, and as I couldn't walk because of a slight injury, they had to carry me back up here. We are waiting for the doctor

to come from Krummhübel (the nearest large village) in a
few hours. Don't worry about me. But I am never going to
go in for tobogganing again. My rescuer was a young
assistant judge (titled) and already engaged to be married.
As always,

Your Sophie

Schloss Adamsdorf, January 25

Two telegrams from Uncle will have reassured you about my
condition. There's no question of any danger any more. I've
broken my thigh. In four weeks—six at the most—I'll be
dancing again. The doctor is excellent and very tactful. He's
a weaver's son from the neighborhood (Therese please
note). My rescue, as I think I told you, was entirely due to
the assistant judge; he's a lieutenant in the reserve, of
course, and if there's a war he intends to stay in the army.
He hates paperwork, and his chief, the district court judge,
smilingly acknowledged the truth of this declaration. I
should find it trying to lie still for so many weeks if the
doctor had not given me permission to move my arms as
much as I want. Aunt immediately had an easel set up for
me so that I can write and draw comfortably. I am making
copious use of it and producing sketch upon sketch. And so
the time has probably come, my dear old thing, to tell you
about the new project I hinted at briefly just after my arrival
a few weeks ago. Instead of painting crests on plates—now
listen and marvel—I am to be entrusted with decorating the
interior of the Protestant church (as in nearly every village
round here, there is a Catholic one as well). The idea is to
have biblical scenes painted on panels going all around the
lower edge of the gallery. Each panel is to be about the size
of a folded card table—rather an odd way to describe size and
measurements in the case of a church, when you come to think
about it. Of course it won't be a great work of art—there's
no fear of that—but it won't be despicable either, and what
makes me happiest of all is that I shall try to solve the problem

in a completely fresh way. So: Joseph Sold into Egypt, Judith
and Holofernes, Samson and Delilah are all out. Instead I
am going to find stories where the landscape is the most
important element, and at the moment I am searching
through the Bible for scenes and material with suitable set-
tings. When I find something I try and hold it down with a
few strokes as best I can in my present position.

You can tell from the length of this letter that in spite of
everything I am very well. Manon may disagree and point
out that as letters are written by hand, no conclusions can be
drawn as to the condition of one's leg. But she is wrong. If
your big toe hurts—really hurts—you can't write any better
than if your thumb hurts.

Write to me with every detail of how you all are. And ask
Friederike to write too; letters from servants are always so
charming, quite different from educated letters. Educated
people don't write so well because they're less natural; anyway, that's how it usually is. The heart is what counts. True,
is it not, my dear old thing? You know that better than anyone. And Therese is to describe the soirée at the Bronsarts,
and whether they had tableaux vivants, and if so, what they
were. And Manon must write about the Bartensteins and
their ball and whether she danced and who with. And what
she wore. Manon knows how to make a fairy dress with a
bit of net and a pink ribbon. And now farewell. Aunt wants
to add a few lines (perhaps to report on my progress).

> As always,
> Your very loving daughter,
> *Sophie*

11

During the weeks of this correspondence between Berlin and
Schloss Adamsdorf there was also a correspondence between
Berlin and Thorn. Leo began it with a postcard to Manon,
which, after writing it, he wisely slipped into an envelope.

Thorn, January 8

Got back three days ago. Copernicus still stands. The whole town smells of fish stewed in beer, though actually that isn't quite true because here they cook their carp with ginger-bread and Hungarian wine. In these matters we are superior to you, though I must say it's carried a bit far.

Wendelin met me at the station, fearfully polite, but very gracious as well. He overdid it: a patronizing air, General Staff all over. And he isn't even on it yet. But of course he will be one day. The state couldn't possibly let so many virtues go to waste. Forgive these catty remarks, but when one feels so invisibly small, one is driven to such malice in order to hold up one's head before oneself and others. The worm turns. I'll write again tomorrow, perhaps today if drilling recruits doesn't deprive me of the breath of life. "Dobry, dobry" and every now and then "fathead!"

A thousand good wishes,
Your Leo

A postscript was scribbled along the edge of the card:

Just had an invitation for tonight: innermost circle. I need hardly say where. Incidentally, I saw Esther at her window this morning, very grand, pomposissima almost, which is a bit frightening. Because she's only eighteen. What will it lead to?

Three days later Manon replied.

Berlin, January 12

My dear Leo,
   Thank you for your lines, which gave me much pleasure because they were so exactly like you. Your card (fortunately inside an envelope) arrived by the same post as a letter from Sophie. You could tell the difference at once. Sophie always

writes as it were with the palette in her hand: always as the
artist, always full of feeling and gratitude. The latter quality
especially is something no one could reproach *you* with.
Your elder (and better) brother makes a fuss of you, and you
make fun of him. Come, come! Such behavior is certainly
not Poggenpuhlish. The Poggenpuhls are full of reverential
feeling. I believe you must have caught your tendency to
mock and sneer from somewhere; it's the influence of your
environment, or—which comes to the same thing—the tone
you find in the home of the very grand Esther, your Pomposissima, as you call her. I know that tone from the Bartensteins, although they themselves don't use it and get
embarrassed when it raises its head. But even the Bartensteins
can't quite prevent it happening; given the peculiar composi-
tion of their society, things aren't entirely in their own
hands. To give just one example: their relatives who gather
together there every Sunday always belong to two quite different worlds: one uncle may have spent thirty years in
London or Paris, and the other in Schrimm. And there's no
denying that it makes a difference. I mentioned the influence of environment: it exists. I feel its power myself, and
when I look at Therese, I see the same power from another
direction, like a perfect textbook example. Because
Therese—even if one might prefer her to be different in
other ways—always knows what is right and proper, and she
owes that to the air of the Wilhelmsstrasse, which, for better
or for worse, is the air she breathes. I don't know what
street Esther lives in (perhaps it's a Wilhelmsstrasse too), but
I do know that in our Wilhelmsstrasse there are no Pomposis-
simas. Here I must stop. I just heard the bell, and from
Friederike's conversation in the passage I can tell that Flora
has arrived and gone in to Mama. I expect she wants to
invite me over. More about the other subject next time. Your
whole future—it becomes clearer to me every day—is contained in the question: Esther or Flora. Flora is blonde, thank
goodness, a pale, reddish blonde, in fact. Farewell.

> With unchanging love,
> *Your Manon*

Dear Leo:

You replied to my first letter at once, without waiting for the second, which was meant to complete it. That was very nice of you, but unfortunately also a bit worrying; the very prompt-ness of your answer was disturbing to me, and several of the remarks you made in your letter even more so. I hope the invitation for the evening of the eighth which you mentioned on your card did not turn out to be fateful. I know that dark complexions have always been your downfall. And Esther! It is strange how some names seem to carry a mystic power, a sort of spiritual fluid which works in a mysterious way. Pull yourself together, be stronger than Ahasverus was (I mean the Persian king): he succumbed to an Esther too. I have just glanced through your letter again, and again I got the im-pression that you had already given your word. If it is so, I know it won't be the end of the world, but it will be the end of your career. Because in the provinces, and especially in yours, religious feeling (or, as the Bartensteins always say, denominational considerations—they are fond of using curi-ous convoluted expressions like that) is much more stub-born, and her parents will simply forbid her conversion. In that case it would have to be a civil ceremony for you, and, broad-minded as I am, I find that a positively horrifying idea. Such a step would exclude you not only from the army, but also, even more important, from society as well; you would have to roam the world as a stranger, rejected and with no resting place. Then we'd have the other Ahasverus. Don't do such a thing to us. Therese would not survive it.

Your Manon

Berlin, January 18

My dear Leo,

Thank God! Now everything may still turn out all right. I can't tell you how relieved I feel that this storm has blown over—for us all, but not least for you. You make fun of my scruples and tease me, and ask what—if it really had happened—the difference would have been between the de-spised Blumenthals and the enthusiastically recommended Bartensteins. Yes, you add that Blumenthal has been a Commercial Councillor for years, and you say that such a sign of approval from the state, which is, after all, a Christian authority, even though it may not actually be baptism, is almost as good, and that therefore the house of Blumenthal is really a step ahead of the house of Bartenstein. Oh Leo, it sounds quite good and I'll gladly accept it as a joke; but the true state of affairs is quite other, after all. The Bartensteins have received the Crown Prince, Bartenstein is the Roma-nian Consul, which is higher than a Commercial Councillor, and Droysen and Mommsen have been to their house (yes, and just before he passed away, Leopold von Ranke was there too); they have several paintings by Menzel in their gallery, one is a court ball, I think, and the other a sketch for a coronation scene. Well, my dear Leo, who else has things like that? Frau Melanie (that is Frau Bartenstein's first name) has sat on a ladies' committee for the Magdalenum[13] for several years, Drysander[14] is always singling her out on every possible occasion . . . And then Esther and Flora them-selves! There is a difference, there *must* be. And I implore: think it over! But above all—and I cannot emphasize this enough—above all do not deceive yourself into thinking (just because I secretly wish it so very very much) that they are waiting for you here with impatience and anxiety! There is not doubt that both her parents' wishes, and Flora's too, are directed toward the nobility; but they are very choosy, and if, for instance, it fell to Frau Melanie to decide, I know for certain that she would not be very pleased with less than an Arnim or a Bülow. So you can work out the Poggenpuhl chances for yourself. In spite of Therese they are not exactly overwhelming, and in the end your personal charm would be far, far more decisive than our historical importance. All the same, that too is a factor to be taken into account, especially as far as Flora is concerned: unlike both her parents, she has a distinctly romantic turn of mind, and only the day before yesterday she assured me once again that when she saw the grenadier caps of the first regiment of guards in Potsdam the other day, it brought tears to her eyes. Altogether, Leo, you still have no clear conception of what or how much is at stake: in spite of my good relations—I might say my very intimate relations with them—there is still a lot of trouble and effort ahead before you can hope to win the bride. So don't be proud and don't turn down the proposal I am about to make to you: that would be a folly from which I hope your good sense and your financial difficulties would equally protect you.

But here comes Flora to take me "shopping" (she likes to use English expressions), and so I must stop without having told you the details of my plan, which is, oh listen and marvel, that *you* should write a family history of the Poggenpuhls. Only this much: Wendelin will have to do most of it, and then Uncle Eberhard, of course. Think about it! But above all—courage and silence! Flora knows nothing, suspects nothing. As always,

Your Manon

Leo replied by return of post.

Thorn, January 19

My dear Manon,
I feel quite shamed by your love and concern. An excellent plan, positively stupendous. But, but . . . Alas, this only puts me into a rather melancholy frame of mind. Wendelin— who, after all, is the one who's got to do it—Wendelin doesn't want to. He thinks it's simply ridiculous. Because in his honest opinion the Poggenpuhls don't begin with the Crusades, but simply with Wendelin von Poggenpuhl. All the deeds that were done for hundreds of years by people like the Sohr and Hochkirch majors he considers very run-of-the-mill stuff; to stand out in front and shout hurrah means very little to him; strategic thinking is what counts.

Anyhow, he puts himself before the family. It's true he always helps me and in many ways he's an excellent fellow,
but he always has to appear to his own advantage and glory
in the eyes of the world; as soon as he thinks he might upset
one of his high-up chiefs or, worse still, appear in a ques-
tionable light, then all his family feeling and his readiness to
stand by us evaporates. His name is Poggenpuhl, but he
isn't a Poggenpuhl; or, if he is, then it's in his own way,
which is quite different from ours. But not a word to Mama;
she's quite capable of putting it in a letter to him, and then I
shall be in the stocks. As it is, I always feel uneasy when he
comes into my room. He's got such a damned superior smile
and I'm supposed to knuckle under. Altogether—and that's
what's so rotten about one's whole career—one's continually
having to knuckle under. But enough of this confession,
and let's get back to the main topic, which is this pamphlet
about our glory that we're supposed to be writing.
Wendelin, as I said, won't do it, and I can't—can't and
couldn't if it were a question of winning the Queen of
Madagascar for my bride. Oh, Manon! . . . "far in the east
over Madagascar the morning breaks"—yes, that's where I
shall have to go, that's how it will end, it must. For I shall
never call Flora my own (that's how some people like to put
it) if it depends on writing the family history. And besides
—and this is the worst of it because it's so humiliat-
ting—I have considerably overestimated Esther's
passion for me. Or perhaps a rival has turned up overnight,
a more favored suitor. In that case I should be forced to hate
Esther. And so as to hide nothing from you: that Quitzow
evening which promised so much or at least ended so
promisingly—almost nothing of that is left at the end of the
week. What a dismal life, and it's thawing outside. I could
recite Hamlet's soliloquy, but I will settle for "Nymph, pray
for me"; it's shorter. I've probably got it wrong. Most
quotations are wrong.

Your Leo

12

The correspondence between the younger brother and sister continued into February, to the disgust of Therese, who occasionally read one of Leo's letters and then bewailed the fact "that a Poggenpuhl could go so far astray," though she cast the blame chiefly upon her sister. "In my opinion," she regularly remarked when the subject came under discussion, "the whole correspondence is superfluous; but if it is to be carried on, then I should prefer it to have a different content. You will end up by dragging him right over to your side, into that social sphere which you unfortunately seem to enjoy—and to enjoy increasingly. You will not acknowledge that the world which in your flippancy and arrogance, and simply in order to sneer, you refer to as the Germano-Christian world—that this world is worth more than half a dozen Gersons (I assume that there must be that many of them by now). What matters is the inner life, not the outer; the prettiest apple usually has a worm inside."

"Whereas gray russets keep the whole winter through."

Therese shrugged her shoulders and broke off; nor did she seek to return to the subject, especially as the prophecy that her mother had uttered to pacify her was soon fulfilled: "Never mind those two," was more or less what the major's widow had said. "You ought to know Leo and realize how little it all means. Today he wants one thing and tomorrow another. Three weeks from now they will have stopped scribbling of their own accord." And that was how it turned out. Before the end of January, Leo had taken up with a Catholic priest, who cheerfully combined strictness in matters of dogma with games of skat and a merry nature, and this new acquaintance immediately proved fatal to the continuation of the correspondence, which promptly died down.

Yes, the correspondence with Thorn soon came to an end, but Sophie and Manon continued to write to one another, and hardly a week passed without a letter from Adamsdorf, usually accompanied by a carefully packed box. Every time she unpacked it, Friederike greeted its arrival with the same speech, "Fresh eggs again, and all wrapped up and packed in chaff too! Well, I've no objection to *that*, ma'am. Because first of all you can't buy them fresh, even if it says so, and secondly eggs are always better than fresh-killed meat. Ducks aren't too bad, because ducks are fat; but it starts with chicken, and when it comes to veal, that's always a bit off . . . And I'll boil one for you right away, ma'am; it's time you gave yourself a treat. It's true you've got your pastilles, but there's not goodness in them, and they're only on account of your cough."

Sophie's letters could be divided, according to the period they were written, into those dealing with her recovery and those which, when that was complete, dealt with her painting activities. It was always a pleasure to read them, and sometimes Manon took one to the Bartensteins in order to read it aloud, though usually only when the old gentleman was present; he liked hearing that kind of thing, while the ladies really only listened from politeness. Flora—possibly because she was learning modern Greek in preparation for a trip to Olympia—was inclined to find everything "insignificant"; which finally caused Manon, enamored as she was of her friend, to be a little more reticient in her communications.

One of the letters went:

I have just got to the Flood, which, if one likes to look at it that way, is a landscape subject. For water is nature, and nature is landscape. And can you imagine what my Flood looks like? Quite different from any other; and I can say that without immodesty, because it wasn't my idea but Uncle Eberhard's. And not really his either, as you will hear. Last week, when I announced at tea one day that I was going to start on the Flood, Uncle said, "Well, Fiechen, and how do you imagine it looked? Or rather, I don't want to know, I'd rather tell you how *I* imagine it was and how I'd like you to do it. When I was still in Berlin with the Alexander,[15] I once went to a village church nearby where there were a lot of paintings, including a Flood. And there, sticking up out of

before after it had ceased to be a monastery, but then they
lost it. He was a perfect gentleman, and our marriage was a
very happy one; as to our respective wealth, we soon
changed places. My money was lost, and we should have
been forced to give up Adamsdorf, if it had not been for a
number of deaths through which my husband unexpectedly
inherited a considerable fortune. That is how we were able
to stay on here. But everything we own therefore became
Leysewitz property again, and must pass to the Leysewitzes;
your uncle knew that from the start and approved of it. I
have had the rare good fortune to have made two marriages
with two equally excellent men. Everything has turned out
well for me, but I must not forget how it came about, and
must live accordingly. This is how things stand; we have
only the use of everything you see here. The house, the
estate, the money, everything is entailed, and because that
is so I have learned to economize. And you—you are a good
and intelligent child and you can follow all this. Therese
used to listen with only half an ear when I touched on these
matters, and she didn't want to believe them. That's how it
always is; nobody wants to believe what they don't like to
hear."

Yes, dear Mama, that is what Aunt wanted me to know. It
will be quite a good thing if Therese finds out too. All the
same: even though I think I was told all this in order to pass
it on to you, please don't mention it in your reply. I always
read aloud my letters from you and my sisters at breakfast,
and if you made a reference to this I should feel embarrassed.

By the way, I haven't heard anything from the boys for
many weeks. In Wendelin's case that doesn't matter much;
he only writes from duty. But Leo? Sometimes I feel anxious
and think his next letter will be from the Cameroons or
Namaqualand. Until his affairs are in order he'll never settle
down. But where is order to come from?

It was the end of May when Sophie wrote this letter, and
she wisely refrained from mentioning the subject again. She

was content for the letter to take its effect and to change her elder sister's unfair carping for a more just appreciation.

Meanwhile the quiet life at Schloss Adamsdorf continued and only changed with the arrival of summer. Sophie's Aunt was a passionate lover of her native Silesia, and she insisted on weekly expeditions into the mountains. They would drive either to Schreiberhau or to Hermsdorf or to Krummhübel, and from there they would climb on foot higher into the mountains, to Kirche Wang or the Mittagsstein or even to the Schneegruben. Sophie would sketch some scene or other for her Old Testament pictures and say, "This is Abraham's tomb, this is Mount Sinai, this is the Brook Kidron." But her greatest pleasure always came on the way home when they halted for a final rest at the place where they had left their conveyance, and watched the doings of the "trippers" from Berlin. These always gave scope for amusement on the drive home, and Uncle Eberhard never tired of declaring, "Yes, those Berliners, you may love them or hate them; but they *are* entertaining, and watching them like that is just like going to the theater. And actually it *is* something of the kind, because they always look round to see if they've got an audience worth raising the curtain for."

Sophie worked hard all summer at her pictures for the church. By the end of August she had already got to "Saul in the Cave" (she had discovered a suitable cave near the Kräbersteine), and Saul himself was partly Uncle Eberhard and partly the proprietor of the dram shop, who wore a long beard and had the evil eye. David, on the other hand, was the assistant judge. Uncle Eberhard was genuinely delighted with the progress of the work, and every day he would declare that he would never have thought that such a thing could give him so much pleasure. He would then indulge in well-meaning remarks about the artistic life in general, and take back what he had said about it in his earlier days. "You may laugh, but all the same, it's a small act of creation of a sort. And creating is fun. At least, I can't imagine that God created the world in a bad temper."

"Some people look as though He had, Uncle."

the water, was not just the usual Mount Ararat with the Ark, but a bit further back there was another mountain, and on this second mountain there was a church. And this church was the spit and image of the little church in the Mark in which we were standing, with its lantern tower and even with a lightning conductor. And that made a great impression on me at the time, and I want you to do the same thing and put in two mountain tops with the Adamsdorf church on the second one. The Protestant church, that is. And if the Catholics don't like it, they can have their own church painted too. I believe in Martin Luther and the pure doctrine. In that I think I'm an unshakable Poggenpuhl." At first I was a bit taken aback when Uncle said that, because I'd imagined it all quite differently; but as there was no getting out of it, I fell in with his idea, and now that it's nearly finished I have quite fallen in love with it. At first it struck me as childish, and it still does, but at the same time it has a deep meaning. When the old sinful world had gone down and a new and better world was emerging, the first new thing to appear (because the animals belonged to the old world) was the church of that little village in the Mark, and now the Adamsdorf church as well. It was as though the first thing God did was to put them there. Of course you can laugh at the idea, but it can make you rejoice too. And you, my dear Mama, who, thank God, come from a devout clerical family, you will see the beauty of it and be fonder than ever of Uncle Eberhard. He really is a splendid man. That's all about the idea for the painting. And now you will wonder how and where, never having seen the sea, I got the idea of what it should look like for my Flood. Now listen. You must remember our expedition with the Bartensteins last autumn, when we all went third class, which amused them so much. Third class on the Ring Line we went, as far as Stralow station. And when we got out, the station was high up like Mount Ararat over the Rummelsburg Lake and the Spree, and both together they looked like a mighty expanse of water. That's the panorama I used for my picture. The station is Mount Ararat, and the Rummelsburg Lake is the Flood. As I was only doing the end of the Flood, I thought I could manage without any kind of stormy movement of the water without being unfaithful to the text.

Similar letters arrived frequently; the one describing Sophie's "End of Sodom and Gomorrah" found special favor with Herr Bartenstein. "It's a warning," he said to Manon, without indicating, incidentally, to whom he wished the warning to be addressed.

Fiechen settled in more and more, and the longer she spent with her relatives, the more lively an interest she took—when she was not painting—in the domestic affairs of Schloss Adamsdorf and particularly in the character of her aunt. The conversations they had together as they walked around the great lawn in the park would be reported in great detail in Sophie's letters home, whenever the occasion arose.

Yesterday we went for our walk round the big lawn again; there is an enclosure in the middle with a few young deer, charming creatures—I hope to make use of them one day. Then suddenly, I can't remember in what connection, Aunt said, "Yes, your sister Therese. She can't have been very pleased with me, and perhaps she complained of me to you, because when we were in Pyrmont that time I wasn't very keen on being presented to the Princess of Wied, which she was always urging me to do. Once when there was a carriage parade I wouldn't take part, let alone decorate the harness with rose garlands. It all seemed unfitting to me, and I told her so quite frankly. Therese, as so often happens, had a false idea of my financial position; it was once very brilliant, but is so no longer. I particularly want you to understand these rather complicated matters. I come from a simple, middle-class family which started small and poor and only later acquired wealth. Then my first husband married me; he had nothing at the time, but afterward he bought Schloss Adamsdorf. It had been in the family once

"Yes, Fiechen, you're right there. Some people do look like that. But just think of all the things that happen! A single instance proves nothing. People nowadays are terribly inclined to make the exception the rule. And if they'd only choose nice exceptions! But no, it has to be something really nasty. True, thirty years ago it was not much better. I can still remember when that ape business came up, and some orangutan or other was supposed to be our grandfather. You should have seen how delighted everybody was! When we were descended from God, we weren't up to much, but when that ape business came into fashion, they all danced as if it were the Ark of the Covenant.

It was the second of September when Uncle Eberhard and Sophie held this conversation in the attic room that the owners of Adamsdorf had furnished as a studio for their niece. An hour later Uncle Eberhard set off for Hirschberg, where the anniversary of Sedan was to be celebrated in the customary manner. Naturally there had to be a speech about Bismarck, and naturally this had to be made by old General von Poggenpuhl, although the thought of it made him feel worse than he had at the very damnedest moment at Saint Privat. At other times when he drove through the lovely valley, the fields would smile at him in all their bounty, but today he did not notice how the oats were doing; he say nothing at all, and just kept memorizing and saying to himself with increasing anxiety, "It's one o'clock now. In another three hours I shall start living again, and even my appetite may come back. But until then I'm just no good." And he had a headache too, and a slight ticking sensation in two places, which naturally got worse as he kept repeating the question to himself, "What if I dry up?" But finally he came to terms with the idea, or at least resigned himself to it. "And if I really do dry up, what does it matter after all? In my day nobody knew how to make a speech, and all the sensible people there will know that. Besides, I've really got the introduction pat, and if I notice I'm getting in a muddle I shall simply say, ' . . . and so I ask you, all you who are assembled here today: are we Prussians? I know what your answer will be. And in that spirit I call upon you . . .' And then we'll have three cheers."

This more or less restored his composure, but he remained somewhat feverish, and the feverishness continued even after the dreadful moment had come and gone. Perhaps it was because, right after the cheers, he had downed a large glass of dry Hungarian wine. After coffee he felt dizzy. But the feeling passed, and he finally set off for home in the best of spirits. The stars sparkled in the sky; and the air had an autumn freshness in it, and he shivered. "Listen, Johann," he said, "haven't you got a rug?"

"No, sir, but I'll take off my coat."

But that was not at all well received. "Nonsense, man; take off your coat! Me, a Poggenpuhl!" And for a while he muttered on in the same manner.

It was one o'clock when they drove into the village street. An old servant was still up at the Schloss, and Sophie too. As soon as he entered the hall, she could see how changed he was. "Uncle, you're so cold, shall I make you some tea or a hot water bottle?"

"Nonsense. General Poggenpuhl . . ."

He sounded so strange that Johann said to Sophie, "Oh Lord, miss, he keeps saying that. I'm afraid he's very ill."

He was very ill. Next morning they called Doctor Nitsche, who said to Frau von Poggenpuhl, "We must hang up damp sheets, shade the light, and give him complete rest." But to Sophie he said, "It's typhus."

"Will he get better?"

The doctor shrugged his shoulders.

13

Their fears were soon confirmed. In spite of the doctor's objections, Sophie took charge of nursing her uncle. Every evening she wrote a postcard home, always emphasizing that there was no danger yet—largely because their aunt might read what she had written. But the danger was all too great, and on the seventh day after the onset of the illness Sophie's mother received a letter which read:

Uncle Eberhard died at noon today. He was very restless
during the night, then in the course of the morning he fell
into a state of apathy, and just before twelve he fell asleep.
There was very little hope from the beginning, less than I
cared to tell you. I have lost a great deal in him. But not only
I—we shall all miss him a lot, except for Wendelin perhaps,
who will make his way anyhow. I will tell you more when I
see you about some of the things that happened in the last
few days. I look forward to seeing you all, you especially,
my dear, sweet Mama. I am assuming that you will come.
Aunt wishes it very much, and I think we should respect her
wishes. First for our own sake, and then because she deserves it so much. She asks you kindly to accept the enclosed from her, and hopes it will be enough for the journey
and everything else. What I need will be sent from Breslau.
It would be best if you left the day after tomorrow in the
evening. Then you would arrive early in the morning on the
twelfth. The funeral is at noon.

Your Sophie

When Manon finished reading out this letter, all three
ladies were more than a little affected, but their feelings were
of very different kinds. The mother was filled with heartfelt
grief, which would have been even purer if it had not been
mixed with many an anxious thought about the future;
Manon, in spite of her love and reverence for her uncle, was
sadly stricken at having to miss a soirée that the Bartensteins
were giving on that very twelfth; while Therese was domi-
nated by the idea of the funeral, which to her was a function
of immense public importance. She not only immediately saw
herself in the front row of mourners; she was animated by the
proud sense that she, and she alone, would be the chief rep-
resentative of the Poggenpuhl family—the two old ladies who
had only married into it scarcely counted. Her pride was
mitigated for a moment or two by the thousand mark note
that accompanied the letter, but on the other hand the advantages of this were so obvious that any sense of oppression

was soon dispelled, especially when it was agreed that
Therese should go into town and buy their mourning attire.
Apart from the burial itself they all felt that this visit to the
funeral outfitters was the most significant event of all, and the
expression with which Therese set out on her mission was so
emphatically distinguished that even Manon was moved by it
and succumbed to a feeling of reverence for her sister.

The feeling rapidly gave way to the opposite when Therese
returned from her expedition. The dresses, she reported,
would be delivered by the following morning: they could
easily make any small alterations that might be needed. All
the rest she had bought on the spot and brought back in a
large box. It contained three crepe hats, long black veils, and
three mourning caps with a widow's peak in front.

"Are you proceeding on the assumption," said Manon,
"that we are actually going to wear these peaked caps?"

"What a strange question."

"That means yes."

Therese nodded.

"Well then, permit me to say that I shall refrain from joining you."

"That you will not. On such a day as this at least you will
remember the duty you owe your name."

"I know the duty I owe my name."

"And what is that?"

"To refrain, as far as possible, from making myself an object of ridicule."

"And what, in your opinion, would constitute that?"

"To insist on getting ourselves up as royal widows. We are
simply the nieces of an old general."

"Of General von Poggenpuhl! I, at least, will follow the
good old tradition."

"But not the dictates of good taste."

They grew more and more heated; at last they wanted their
mother to decide. But she refused. "I am not sufficiently experienced in such matters, and I don't know whether it
would be suitable or not. I think we should take the box with
us and let Aunt decide."

To this they agreed. Next morning the dresses arrived. They "fitted like a glove." The sisters stood before the tall, narrow looking glass, studying their own appearance and approving one another's, and it was here that peace was concluded once more between them.

"What a marvelous man he was," said Manon.

"He was, and may his memory be blessed. His picture will always have a place in my heart."

The night train left at ten o'clock from the Friedrichsstrasse Station. It was not yet nine when they stood ready in their travelling clothes, and Manon, who looked very good, found it hard to resist the temptation to complete her costume with a pair of binoculars that happened to be lying about. But she said it would show "lack of style" (this was one of Flora's favorite expressions), and, once this redeeming phrase had occurred to her, she found it easier to renounce the binoculars. Friederike was in the front room with them to help when the moment came for putting on their coats; but it was still much too early, and they began to wonder what to do to pass the fime. The major's widow used it to deliver an urgent speech.

"All I can say to you, Friederike, is: be careful and remember all the things that happen every day. Only yesterday there was something in the papers again."

"Yes, I know, ma'am. But it's not as if I was a child."

"And if the bell rings, don't open the door at once. You'd better get a footstool and climb up and look through the fanlight, so that you can see who it is . . ."

"Yes, ma'am."

"And when you open the door, keep the chain on and only speak through the crack . . Only the other day they killed another widow, and if you fling the door open like that, it could happen to you too, or they'll throw snuff in your eyes, or they'll gag you so you won't even be able to scream. And then they'll clear off with everything . . ."

"Lord, ma'am, they always know where to go, they'd never come here."

"Don't say that. *They* know every mickle makes a muckle. Better safe than sorry."

Friederike promised to do everything she said, and then they left.

A cab was already waiting at the door—the porter's wife had condescended to fetch one. They all said good-bye to Friederike once more, and then they were on their way to the Potsdamer Strasse.

Next morning, just after five, the train arrived at Schmiedeberg, and from there it was barely an hour's drive to Adamsdorf. Johann was waiting at the station with an open carriage. The big trunk was put on the box; the major's widow sat on the back seat, with Therese beside her. Manon, across from them, sat facing backward and enjoying the scenery. The sun had not yet risen, but the mountains all around were turning pink, and a fresh breeze was blowing. Everything promised a beautiful autumn day.

Therese too was quite carried away, and as the contours of the mountains grew sharper and clearer she pointed to them and, rising in her seat, she said, "So that is the Riesengebirge?"

The question was addressed to Johann, but he could not immediately adjust to the unfamiliar words and therefore said, "Yes, over there on the left, that's the Koppe."

"The Schneekoppe?"

"Yes, the Koppe."

Manon was amused by the fact that the coachman was reluctant to follow her elder sister's educated speech, while Therese happily indulged in her favorite train of thought about the inferior intelligence of the common people.

It was just six o'clock when the carriage stopped before Schloss Adamsdorf. A manservant helped the ladies to alight, and right after him came Sophie, visibly pleased to see all three—including Therese, although the latter appeared rather reserved. This was because their reception had not turned out as she had expected, and she particularly missed the presence of her aunt.

"Where is Aunt?" she asked. "Not ill, is she?"

"No, she's not ill," said Sophie, immediately guessing what was going on in Therese's mind. "The last few days have been very hard for her. So she wants to rest as long as she can. She asked me to make her excuses."

"Poor relations," Therese murmured half audibly.

After that they climbed the wide stairs to the first floor, where two communicating guest rooms had been prepared, one large and one smaller, with the door between them open and covered only by a heavy curtain. The large room was for Manon and her mother, the smaller for Therese, who was half mollified by the distinction inherent in this arrangement.

"And now you have two whole hours to rest," said Sophie. "Or would you like me to send breakfast up to your rooms right away? Then you can walk in the park until Aunt comes. It's at its best in the morning."

Manon and her mother seemed to hesitate, especially Manon, who had an exalted conception of "morning walks in the park." But Therese thought it unwise to make too much of such things and to behave as though one had never seen anything of the kind before. After all, the Pomeranian estates with which she was familiar also had their parks, and so she said the best thing would be to follow their aunt's example and to gather their strength for what still lay ahead.

14

At half past eight the ladies made their appearance downstairs in the great hall, where a fire was burning although the air outside was almost summery. The general's widow greeted them warmly and at the same time with so much breeding in her manner that Therese was somewhat surprised. At Pyrmont her aunt had struck her as very middle-class, and that had been the cause of all their disagreements and little tiffs. And now she was so different. Was it the feeling of being on her own home ground here at

Adamsdorf? Or was it simply that grief had ennobled her? Therese decided in favor of grief.

They did not spend long together over breakfast; only a few hours remained before the funeral, and the local nobility would probably appear a good deal earlier. Frau von Poggen-puhl asked whether she might see her brother-in-law once more; her request was refused because the coffin had already been nailed down. Manon and Therese expressed their re-gret, but actually they were relieved and consoled themselves with the phrase, "We will remember him as he was in hap-pier times."

By ten o'clock the courtyard in front of the castle began to fill with villagers. The old, men and women alike, were sol-emn and much affected because they had loved and revered the general; but the young people regarded the occasion more or less in the nature of a fair; they giggled and whispered very un-other-worldly remarks to one another. At eleven the coaches arrived, and half an hour later the two village clergy-men, the Catholic as well as the Protestant; and at twelve the procession set off for the church, singing hymns as they went. The parson gave an address; and after him the old Catholic priest spoke in his private capacity "just to express his thanks for the fine sense of justice which had always distinguished the deceased." After that came the blessing, and then the coffin was lowered into the crypt. Therese was grieved to think that a Poggenpuhl should be fated to lie among the coffins of a strange family, and she expressed her sorrow by a severity of bearing which was noticed by all those present. Some of them approved, but others—members of the Silesian nobility—thought it ridiculous and whispered to one another, "Typical Pomeranian Junker pride." For the Silesians have no Junkers. Or at least no authentic ones.

Everyone, incidentally, was pleased with the ceremony, except for a church elder who could not get over the fact that "the ole Cath'lic" had spoken. If that kind of thing were allowed to take hold, they would soon be in trouble and simony would raise its ugly head. What he meant by this was never fully ascertained.

Refreshments were served immediately after the church service. There was no luncheon as such, and when the visitors had gone, the two old ladies, the general's widow and the major's widow, retired to their rooms. They needed rest and wanted to be alone. Sophie still had things to do in the household, and so Manon and Therese were left to themselves. They soon decided on a walk around the outer edge of the park, which was bordered by a little stream. It must have been about four o'clock; the sun was already sinking and shone through the tall Lombardy poplars. Not a breeze stirred, everything lay quiet; the only sounds to be heard were the hammering and clinking from a nearby smithy and, later, when they had almost reached the fields, the tinkle of a scythe being sharpened. Small white birchwood bridges crossed the stream, and every now and then the wooded path widened into little openings and embrasures with seats in them. The birds had stopped singing, but a squirrel ran across their path. Therese abandoned her critical mood and condescended to sprinkle her conversation with approving remarks about the Silesian nobility. "Everything here is richer," she said. "You can feel it; nobody thinks about saving money. With us everyone does, even people who can afford not to. Look at this seat—granite, and faced with sandstone. At home it would be made of wood."

Manon really agreed with this. But the chief form of conversation among the Poggenpuhl sisters consisted of one contradicting the other. And so she said, "You always overdo things, Therese. When we arrived there was nothing you didn't dislike, and now everything is beautiful and rich and superior to what we have. I can't agree. I much prefer the Tiergarten."

"How can you say such a thing, and all for the sake of contradicting! All right, the Tiergarten is not too bad but it's public, and anything public is always vulgar. And some of the things you see in the Tiergarten are positively cynical."

"Cynical?"

"Yes. You see statues and reliefs that are shamelessly cynical. I choose the expression deliberately. It's this predilection for the natural that modern art thinks it has a right to. I, on the other hand, believe that art should throw a veil. However, be that as it may, I don't want to discuss it. When I deliberately used the word 'cynical' just now, I was thinking more of the living pictures and scenes—of the people you come across there. On every bench there is a couple whose attitude is offensive. And when you finally feel like sitting down somewhere where there doesn't happen to be a couple, it's still impossible, because you never know who has been sitting there before. The Tiergarten especially is supposed to be full of dreadful people."

"I always sit where there are children playing."

"You shouldn't do that, Manon. You can't be sure even there—there least of all, sometimes. And anyway, the magic of the unpolluted is totally absent. Here I know the air I breathe is pure. Look how the water flows; at home it's all murky puddles."

Therese went on talking in this vein and was so far carried away as to speak with the highest esteem of their aunt. "Sophie did not exaggerate in her letters. A woman whose past has been totally eradicated. Not everyone can claim as much. Now, when I think of Mama . . ."

"You shouldn't speak ill of Mama. Mama is good and has had much to bear, and has borne it. Not everyone can claim to have done that either."

It was not until tea that they were all reunited. Manon talked about the guests, about various incidents, and finally about the address. The vicar had said a lot about the Resurrection, and the general's widow asked Sophie whether the Resurrection could not also be illustrated by some incident from the Old Testament. She would be glad to know that it could.

"Yes," said Sophie. "There is a story in the Old Testament which is thought to signify the Resurrection."

"And which is it?"

"It's when the whale spews up Jonah. You must admit it's full of significance. But I don't feel I could do it justice."

"Thank goodness," said Manon with a sudden attack of mischief.

"Don't say that, child," said her aunt. "It sounds funny to

you. But what has been regarded with solemn reverence for
centuries has always seemed to me something we should
respect."

Manon blushed; then she rose and kissed her aunt's hand.

They retired early, assuring one another that they would all
be down to breakfast next morning by seven at the latest.
There were still a number of things to discuss. And they
agreed that after all this time in semi-isolation, Sophie should
accompany her family to Berlin, though only for a short stay.
Sophie, said her aunt, was so good and wise and unassuming
that her presence had become a necessity to her. Of course
she must go and have a vacation in the city, but the sooner
she returned the better she—her aunt—would be pleased.
She decided that Sophie was to be back in Adamsdorf by the
middle of November. There would probably be no more
painting at that dark and foggy time of year, but that did not
matter; if Sophie would only sit beside her looking into the
fire and thinking of the dear departed, that would be better
than any painting. As she said this, she reached for Sophie's
hand, and they were all glad that such a warm relationship
had grown up between these two. Even Therese was pleased;
her family feeling was stronger than her personal pride, and
she regarded the whole thing as a victory for the Poggenpuhl
spirit—with which Sophie too was imbued, albeit in a manner different from the others, especially from Therese herself.
Sophie had the loving, friendly, humble characteristics that
dear Uncle, after all, had also possessed.

After these arrangements had been made, the girls retired
to call on the vicar and his young wife, who was supposed to
be a beauty—and was. Only the two old ladies who bore the
name of Poggenpuhl without being Poggenpuhls remained
behind on the veranda. The servant came to clear the breakfast table. "Wait awhile, Joseph," said the general's widow;
and when they were alone once more they both looked across
the center bed of the garden, and then across the ivy-covered
wall to the place where the green copper roof of the church
stood out among the other roofs in the village street. The

thoughts of both went in the same direction: they thought of him who now lay in the silent crypt over there.

A few minutes went by without a word being spoken; then the general's widow took the major's widow by the hand and said: "Dear sister-in-law, I have to make something clear between us, a business matter; and I think you will agree with what I am about to propose."

"I am sure I shall. I think I can say that without knowing what it's about. I know only too well how kind you are."

"All right then, I won't beat about the bush. You know from Sophie—she confessed to me afterward that she had told you—how I am situated as regards the property. Adamsdorf is mine as long as I live, and then it reverts to my first husband's family. The fortune I brought him has been lost. You will know about that too. But I was able later to make good this loss, at least up to a point. Poggenpuhl paid for his little hobbies out of his pension, we lived economically, and so I am in the happy position—in spite of bad harvests—of having collected another modest private fortune. I am free to do as I like with that, and before you leave Adamsdorf I want you to know how I have decided to dispose of it. At the moment the sum itself does not amount to more than seventeen thousand talers—I still reckon in talers—twelve thousand of which are deposited in five percent shares with my banker in Breslau. From the first of October onward you will receive the quarterly interest on those, so that your annual income will increase by about six hundred talers. The capital is not redeemable. Only in the event of one of your daughters marrying, her share will be paid to her. If all three get married, you, sister-in-law, would not have much left, but you would then get the whole of the pension I have from the state; and I know how modestly you manage to arrange your life."

Frau von Poggenpuhl was so touched that she sat in silence looking straight ahead, while the general's widow continued, "Then of course there are your sons, and they are not to be forgotten. But that is a private matter, nothing to do with the other; they will have to be content with just one small out-

right gift each. I intend to send a thousand talers to Wendelin, who is a good manager and understands the value of
money. Leo will get five hundred. He will blow it; he's a
harum-scarum, but I don't mean that as a moral judgment. I
like harum-scarums, as long as they preserve their decency
and their convictions in spite of their way of life. As for my
beloved Sophie, I shall make some special decisions about her
later. That was what I wanted to tell you before you leave, my
dear sister-in-law."

The sun's rays shone muted through the trees, which were
still thick with leaves; but its full light fell on the center bed
and on the borders along the veranda, where it made the few
verbena and balsamine still flowering glow more intensely
red or white. Pigeons rose from the farm buildings and flew
high above the garden to the church steeple, where they
circled before alighting on its copper helmet or on the ridge of
the roof.

Frau von Poggenpuhl tried to kiss her sister-in-law's hand,
but the latter embraced her and kissed her on the forehead.

"I am happier than you," said the general's widow.

"You are, indeed. To make others happy is the greatest
happiness. It has not been my lot. But to know how to
receive with gratitude is happiness too."

15

On the day the Poggenpuhls were expected back, not only
Friederike but also the porter's family were in a state of considerable excitement. In the case of the Nebelungs this was
due to a fortuitous circumstance: a Free Conservative privy
councillor on the second floor happened to be away, but his
newspapers continued to be delivered to the porter's apartment; and Nebelung, who was both inquisitive and lazy (his
wife had to make up for it by working her fingers to the bone)
studied them carefully or just glanced through as the mood
took him. Among these papers was the *Post*, and on this

particular day the morning edition carried a mention of the death of Major General von Poggenpuhl, accompanied by the words, "See also Deaths." Nebelung immediately pounced upon the deaths column, and, when he had found the black-rimmed announcement, he read it carefully. A strange grin spread across his face as he pushed the paper toward his fourteen-year-old daughter Agnes, who was just having her afternoon coffee with her two brothers. "There, Agnes," he said, "read that. The bit with the thick black border." And Agnes, who was not only anemic but also destined for the stage on account of her figure and her passion for *The Maid of Orleans*, read out loud while the rest listened:

Today our dear husband, brother-in-law, and uncle,
   Major General (retired) Eberhard Pogge von Poggenpuhl,
Knight of the Iron Cross (1st Class), Knight of the Order of
Albrecht the Bear, passed away, aged sixty-seven, at Schloss
Adamsdorf, Silesia. No individual announcements will be
sent by the sorrowing relatives:
   Josephine Pogge von Poggenpuhl, née Bienengräber,
      widow of Freiherr von Leysewitz, widow
   Albertine Pogge von Poggenpuhl, née Pütter, widow of
      Major von Poggenpuhl, sister-in-law
   Wendelin Pogge von Poggenpuhl, First Lieutenant
      in the Trzebiatowski Grenadiers
   Leo Pogge Von Poggenpuhl, Second Lieutenant   Nieces
      in the Trzebiatowski Grenadiers   and
   Therese Pogge von Poggenpuhl   Nephews
   Sophie Pogge von Poggenpuhl
   Manon Pogge von Poggenpuhl

Agnes's somewhat sallow complexion had turned quite red with the effort of getting out all these names—the only one she could not quite manage was the Polish name of the regiment. As she put down the paper, the old man said, with most obvious relish, "What a lot of Pogges.[16] I can positively hear them croaking." This joke was greeted with howls of gleeful applause by his sons, true Nebelungs both, but his daughter had expected quite another response to her dramatic rendering; she rose and left the room. As she passed her mother, who was sitting a little apart, she said, "I don't know, but Father is being so common again today." Her mother, a sickly and perpetually bad-tempered woman, corroborated this remark with several nods. But Nebelung himself called after his daughter as she disappeared through the door, "Don't be so impudent, toad; you're not on the stage yet."

In one sense Agnes had been unjust to her father. In the depths of his soul Nebelung was not completely unmoved by all these things; but being a true Berliner he had tried to joke away the impression made upon him by the enumeration of so many glorious names. On the other hand he was genuinely annoyed because "those paupers up there" were now being forced on his attention as being something very special. Ridiculous; all rubbish. All the same, even as he protested, he was willing to put a good face on it, and the occasion soon arose.

It was about half past four (the boys had just returned from school) when the quarrel took place between father and daughter; barely an hour later a cab loaded with luggage came up the Grossgörschenstrasse. The whole house was waiting. Like Friederike, the Nebelungs had planted themselves outside, albeit adopting very different attitudes and occupations. The two boys were leaning against the wall, half curious and half lolling because they did not want to compromise their status as free German citizens; Nebelung himself, a sort of fez on his forehead, was patrolling the sidewalk while Agnes stood slender and upright in the open doorway as though she were impersonating Mondecar or some other lady of the Spanish court. When the major's widow walked past her, she dropped a well-rehearsed court curtsy, which she repeated even more emphatically when Therese appeared a moment later. For Therese was the only member of the family still wearing the long mourning veil: together with her funereal bearing it had already earned her a measure of homage on the journey. She had been taken for the young widow of an officer who had died in a Silesian spa.

The cab was still standing by the pavement, and Manon and Sophie were arguing with the driver—a sly-looking man—about carrying up the luggage. He couldn't leave his horse, he kept saying, otherwise he would be fined. At this awkward moment, Nebelung, usually so aloof, approached the young ladies, lifted his fez with an obliging air, and declared himself willing to carry the big trunk up to the flat. "Oh, Herr Nebelung..." said Sophie. But he had already grasped the trunk and skillfully hoisted it onto his shoulder; he was not deflected by the cab driver, who, his diplomatic maneuver having miscarried, now sneered after him, "Look out, or you'll do yourself an injury!"

But no injury befell him, because the trunk, though large, was not heavy, and Nebelung seemed scarcely out of breath when he reached the top of the stairs. Friederike relieved him of the trunk, and at the same moment Sophie said, "Please, Herr Nebelung, ... I want to thank you." And when he returned to his lodge, Nebelung threw a bright new mark piece on the table and said, "There, Mother. We must put that in the money box. Pogge von Poggenpuhl... And from little Sophie too... Virgin money. That breeds."

Agnes caught only the last words, and she turned contemptuously aside.

Upstairs half a sheet of paper with the word "Welcome" in Friederike's own hand hung over the door. Perhaps because she was uncertain of her spelling, or possibly from economy, the letters were barely filled in with ink and consisted only of double lines. The flower bowl under the Sohr major held red and white asters from the market. Some of them had been intended for the Hochkirch major: Friederike was going to stick them under the frame. But she abandoned the idea with the observation, "I know that one. Just touch him and he falls down."

"Well, you're still alive," said the major's widow as Friederike dutifully took her coat. "Are you sure you haven't been stinting too much? You mustn't do that. I know you always boil up the old coffee grounds. You'll never get fat like that."

"Oh, I'll get fat all right, ma'am."

"Well, I hope it's true. But now bring us some coffee. The cups are out already, I see. I must say, I'm half frozen. There was a lady who kept opening all the windows."

"Yes, Mama, that's what everyone does nowadays."

"I know it's what everyone does. And it may be a good idea. But not for everyone. When you suffer from rheumatism . . ."

Meanwhile Sophie too had made herself comfortable. She threw herself into a corner of the sofa with a certain relish, and studied first the room and then all the little objects scattered about that she had held in her hands so many times.

"Come, Mama, you must sit beside me. Or I'll move up a bit—this is your corner. Goodness, when I look at it all! It's really very nice here in your apartment."

"You might say 'in our apartment,'" said Therese.

"Of course, of course. Of course I belong to you and I always shall. But it's been such a long time. Nine months or very nearly. And then I'm supposed to be going back."

"And do you want to? Do you really want to?"

"Of course. And it's settled. And even if it weren't settled, I like being at Adamsdorf and I like being with Aunt."

"Who wouldn't," said Therese. "The park and the crypt where our uncle the general now sleeps. Everyone must feel the draw of that. And that woman has much to forgive me; I thought her enslaved to her middle-class origins, but she has quite the manners of society. It's a pity that such metamorphoses are so rare."

Sophie and Manon glanced at their sister with the obvious purpose of diverting her from this delicate topic. But though they meant well, it was quite unnecessary, for their mother felt no bitterness on the subject. She merely smiled sadly with the quiet assurance that comes from having lived and from knowing that one has fought life's battles honestly through to the end. "Ah, my dear distinguished daughter," she said, "there you go again."

"I didn't mean to hurt you, Mama."

"I know. And I'm not hurt. Once I had my self-esteem too and my own pride, but life has eroded all that and worn me down . . . What you said about Aunt—yes, there you were right. An excellent woman, and—if that's how you want it—a *noble* woman too. I've always known that, and since this last visit I know it even better. But—and it's hard that I should have to keep proclaiming it to my own daughter, who ought to realize it without any assurance from me—I too could have turned out like her if life had given me the opportunity; but it didn't. To live in a castle and to be able to make hundreds of people happy—and then to be able to punish them by withholding their happiness—that's a different school of life from having to watch Herr Nebelung's expression and to beg favors from him. All I have been taught is care and want. That has been *my* school. It hasn't made me very distinguished, but it has taught me humility. God forgive me if what I say is wrong, but real, genuine humility is a virtue that need not be ashamed of itself even among the nobility."

Sophie slid softly from the sofa to her knees and covered the old lady's hands with tears and kisses. "You have much to answer for, Therese," said Manon and went to stand by the window.

But Therese herself calmly cast an eye over the "gallery of ancestors" above the sofa, and that eye seemed to say, "You are witnesses that I said no more than I had a right to say." But then another, better feeling overcame her, and that too she put into words. "Forgive me, Mama," she said, "Perhaps I was wrong."

It was not in the nature of the family to allow such a scene to disturb their good humor for long. The mother had learned to bear harder trials and was always ready to pardon and give way, whereas Therese, although fundamentally she persisted in her views, was not really obstinate and felt an urge to mitigate what she had said. A conversation with Manon seemed the best way to do that. So she took her sister's hand and led her back from the window to the coffee table. She drew her down beside her on a footstool and said, "Many things will have to change for us now—and for you too. You, my dear little scamp, are farthest from the right path. What do you think about your future now?"

"Future? . . . Oh, you mean marriage?"

"Yes, that too, perhaps. But first of all I mean the company you keep, the society you move in. What do you think about that?"

"Well—exactly as before. I shall keep the company I've always kept."

"You ought to think it over all the same."

"Think it over? I ask you . . . I'd like to see old Bartenstein's face if I suddenly remembered my ancient lineage just because I've got an income of two hundred talers. If it was more he might forgive me. But . . ."

"So everything is to go on as before?"

"Yes. And as for marriage! We mustn't start having silly ideas like that; we shall still be poor girls. Mama will eat better and Leo won't have to go to the Equator. Because I imagine he'll be able to pay his debts now, without the Blumenthals and even without Flora. But Flora herself will still be my friend. That's what *I* want. And so we shall live happily ever after until Wendelin and Leo have really got somewhere and we have a few more celebrities in the family like the Sohr and Hochkirch majors."

"You forget the third—your father," said the major's widow, who felt the Poggenpuhl spirit rising in her for the first time at this omission.

"Yes, my father—I'd forgotten about him. Funny, fathers are nearly always forgotten. I must talk to Flora about it. She was saying something of the sort the other day."

NOTES

The Woman Taken in Adultery

1. German *Kommerzienrat:* an honorific title bestowed on a businessman (see Translator's Note).

2. Quotation from a poem by Emanuel Geibel (1815–84).

3. Manasse Vanderstraaten was a character in the tragedy *Uriel Acosta* (1864) by Karl Gutzkow. Both Vanderstraaten and Acosta were Jews.

4. Ezel is the German form of Attila.

5. A ball at the opera house. Those wishing to attend had to pay a fee in order to be entered on the list.

6. Wagner had referred to the legend of Wayland the Smith in *The Work of Art in the Future* (1850). At the same time he wrote a plan for a play on this subject, which was published in 1872.

7. Wagner.

8. Helmut von Moltke, Chief of the General Staff.

9. A Low German folk tale. The poor fisherman and his wife are granted a series of wishes by a magic fish, but they lose their good fortune almost as quickly as they win it by the exorbitance and silliness of their wishes. The story ends, "So there they are, back in their pisspot."

10. Wagner.

11. Vilma von Voggenhuber was a Wagnerian singer at the Berlin Opera.

12. "Gold is only a chimera" is a line from Meyerbeer's opera *Robert le Diable,* which also contains a ballet of nuns.

13. A novelist from Mecklenburg, who wrote in Low German.

14. Bismarck.

15. Poem by Goethe.

16. Baron Stoffel was the French military attaché in Berlin from 1866 to 1870. He warned his government about the Prussian preparations for war, but was not heeded.

17. Sattler von der Hölle: literally, "saddler of hell."

18. Himmelpfort: "Gate of Heaven."

19. Quotation from the patriotic song *The Watch on the Rhine*.

20. See note 17.

21. Quotations from the ballad *Lenora* (1773) by Gottfried August Bürger.

22. Trakehnen was a famous Imperial stud.

23. Gabler: literally, "forker."

24. Opening line of a poem by Ferdinand Freiligrath, set to music by Robert Franz.

25. *Rotraud* (1838) is a poem by Eduard Mörike. The refrain is, "Be silent, my heart."

26. See note 25.

27. "One doesn't...trees": quotation from Goethe's novel *Die Wahlverwandtschaften*, part 2, chap. 3.

28. The tune is Papageno's aria from *The Magic Flute*, "Ein Mädchen oder Weibchen." The words are by Hölty.

29. The hero of a novel by George Sand.

30. There is a legend that when Maximilian I (1493–1519) had lost his way on the Martinswand (a mountain face), he was rescued by an angel.

31. An island in the Tiergarten.

32. "Everything has its price, and you pay twice for happiness."

33. reference to Bismarck's anti-Catholic policy.

34. Quotation from the harpist's song in Goethe's novel *Wilhelm Meisters Lehrjahre*, book 2, chap. 13.

35. A reference to Schiller's poem *Der Jüngling am Bache.*

36. Toussaint L'Ouverture was the leader of the Negro uprising in Haiti (1791–1801); Toussaint-Langenscheidt is a method of learning languages and the name of the most commonly used foreign-language dictionaries in Germany. Melanie has confused them.

37. See note 35.

38. A Christmas custom in which a present arrives mysteriously, often left outside the door or thrown in at the window.

The Poggenpuhl Family

1. Gerson Bleichröder 1822–79 was a Jewish banker generally regarded as the richest man in Berlin. He was banker and financial adviser to Bismarck.

2. A popular amusement place.

3. "Canoness" is the nearest English word for *Stiftsdame. A Stift* is a foundation for unmarried daughters of the Protestant aristocracy. It retains the structure of a pre-Reformation convent, but the inhabitants are not bound by vows.

4. *Schloss* is untranslatable: it can mean a castle, but more often, as here, it means an unfortified building of any size between a large country house and a palace.

5. Litfass columns are still found in Berlin. Their purpose is to carry advertising, and they are pasted all over with public notices, theater programs, and advertisements.

6. A public entertainment palace founded in 1844 by Joseph Kroll. It contained a theater and concert hall.

7. Patriotic play by Ernst von Wildenbruch (1845–1909).

8. Officers received their discharge from the War Office in blue envelopes.

9. Serious offenders in the army were put into punishment cells with nothing to sit or lie on and sharp slates nailed all over the floor.

10. Quotation from Schiller's poem *Hoffnung* (Hope).

11. Medieval family of Polish rulers.

12. Unusual, affectionate diminutive of Sophie. It is pronounced exactly like "Viehchen" which would mean "little animal."

13. Home for delinquent girls.

14. Ernst von Drysander was the court preacher.

15. After the Napoleonic wars the first regiment of Prussian Grenadiers was named after Czar Alexander I.

16. *Pogge* is a dialect word for "frog."